SMUGGLED

SMUGGLED

Christina Shea

Black Cat
New York

Published simultaneously in Canada
Printed in the United States of America

FIRST EDITION

ISBN: 978-0-8021-7086-6

Black Cat
a paperback original imprint of Grove/Atlantic, Inc.
841 Broadway
New York, NY 10003

Distributed by Publishers Group West

www.groveatlantic.com

11 12 13 14   10 9 8 7 6 5 4 3 2 1

To JSL

Did I request thee, Maker, from my clay
To mould me man? Did I solicit thee
From darkness to promote me?

—*Paradise Lost*

Did the dove go astray, could her ankle-band
Be deciphered? (All the
Clouding around her—it was legible.) Did the
Covey countenance it? Did they understand,
and fly, when she did not return?

—*Paul Celan*

Cover us with your big wings, vigil-keeping evening cloud.

—*Miklós Radnóti*

SMUGGLED

I

1943

THEY WOULD SLIP HER BETWEEN the seams of the two countries. Eszter made the chain stitches binding the thread into a
knot, then she cut the thread close. Straightening up against
the chair back, she reached to turn up the lamp. She had done
the stitching by hand, not trusting the machine. The money lay
flat beneath the coat's lining. The sewn in pocket was barely
detectable. She shook the coat out, then clutched it to herself,
shutting her eyes. When she opened them again György's hand
was on her shoulder, pressing. "Darling, it's time. We must."

She had to believe in the hiding place. Believe in order to
risk the only thing that mattered to her now. She had told Éva
the plan that morning.

"But when will you fetch me, Mama? After the war?" Éva
had asked.

Her mother nodded. She had explained so many things to
her this way. After the war they would have sugar in their tea
again, after the war Éva could go to school.

"But you must not sulk or pine, Éva. You mustn't burden your Auntie Kati," Eszter cautioned. Her voice had been fraught, her thoughts at an impasse. "Listen, Éva, for once you do as you are told!" Her words were a declaration. All instructions she delivered with the same fervent insistence. There was no other way to suppress Éva. She was fearless.

It was all because of her hand, Éva felt. Nothing would ever be the same. Her mother had given her several spoonfuls of cough syrup before bed. She awoke from deep sleep on her mother's lap in the passenger seat of György's car. She was buttoned up in a strange coat. Éva stared through thick fog at György driving. She thought it must be Tuesday since her father was there.

At the train station, György took her swiftly in his arms and they hurried up the narrow flight of stairs and along the darkened platform. He drew up short beside the controller's booth. She slid into her mother's arms and was cradled like a baby and her forehead was warm with kisses. György held open the flour sack. They lowered her into it. The blackness swallowed her.

From the bottom of the sack she looked up at her mother's face, a grave moon. Mama! But she shouldn't speak or cry out. She must hide herself. She carefully pulled her broken hand out of its sleeve, nestling it inside the coat.

The moon came close. Her eyes shone. "I love you, my Éva," Eszter whispered.

Then György tied the sack tight.

*   *   *

Kati crouched, waiting in the field adjacent to the tilled no-man's-land at the border crossing. She listened for her husband's boots on the frigid ground. When she heard him approaching she stepped out of hiding. Ilie set down the sack, and Kati leaned in with a kitchen knife and carefully tore the seam. The child slid out, coated in flour dust, and slumped heavily onto the ground.

"Come, we must hurry," Kati urged, shaking the child's shoulders.

The girl's eyelids fluttered open as Kati lifted her to her feet. She rocked unevenly on her thin legs and blinked, peering at their faces in the early dawn. She looked frightened, and Kati hastened to hush any outcry, pressing hard fingers over her lips.

"Carry her," Ilie whispered. "She's half asleep."

He had to return to work. He couldn't be gone long without attracting attention. He took the rake Kati had brought and retraced his exact path, working to erase his tracks.

Kati stared down uncertainly at the forlorn child. There was no time to waste. "Come," she said, reaching for her hand, attempting to pull her. The child stumbled forward on rubbery legs. Kati panicked: the sun would be shining before they got home! They should have left her in the sack! Squatting, she took the girl by the arms and hoisted her onto her back. She straightened up carefully, steadying herself under the surprising density.

She went as swiftly as she could through the corn and

tobacco fields. Dogs began to bark at the farm. Kati hurried, breathing heavy clouds in the cold morning air. Climbing the embankment to the road, she stumbled and fell on one knee. She pushed herself up, gritting her teeth, her back on fire from the child's weight. In the distance she could see the house silhouetted against the sunrise. She crossed the road, stepping clumsily through an opening in the old sheep fence, and trudged doggedly across the last field, inwardly muttering her paternoster. At last she came to the hedge that bordered the garden wall. "Close your eyes," she whispered to herself and pushed headlong through the privet, emerging on a small footpath. She groped for the key inside her pocket and fit it into the lock of the wooden door in the wall. The gate swung open. She stumbled in and, finally, exhaling, set the child down.

The dormant garden was covered in frost. Icicles hung from an arbor. Kati looked at the waif beside her. Her blood was still pumping. She extended her hand and, when the child didn't respond, she took her firmly by the sleeve, up the pathway, into the shadow of the house.

Kati struck a match and lit a candle. "Godspeed," she said, turning to the child, her breath evening out now that she was home. "I am Kati." She clasped her hands together nervously and said, "Auntie Kati. Your father's sister." She hurried to hang up her coat and, tying on an apron, stoked the fire back to life. She was broad-backed and plainly dressed, her hair pulled back severely. Her face glowed over the coals. "I'm married to Ilie Balaj, a Romanian. That is who carried you from the train." She set aside the fire iron and closed the stove. "You're in Crisu now."

She helped the child out of her coat, wrinkling her nose. She had soiled herself. Kati shook out the coat and coughed as the flour rose like smoke. She ushered the child across the room to the bath.

"I heated the water before setting out for the border," she explained. She lifted the kettles, pouring them into the tub.

The child stared with glassy eyes at the steaming water.

"It's good and warm," said Kati, shaking the droplets from her fingers. "Go ahead, get undressed."

When the girl didn't move, Kati held her breath against the stench and stripped her down. She was terribly thin, small for her age, but long legged like a crane. The wild mop of hair on her head had gone stiff and hoary in the flour sack and her skin was coated in the pale white dust. Kati watched her climbing into the basin, the flour dissolving into parting rings on the water's surface. A strange, ethereal child, Kati felt.

"You're shivering. Sit down," she urged. She slopped the washcloth over the girl's bony shoulders, studying the goose bumps on her skin. She began to feel troubled by how dark she seemed.

The child was coming awake in the water, blinking her eyes and looking around the room.

"Your father and I grew up in this house," Kati said to her. "This village was part of Hungary once, called Körös. Crisu is the Romanian name. The whole region, all of Transylvania, was once

Hungary." She sighed. She was talking to herself now. "At Trianon, they took it all away from Hungary, but with the Germans they have redrawn the boundaries." Kati didn't lament that Crisu had been left behind in the partition of 1940. She didn't care what country she was in as long as she was in this house.

"Tip your head back so I can rinse the hair." She nudged the child's chin. The hair fell away from her face and fanned out around her as her head touched the water. Kati paused in astonishment over her upturned features suddenly exposed. The waterline crowned her—a delicate island, a floating jewel.

Their plan was to provide her with a new identity. It would be risky, but not impossible. The population wasn't without empathy for the casualties of war, especially children. As long as they weren't Gypsies. And the Jews were gone, purged from the villages on the Hungarian side after the border shifted, in a roundup of "aliens." A final sweep had been done in Crisu only recently, conducted with uncharacteristic organization—every house, every barn. Everyone said that Antonescu was trying to impress the Germans so that he could get Transylvania back. When Kati wrote to her brother György, agreeing to his offer, she'd explained that Crisu was relatively safe now, isolated, cut off since the road closing, just the mail train going back and forth.

Now that the child was actually here Kati was filled with dread. She was wrapping the girl up in a towel afterward, still ruminating over her olive tone. Anyway, she was too dark to be Hungarian! She would be an internal refugee, Ilie's side of the family. Of course, they would have to hide her until she learned the language, but they could also lie about her age. She was petite, even smaller from poor nutrition. She was five years old but might pass for three. The thought of not having to acknowledge her own blood tie was a quiet relief to Kati. Ilie didn't care. He had no shame. He had been persuaded by the sum of money that György was paying. As for Kati, even though she had given up longing for a child of her own and was now rather too old for it, smuggling this girl over the border had seemed less a risk than a chance at something.

Her face was pink from the bath and from having her hair combed. She was buttoned up in woolens Kati had bought in anticipation of her arrival, seated at the table. Kati set a fork and knife down in front of her and a plate of stew and sliced bread. The plate was one of Kati's, painted with ocher and indigo roosters. Similar painted pottery decorated the walls and shelves of the room. In the far corner were more shelves lined with trays of unglazed earthenware. Kati's potter's wheel was draped in a sheet.

Kati was rather frantically searching the inside of the wool coat the child had arrived in. At last she found what she was looking for. She slashed the lining with a scissors and began counting the reich marks from György. She glanced over at the girl. With a flush of color she tucked the roll of bills inside her apron. She reached across the table and nudged the plate of food.

"Aren't you hungry? Eat something!"

She could barely manage the fork in her right hand. Her other hand was curled inertly in her lap.

Kati looked on curiously. "What happened to that hand? Are you a cripple?"

She looked timidly up at her and for a second they studied each other.

"It's good," suggested Kati, "if people will pity you."

The old cat had one green eye, one blue. At night, the cat slept wedged between Éva's back and the old smoke chimney, deaf to the mice that ran along the pickle shelves. The calico cat was the mouser, too tough to be cuddly, but she had Auntie's respect. Auntie left the pantry door open at night so that the heat from the stove could reach her. She lay in the fold of a down quilt on the pantry floor, her knees drawn up to her chin as if she were still inside the flour sack.

"Anca," Auntie had said to her. "That's what we'll call you. Do you understand? Anca Balaj is your name now. You must forget Éva."

When she closed her eyes it was just a dream. The numbness and shock gave way in her sleep, and she could see her mother's pretty face, yearning it into being. She was wrapped in Mama's warm arms, her cheek pillowed against her bosom, the worn fabric of her blouse, the fading cherry bouquets. At the first signs of morning consciousness, she held her mother tightly, with two good hands, never letting go. Still, when she opened her eyes in the morning, Mama wasn't there.

After one week, Auntie Kati stopped speaking to her in Hungarian. Only Romanian was permitted.

"It's the only way," Auntie insisted. "You'll learn quickly. It's not so difficult, you know. Even I have managed to pick it up and there wasn't a Romanian school when I was growing up. It's easier than Hungarian."

There was constant confusion for her, beginning at breakfast. Auntie stood over the table, repeating her words. It was something about the milk. She looked cautiously at her cup. She despised the hot milk that Auntie served.

Auntie Kati tapped her foot, expecting an answer. "A mute child will not be understood even by his mother," she interjected thoughtlessly, in Hungarian. It was an old expression. Auntie's voice grew louder, returning to Romanian. She was asking her question again, her pitch rising. But she spoke so quickly! Was she asking if she liked the milk? She nodded politely at Auntie, and then looked on in wonder as she whisked the cup away, dumping the milk back into the pot to be reheated.

"There. I warmed it more. Now, drink it all up," encouraged Auntie Kati, returning the cup to her.

She gagged on the scalded taste, swallowing shamefully.

All day long she was immersed in the strangeness of the new language. Her tongue would never get used to putting "the" at the end of the word. In Hungarian, you said things the way you meant them but in Romanian the order was always the same. She was continually forgetting this. Auntie would shout, reverting to Hungarian in her exasperation, sometimes banging her palm on her potter's wheel. She was terrified, and struggled for control. Romanian sounded so angry. "Anca" itself was such an ugly name—like glass breaking. Her head throbbed with foreign noise.

At night she lay desperate in her bed, too tense to sleep despite her exhaustion, feeling helpless against the invading Romanian. She peered up at the little window for a glimpse of the moon. The cat purred at her back. In the next room Auntie Kati stayed up late working. Light from her lantern flickered on the pickle jars. Leaning in to center the clay at her kick wheel, Auntie sang to herself in Hungarian. Even if she couldn't make out the words over the whir of the wheel, the rhythm and tone were a comfort.

She had never before been on a farm, and knew of village life only from picture books. Auntie and Uncle's house was a different world. Besides the hens out in the yard, they kept a goat that they milked, and a pig, and a vegetable garden. Even though it was winter they were not hungry like she and her mother had been. Auntie added vegetable peels and table scraps to the pig feed every afternoon. She looked on from the window. As long as she stayed behind the curtain Auntie didn't object. Auntie was friendly with the pig, patting its rump and talking to it. The pig would lift its snout from the trough and flash bright eyes.

On Christmas Eve, two months after her arrival, Uncle and Auntie invited her to go outside with them after dark. She didn't catch their words but followed them out into the frozen yard wrapped in a shawl. She watched in horror as Uncle sliced the pig's jugular and the blood pulsed out and into Auntie's waiting bucket. An acrid smell filled her nostrils, her head reeled, and she vomited in the snow. Auntie looked askance. "It's Christmas Day dinner. Come stir," she urged, handing her the long wooden spoon, explaining, "The blood has to be stirred so it won't separate."

They would make blood sausage, *véres hurka,* but first Ilie poured a steaming cup out in the garden. "It's the Romanian custom to sacrifice some blood to the gods," said Auntie.

"The gods?" scoffed Uncle. "It's for my dormant grapes!"

It was the first time she had breathed fresh air since coming to Crisu. She felt wide awake. Uncle was in a bright mood, making short work of the butchering. His expression was intent, his face glistening with sweat despite the frigid air. His sleeves were rolled and his apron was splattered and smeared with blood. He scooped the innards, depositing them in a basin of water. Auntie washed off the guts. Then came the all-night stuffing of sausage casings and the cooking of scraps for headcheese, with Auntie explaining the differences between the Romanian and Hungarian ways. "Romanians mix rice together with the liver, and sometimes mix rice with both the liver and the lungs . . ." assuming that she had tasted such delicacies before, but her mother had never served pork.

"Pay attention," Auntie said sternly, handing her a bowl with the cleaned pig's liver in it. "She's busy looking up at the stars," she remarked to Uncle.

He was tending the cooking fire. "Maybe she'll be an astronomer."

"Or a dreamer," said Auntie, "like her uncle."

Auntie Kati was a devout Catholic but she couldn't leave Anca's Romanian Orthodox education to an atheist like Ilie. She taught her to make the Romanian cross over the bottom of a loaf of bread before cutting into it. She called her to the window as a funeral procession was passing, on its way to the Romanian cemetery. It was the second one that week.

"See the open coffin, and the linen cloth over the soldier's shoulders?"

She nodded solemnly, her eyes wide. The mourners were dressed in black, including the priest who had a long beard and was swinging a censer. In the late winter air, the smoke appeared lined in silver. Several people carried tall candles decorated in winter greenery and berries.

"The candles are larger and thinner and darker yellow than the candles Hungarians use." Auntie went on as they looked out the window, "And the wax smells differently, bitter." She thumbed her nose. "I don't know why they prefer these." Auntie tended to dwell when comparing. She glanced over at Uncle, who snorted, overhearing bias.

At first, she had believed that good behavior might restore her mother to her. Her mother could not deny her if she did everything she was told. But she would never like warm milk. And Auntie Kati's language drills would never end! She was frequently distracted, looking out the window at the bare haw-thorns and the blank gray sky, another funeral passing.

Auntie Kati was waggling a finger in her face. She didn't like to have to ask a question twice. "What is your name, little girl?"

This was the dialogue she liked the least. It wasn't just that she was tired of it. She paused, feeling sullen. Up until this moment she had been such a good girl—but what if Mama never came for her?

"I don't know," she whispered in Hungarian.

"Don't know? Of course you know your own name!" Auntie insisted in Romanian. She stood arms akimbo now, frowning in consternation.

Sensing Auntie's threshold, she was suddenly emboldened. "I am Éva, not Anca," she insisted.

"What?" Auntie threw her hands up. "Are you thick as the dark of night?" She looked to Ilie, seated at the table reading the paper.

He set the paper aside and slowly pushed back his chair. She tensed at his approach. He got down on one knee and she quickly lowered her eyes. His breath smelled of stale coffee. "It will be a good day if the police do not put a bullet through your head before our very eyes," he told her in a low tone. Cocking his thumb and pressing his index finger into the bridge of her nose, "Éva is dead," he said.

"Enough," Kati admonished him. "You're frightening her."

"We'll all be dead," said Uncle, straightening up. "They'll shoot us all if she isn't careful." He held up a hand to silence Kati.

The Romanian language set seed finally, without her noticing. Simply, one morning in the new year, she was staring up at the dawn through the little window of the pantry, understanding the conversation she was overhearing. Uncle was complaining that his coffee was thin and Auntie replied that she had used twenty beans. The war was on, even for border personnel. Uncle was grumbling, his spoon tinkling as he stirred his coffee. The conversation turned to her own breakfast, which Kati was preparing.

"A child should eat eggs," remarked Uncle.

"But I don't ever cook for breakfast. There's no sense in arousing the neighbors."

He scoffed. "Tell them your husband's hungry!"

"'They'll shoot us all!'" Kati mocked.

"Cook her an egg!" he thundered.

Then came a ruminative silence. "Where are her papers?" Auntie asked finally. "You said it would take just a few weeks."

Uncle made no reply. Then she heard Auntie's hurried footsteps, the back door opening and closing, heading out to the hens.

By winter's end Kati had resumed her customary workday and expected Anca to keep herself busy. But the balls of clay that she gave her to mold quickly lost their novelty. Without her fingers, her left hand was limited, but she seemed to favor it. Her right was certainly clumsy. More than once Auntie Kati had asked her what had happened to her hand, but she acted mute.

"She's useless for doing the washup or the mending," Auntie complained to Uncle. "I don't know what to do with her all day. She stands at the curtain looking out."

"Well, you've got her imprisoned," said Ilie, getting up, tucking in his work shirt. He folded up the newspaper. "There's no reason she can't go outside. I told you. Her papers are in order. I've seen to her registration with the county."

She was in her usual listening place near the back window.

"I worry," Kati said. She was filling Uncle's lunch pails from the pots on the stove.

"About what?"

"'About what?' How can you ask me?" She spilled a little of the soup she was ladling.

"We can't hide her forever," shrugged Ilie.

"What if her papers are suspicious?"

"They're perfect, I told you."

"She'll need a new coat," Kati said, after a moment. She snapped the lids and handed him his lunch. "I've laundered that coat twice now, beaten it with the broom, but it's still sending up flour clouds."

"Cut rags from it," he suggested.

She nodded. "A shame because it's excellent tailoring."

The next day, Ilie brought home a burlap child's coat. "Now there is nothing standing in your way," he told Kati. "Let the stir-crazy child out!"

Kati bundled her up, tying a scarf around her head. She bent down to be at eye level, giving her an abrupt shake. "Keep your hand inside your pocket!" she said warningly. "And if any-one ever asks you what happened to it don't act dumb. Say you were born with it this way."

She made it sound as if there would be people lined up to meet her, but in fact the garden and yard were almost as quiet as the house. Still, the spring air was pleasant and Anca seemed enlivened by it. She lingered in the barn, petting the goat after

Kati milked it. She gamely carried the water buckets up from the well. While Kati hung out laundry Anca roamed Uncle's garden, on the verge of spring. Kati took the clothespins from her mouth when someone she knew passed by and conversed in Hungarian or Romanian, depending.

"She's come to us from Sibiu. Ilie's sister's child, rest her soul," said Kati, stirring the air with the sign of the cross. The postman straddling his bicycle tipped his cap, but she didn't look up. She was cracking the frozen puddles with her shoe heel. "She's a bit withdrawn," Kati hastened to add. "It's understandable."

Kati took the letter he was handing her, her eyes fixing on the Hungarian stamp.

The postman's squeaky wheels grew fainter down the road.

György's letter confirmed what she'd overheard in the market about the organization of a ghetto in Szeged and mass deportations now that the Germans had occupied Hungary. György said that it wasn't possible to travel inside the ghetto confine and the only tram went through without stopping, all the windows painted. He had lost contact with the child's mother.

She stuffed the letter into her apron pocket and looked over at Anca. What had György been thinking? She couldn't imagine it. Her brother György had been the youngest of three (the oldest had died as a result of a farm accident). Their mother had always babied György. He had been everyone's favorite. Kati had envied him, because he'd gone to college and was successful in business, but she didn't envy him anymore.

The child was here to stay, wasn't she? Although this pos-sibility was implicit to begin with, given György's marriage, she felt the weight of it and caught her breath.

Anca had stamped the broken ice into dust by now, the calf muscle bulging in her skinny leg, surpising determination on her face. She was a pretty girl. Everyone could see how pretty she was. She had gained a couple of kilos over the weeks. Maybe she would have the Tóth shoulders.

She waved Anca away from the ice like she was shooing the chickens.

There was to be a wedding in the village, and Auntie Kati knew the family. Uncle would be on border duty, but Auntie had no choice but to accept an invitation, and to bring Anca. The mother of the bride worked in an outlying factory and rode by the garden gate every day. She had stopped to confide her troubles over her pregnant daughter and had met the "orphaned niece," declaring her an unexpected blessing that had befallen Uncle and Auntie. Over several evenings preceding the wed-ding, Auntie Kati went to lend a hand plucking chickens and rolling noodles. It was to be a big party—guests coming from other villages. "You will not be the only stranger, fortunately."

The wooden church sat perched on a hillside, the after-noon sun casting a shadow of the steeple on the green grass. A crowd was gathering. The weather was fresh and it had been a long time since the last wedding in the village. Women carried cakes for the party—flourless, honey-sweetened cakes, precious and lovingly decorated, whose presence transformed the walk to the church into a parade. The bride and wedding party brought up the rear. The young woman was dressed in traditional bridal dress, elaborately embroidered in bright colors. The same flower motif was repeated in the headdress, and symbolic strands of wheat were woven in.

The bride was a homely, chubby girl, her cheeks pocked with pimples. Long ago, when Anca was still Éva, she would have objected, her sensibilities offended by the unattractive bride, but she had only the faintest inkling of this at the moment. Standing on the roadside with Auntie watching the procession, she felt only goodwill for the couple. She was grateful to be out of the house and in a crowd of people, a part of something. She had never been to a wedding.

The bridal group and their invited guests went up the steps of the wooden church while the rest of the crowd, practically the entire village, milled about in the churchyard awaiting the party. She was pleased to be going inside with Auntie. She held Auntie's hand and climbed the steps. The church interior was disappointingly spare, but there was a large candelabrum burning in the center of the wooden altar. She sat down next to Auntie in one of the rear pews. Her eyes lifted from the candles to the large wooden crucifix suspended from the rafters. She stared in horror at the plaster figure, the hands and feet driven through with nails. It seemed very strange that the wedding ceremony should take place underneath that swinging cross but nobody else seemed to think so. She looked around questioningly at the faces in the church.

The groom was just a boy in a soldier's uniform. He also had a pimply face. The priest said the blessings. After a few jabs of Auntie's finger she sat still through the entire ceremony. Only when she thought about it was she aware of a change in herself: Anca was different than Éva. Anca was not so demanding. She recalled how she used to recoil at the sight of the warm milk or yogurt that Auntie set out for her each morning, but now she ate her breakfast with gusto. She delighted in the bride and groom kissing.

The church bell had disappeared at the outset of the war, but someone struck a chord on a violin when the couple led the way out of the church, bound at the wrists with a ceremonial piece of cloth. Everyone made their way to the bride's uncle's house, the second house down from the church, and, with a salt cracker and shot of *pálinka* served, the party got under way. There was a roasting pig on a spit in the center of the yard. Gypsy music was playing on a phonograph. The crowd milled about. She was quickly absorbed in the festivities. Most everyone was speaking Hungarian and the air smelled of sweet pork. Someone handed her a stick and Auntie took it from her and skewered a little cube of bread from the basket, then nudged her over to the roasting pit.

"Here, catch the drips," said Auntie. She gulped, catching herself, and quickly said it again, in Romanian.

Auntie was in a state of high alert after her slip. She insisted they would leave shortly, but the cake hadn't even been served. Slices were just now being passed around, first to the children. Auntie couldn't deny her a piece of cake! She looked longingly at the plates gliding past. Then one stopped in front of her face.

"*Köszönöm szépen,*" she chirped without thinking, making the same mistake as Auntie. She glanced up at the woman serving her the cake.

The woman smiled, remarking to Auntie Kati, "She knows Hungarian."

Auntie looked stricken. "A little bit. 'Please' and 'thank you,'" she recovered quickly. The server moved on and Auntie shot a harsh glance at her, speaking through tight lips. "We leave directly after your cake."

She nodded quickly, trying not to shovel the cake into her mouth so quickly, gazing around at the other children at the wedding. She had not laid eyes on another child in a long while. She also had not tasted sweets. She was enveloped in the happy frenzy and didn't even notice Auntie Kati elbowing her to leave.

Auntie leaned in, meaningfully, "Anca, it's time to go."

She didn't want to leave! People had begun to dance the *csárdás*. The music galloped forward out of the big phonograph horn. She squirmed away from Auntie's sharp pinch. Auntie Kati looked around frantically, at a loss. Just then they heard a motorcycle engine over the music. She and Auntie turned to see Uncle roaring through the village on his motorbike, spewing mud, dogs giving chase. Recalling the imaginary gun he once held to her head, she got soberly to her feet and took Auntie's hand.

Uncle pumped the horn as he went by the party and people waved.

"His position at the border makes him a celebrity," someone said to Auntie.

"It's true, people depend on Ilie," Auntie said modestly.

As they walked away, Auntie loosened her hold. In a little while she began to hum the *csárdás*. She seemed to be in a good mood, despite the mistakes.

"Did you enjoy yourself?" Auntie asked.

"Yes, Auntie."

"'She takes after her uncle.' Did you hear everyone saying it about you?" Auntie looked pleased, the constant crossness in her face giving way to something softer, serene.

Really, her only likeness to her uncle was a darker complexion but it seemed to count for everything. Uncle Ilie was tall and hulking with beady eyes and a wiry black mustache. He was an eccentric with a hard heart, except when it came to his grapes, the sweetest in the village. Although he often ordered her around, he was more patient than Auntie. He discussed his grapes with her, calling on her to test and compare the varieties. She was tireless stomping the grapes for his wine. Even though he could be mean, she was at ease with Uncle. She always felt he didn't care where she came from, even if he acted as if she owed them. He paid no mind to her crippled hand during the meager cereal harvest, demanding she do her share in bundling the wheat in the fields, barking at her to pick up the pace before the crop spoiled.

The Russians were driving the Germans out of Romania. The war was ending, Auntie said, but it was no cause for celebration with Russian soldiers encamped on the edge of town. Even girls of her young age were sent to hide in the haystacks.

In the middle of the night, Uncle carried her out into the field wrapped in a blanket and tucked her in between the bales.

"Don't even sneeze," he warned her. "Understand?"

She cocked her thumb and forefinger, pointing to her temple.

He leaned in, kissing her forehead, and then he was gone until the next night.

It was a tense few days for all of Crisu. At night, she was warm and dry between the straw bales, but during the day she was sweltering. Braiding the straw required concentration she couldn't muster in the heat, right-handed. Her skin itched. It wasn't possible to sit up straight, so she lay curled up on the ground for endless hours. She closed her eyes and went inward.

There had been a storybook that her mother often read to her. She could see her mother's hands holding the book, the identical moons rising on each of her thumbnails. With a rush of blood, she heard the timbre of Mama's voice.

Once upon a time there lived a princess who possessed exceptional vision. She could see inside a mountain. To her, the stars were balls of fire, nothing was lost to her, and no one could hide from her.

She remembered suddenly a woodcut illustration of black boots. They were the swineherd's boots, bestowed on him by an eagle he meets along the journey to the palace. She opened her eyes and the boots went away. Still, she could hear her mother. She was saying to her, "Éva, soon you will have to be my clever swineherd." But she hated those boots. She was the princess!

Her mother's throat was wrapped in a towel because it was sore, and her hair was loose. She had waves of hair. It was when Mama no longer cared if Éva sat at the table for supper. She would tear pieces from what was left of yesterday's bread—the bread she used to feed the pigeons—and they would soften it in their glasses of tea. After supper Mama read to her.

"Éva, darling, the princess is haughty and proud."

She bobbed up and down on the couch, more buoyant with every declaration: "She can see down to the bottom of the sea! She can see inside the fish's mouth!"

"But the princess can't see herself. That's why she can't find the swineherd when he hides inside the rose of her corsage." Mama grabbed her tightly and looked intently down at her. "Don't you see, my darling? You must be resourceful like the swineherd, cultivating friends who will help you hide."

"I can be who I want to be!" Snatching the book up, flinging it clumsily.

She inhaled the hay and stared down at her maimed hand. It was not a dream, it was a memory. If she tried to make a fist with her hand she would feel sharp pain. She did it anyway. Her throat ached from wanting to cry. She consoled herself thinking how she'd gotten used to "Anca," and she was no longer afraid of Auntie or Uncle. They weren't ever unkind, really. She had grown accustomed to Auntie's barking like a farm dog. She wiped away a single tear.

In the growing dark she looked forward to Uncle's arrival. He would come to her with food and to apply an ointment for the rash that had broken out on her skin. Only once, in the few days that she hid, did she hear Russian, someone shouting along the road. Otherwise it was just the Gypsy sisters hiding in the haystack ten meters away. She tried to make out their mixed-up Romanian.

At Yalta, in 1945, Romania's fate was sealed in a handshake between Churchill and Stalin and the Iron Curtain was erected. At the border, everyone sat tight while the powers shifted and Transylvania was restored. During this time, another letter arrived from Szeged, enclosing Éva Farkas's Hungarian identification papers. György must have sent them but there was no note. Kati wasn't sure what to make of it and then, a week later, there was a telegram from György's wife reporting his suicide. Kati went to the post office and sent her condolences to Ildikó, whom she'd never liked.

It rained for days. By the end of the week she could bear Anca's restlessness no longer. The child was bouncing around the house. "Stop it!" she called from the seat of her potter's wheel. "Stop that hopping. I can't center the vase." Kati leaned over the wet clay. She had been wondering all week how to give Anca the news.

"Auntie, it's not raining!" she exclaimed, running to the window.

Kati stared past her. There were deep puddles in the road. She thought of the grove on the ridge. "We'll gather mushrooms," she said. "Get your coat."

A dank quiet had settled under the woodland trees. The mushrooms were plentiful, deep orange with white undersides, striated and velvety. Kati's fingers dug deftly down into the loamy earth, extracting the clump with its root.

"There's been a telegram," she said slowly, sitting back on her haunches, studying Anca. The girl's cheeks were pink from running the entire way, and the curls on her head shimmered with droplets of mist. She held out the burlap for the mushroom and Kati gently deposited it, sighing. She bolstered herself finally. "Your father, my brother György, has thrown himself in front of a train."

Anca looked blank.

"György Tóth," prompted Kati.

Anca asked, "Why?"

Kati paused, then reached out to embrace her. "His heart was broken." It was the truth, she was sure of it. "Your parents are both gone now, I'm afraid." Kati noticed Anca's crippled hand had begun to tremble. "Why is it doing that?" she whispered, feeling spooked. "Hide it, put it in your pocket!" She glanced around at the ghostly fog moving between the trees. She grabbed the burlap and got to her feet.

They walked back through the trees. At the edge of the grove, Kati told her she could run ahead if she liked. She didn't fly away like a dog let off its leash but kept on at Kati's side.

Despite the risk they presented, Kati never could bring herself to destroy the Hungarian papers. After all, György must have sent them to her for safekeeping. She tucked Éva Farkas's identification inside the Hungarian Bible she kept hidden under her mattress.

A week later Kati was in the garden crushing the blackened heads of sunflowers over a seed sifter.

"The sunflowers require two hands," she insisted, when Anca came outside and asked to help. She had too much energy for one small child. Sometimes Kati wished she would just disappear. "Go and pick Uncle's grapes," she suggested.

"They're not ripe yet, Auntie." She wandered off.

Out of the corner of her eye, Kati watched her petting the goat and scattering cornmeal for the hens. She played at tossing stones into an old wine crate. Then she dragged the crate over to the wall for a step stool and scrambled up the side, swinging a leg over.

"Be careful!" Kati called out.

She stood up on top of the wall and flapped her arms like wings. Kati bit her lip. She was not going to watch her hurt herself. She turned back to her work. The sunflowers' withered heads, gathered together and cinched with twine, disintegrated easily, leaving their hard seeds in Kati's fingers.

"Auntie, where is my mother?" She had seated herself now, dangling her feet. She looked down at Kati from a few meters away.

Kati paused and squared herself, a hand at her aching back. The sun was strong, dark crescents had appeared under her arms. Hadn't Anca understood in the forest the other day?

"It's time she came to fetch me," she persisted, legs swinging.

"This is your home now," Kati replied.

"Maybe Mama doesn't know where I am," she suggested, brow furrowing.

"Your mother's gone. All the Jews were killed," said Kati sharply, first in Romanian and then in Hungarian so that there could be no mistaking it. "And, now, György is gone, too. I told you already. They sent you to Crisu to keep you safe. There was no escaping—only for you." She felt frustrated for having to say it all over again. "You're a big girl. You must stop pretending." Kati walked around to the opposite side of the seed tray, turning her back and ignoring the tiny pebbles from the masonry that Anca pelted in her direction. When the pebbles ceased, Kati glanced curiously over her shoulder. Anca was on her feet again. She'd gone back to flapping her long arms and then holding them aloft on a current of wind.

Once upon a time, she had been known as Éva.

"Éva!"

She was inside the roses looking out, crouched beneath the canopy of brambles so that Péter couldn't find her. She was ignoring her mother's calls, determined not to give her hiding place away. Now she could see her mother descending the stair, her graceful profile and languid step, reaching back absently to untie her apron as she went.

"Go away Mama!" she hissed under her breath. Across the courtyard, Péter was searching between the drying racks. She felt tickled by his blindness.

Her mother's footsteps sounded on the courtyard bricks. Soon her face appeared, peeking under the thorns, her long rope of a braid swinging over one shoulder. "Éva, it's time to come inside."

Éva stuck out her tongue in reply. How did her mother always know exactly where to find her? Just then, Péter came running, hard leather soles slapping the cobbles, and Éva shrieked at having been found out. She slipped through her secret hole in the brambles and darted off. Péter gave chase but Éva was the princess, faster, more powerful. She snatched her mother's apron on her way and ran with it billowing. Her mischievous laughter pealed through the courtyard, her heart-shaped face flushed with possibility.

Her mother shook her head in dismay. She wasn't strict enough. She was making a mistake in raising Éva without God. Eszter Farkas was twenty-five years old, a girl herself. She sighed, turning resignedly for the stairs.

Soon Éva was charging up from behind. "Here I am, Mama! See? I'm coming!" Éva flung her arms around her, pressing her moist face into her skirt. "I love you, Mama!"

"I love you, too," she said, gently unwrapping herself. "But next time, come when I call you."

"I couldn't help it!" She glanced back at Péter, who had turned to bouncing a ball.

"Oh? Why is that?" Eszter held out her hand and Éva grasped it. They took the last steps together.

"Because I was the princess and I was hiding," Éva said.

"It's the swineherd who hides from the princess, Éva."

"But that's not the way I play it!" Éva retorted.

"Well, be yourself now," she sighed. "Your father will have dinner with us."

György Tóth was almost twenty years older than Eszter, a married man, already the father of two grown children. She had met him at the tennis club where her mother was an instructor. When she was barred from entering university, she wasn't too proud to accept a job in his coat factory. Within a year she was pregnant with his child. Her parents shunned her. György had secured this rental for her on the city outskirts, a neighborhood of working-class houses where few Jews resided.

Eszter had laid the table and swept the floors. She was in the bedroom pulling on stockings when Éva came from washing her hands and face. She ushered her onto the step stool.

"Do the buttons for me, Dovey?" She owned two evening dresses, both gifts from György, for wearing when he visited. She held her breath as Éva's little fingers climbed the line of buttons up the back. The Germans were demanding reorganization. She had read it in the newspaper that morning. She breathed in her anxiety.

"Did the zipper bite you, Mama?" Éva quickly asked.

"Oh, no. I'm yawning, a little tired, that's all."

Éva stepped down from the stool and stood biting her fingernails.

Eszter smiled at her. "Now, sit while I comb your hair for you?"

She jumped backward, out of reach, hoping to incite a chase.

Eszter brought the wooden comb, seating herself on the edge of the bed. "Come," she said brightly. "I'll tell you the story of 'The Princess Who Saw Everything.'"

She was compliant suddenly, swiveling around, presenting what was left of the morning braid. Eszter recounted the tale from memory. She had read it to Éva countless times. She studied the wooden comb on its downard press through the thick forest of her daughter's curls.

*   *   *

György Tóth had a special knock—one rap, then two quickly; her mother was always right there to answer it. Éva looked on from the living room. Her hair neatly braided, she sat cross-legged on the bare floor. She had been playing with paper dolls. Her mother was helping György Tóth out of his coat, going up on her toes to remove his hat. György Tóth was tall with a barrel chest. He was an old man, Éva felt. He put his hands on each of her mother's shoulders and pulled her to him. His head turned, he had a view through the door, their eyes met. "Good day!" he called in to her.

György Tóth brought them things. There were banknotes and extra rations in a sealed envelope and for Éva a box of chocolate-covered cherries. First she would have to sit politely through the lunch. Her mother called her into the kitchen. She had tied a clean apron around her waist and was ladling the soup into bowls. György was seated at the table, in Éva's usual chair. Éva sat down on the sewing stool waiting for her. It lifted her higher than she was used to. She swung her legs and watched the steam rising from her bowl. They talked in earnest over her head.

"The police came again today," György was saying.

"Yes, everyone on the floor was talking."

"They'll shut the factory down if I don't proceed with the layoff. It's the law now."

Her mother set down her spoon and was up, fluttering again, cutting him another slice of bread. She glanced at Éva. "Drink the soup, darling."

"I'll bring you a sewing machine. You can do the work right here," György suggested. He had rolled up his sleeves. He pulled her mother over to him before she could sit down again. She stood in his arms and kissed him solemnly on the head.

"I wouldn't have to pay Mrs. Somogyi to look after Éva anymore," she considered. "I think she'll be relieved. Éva doesn't mind for her."

"Éva doesn't mind for anybody, it sounds like," quipped György.

Éva could feel György's eyes bearing down on her. She was minding right now, in case he hadn't noticed! She drained her spoon noisily. Still, she brightened at the thought of not having to stay with Péter's mother during the day. Éva hadn't been allowed to go to preschool like Péter because she was a Jew. She was a Jew because her mother was one and that was all she knew about it.

"Mama, may I have my chocolates now?" she asked quietly. Her mother ignored her.

"It's a question of the Kállay regime having any actual power of resistance," György said doubtfully.

Underneath the table, Éva tapped her mother's calf with her toe and again, kicking pointedly. Her mother reached distractedly for the box of chocolates and set it down in front of Éva.

Each one was hand-dipped, a budding breast concealed in gold paper. There were six pieces in all. She selected one and carefully unwrapped it and popped it into her mouth. She sucked the softening chocolate with delight and the cherry flavor spilled out. With her finger she smoothed the golden wrapper, rubbing it to a uniform shine.

Her mother began to clear the table. Their talk had turned
to what was available in the shops. When her mother reached
for György's bowl he pulled her in again. His thick arms wrapped
around her. Éva glanced over at them. Her mother was often
telling Éva that she was getting too big to sit on her lap, but
Mama was seated sideways on György. She leaned into him,
her head resting on his shoulder, her own braid hanging down.
He fingered the bow she had tied at the tassle. They were
quiet, lost in thought together, and didn't notice her reaching
for chocolate after chocolate, devouring the box. She'd have six
golden squares for cutting out later.

That night, lying awake with her stomachache, she listened
to the music they were playing on the radio. In a little while,
inside the waltzing piano, she heard the sofa frame creak, her
mother's moans through the closed door filling her with interest.
In the early hours of the morning, Éva climbed into bed with
them. György's chest was a mountain; she watched it swell and
give way. She felt he was not so impressive with his eyes closed.
Her mother rolled over in the sheets, making room for Éva. It
was warm and lovely lying in her imprint.

Eszter owned a custom left-hand pair of scissors, proper textile
shears that shone like nothing else in the house. Worn down by
Éva's begging, she let her use them for cutting out paper dolls.
She had to admit, she possessed unusual dexterity for such a
young child. It was remarkable how she could wield the scissors.
She would sit for long periods scissoring and it was a welcome
break from her usual restlessness. Eszter was often at a loss as

to how to keep her occupied. She couldn't let her go outside
alone. Eventually, she sewed a fabric ball that she could play with
indoors. Éva took to batting the ball into the air, bouncing it off
the walls or off the palm of her hand, trying to keep it aloft. Eszter
paused at the sewing machine and looked on in amusement. If
she could just bottle some of Éva's energy, she would have a sip
every afternoon when the sun was going down. It was dark so
early now. She would trade cooking oil for extra rations of daylight.

After lunch they usually went outside into the courtyard
for the fresh air. Bundled in her hat and muffler, Eszter stood
beside the barren rose brambles scattering a handful of bread
crumbs for the pigeons that nested under Mrs. Somogyi's roof,
while Éva ran around refusing to put her arms into the sleeves
of her tattered coat, despite the cold.

"It's too small for me, Mama! I've turned it into a princess's
cape."

Wearing only the hood, she ran so that the coat blew
out behind her, and when she veered too close Eszter wailed,
"No, Éva!," in protest, as all the pigeons fluttered back up to
the roof.

György was still coming to the house once a week, Tuesday
evenings usually, but by April 1943 they had grown silent at the
dinner table. György refused any food. One time, tiring of her
insistant offering, he stood up from the chair and scraped the
plate back into the pot himself. He had taken up smoking. They
listened to the radio for purposes of news only, too preoccupied
for the Czech piano masterpieces that aired late at night.

Eszter set aside the wool coat cuffs she was stitching. She had taken to biting her lip, tearing at the chapped skin. She turned to Éva, who was bouncing the ball off the wall, and announced, "I'm going to buy some special crackers for a soup. It's a long way. We'll ride on the tram. Hurry, get your coat."

She was preoccupied, staring out the window of the tram car as the streets became familiar, Éva tugging her sleeve. "Why is it such a long way to buy crackers, Mama?"

She looked down at Éva. She had forgotten to comb out her hair. She reached out, smoothing back her curls. "These are special crackers," she said.

Éva looked impressed.

Eszter added, "I'll make a delicious soup if you behave yourself."

They entered through the back of the building. The line of people extended through the sanctuary, down the staircase to the basement, where the matzoh was being distributed. There were no lights on, but the waning daylight made it possible to view the building's magnificent interior. As hoped, Éva was perfectly silent, in awe, staring up at the domed ceiling. Eszter eyed the door every time it opened and someone new slipped inside. It was dangerous to be here—the restriction of Jews in Szeged included a prohibition against going to synagogue—but she harbored a secret hope that her father might turn up, that he would see her there with her child who looked just like her, that his heart would go out to them. An image flashed of her parents preparing the Seder, a tablecloth unfurling, the rippling flesh of her mother's arms.

Possibly, her parents had already gotten out—but her father was a gymnasium history teacher, her mother a tennis instructor; they didn't possess the means. They had been counting on Eszter to take care of them through a marriage they'd arranged. Her refusal was the first time she'd ever crossed them. Then she'd gone to work sewing coats.

Once she had advanced to the head of the line at the bottom of the basement steps, and bought the matzoh, it didn't seem reasonable to linger any longer, given the risk it was and the curfew. Eszter had overheard people in line whispering of a massacre—Jews and Serbs, by Hungarian soldiers in one of the annexed territories. She squeezed Éva's hand tightly. They went out the way they'd come in, through the rear door.

Her mother was in a hurry now. Éva trotted to keep up. They were rounding the corner of the building when two men stepped out from under the yew trees. They wore uniforms like policemen, or soliders, and they had armbands.

"Show your papers! Identify yourself!"

Her mother stopped short, clutching Éva to her. She rifled inside her coat but, in her effort to keep the matzoh concealed, dropped their identification. Éva lunged for the papers on the ground, but one of the soldiers sprang at her, stamping her hand down under his boot. He kept her fingers pinned and she cried out.

"Hush, darling!" Mama admonished.

Éva bit her lip, flashing astonished tears. She was filled with rage. She groped for the identification papers with her free hand, twisting herself around and pushing the papers at the second soldier.

"What a clever girl!" he sneered, snatching the papers.

The first one ground his heel down harder. Éva went white from the pain. She hung her head, whimpering.

"Please," her mother whispered, trembling, "release my daughter."

"She's a bastard Jew," the second one reported, flinging the identification.

The first one struck Éva across the face with the back of his hand without lifting his boot. The force knocked her down.

"Please!" her mother pressed. She was hurriedly unbuttoning her coat, letting the matzoh drop out. "Release her," Mama whispered, gathering up her skirt revealingly. "Take me."

The officer lifted his boot.

"Go," she hissed, yanking Éva to her feet. "Go now!"

Of course there was nowhere Éva knew to go. She stumbled into the shadows and hid behind a tree as they shoved her mother to the ground. Only Mama's elbows inside the coat sleeves were visible, and her splayed legs in the torn stockings. She made no sound. It was just a few minutes and then the second one turned her mother over roughly and climbed on top of her, baring horrific gray buttocks. Her mother let out a small wail and it scorched Éva's ears.

The men had gone. She stepped out cautiously from behind the tree. She gathered up their papers and her mother's crackers with her uninjured hand. She hurried to her side.

"Mama?"

She was sitting up. There were pine needles in her hair and dirt on her face. She was breathing hard. She reached for Éva's injured fingers, cradling them gently, kissing them with bloodied lips. She struggled to get to her feet. Éva handed her the matzoh. She tucked it back inside her coat with the papers. She took Éva's good hand in hers and they continued down the street.

The Jewish doctor she had taken Éva to on occasion was no longer employed by the hospital and no other doctor had time for them. Mrs. Somogyi brought up herbs for a poultice and a bottle of *pálinka*. Eszter uncorked the bottle, forcing a spoonful on Éva. She yowled in protest, but in a little while she was dozing off against the cushions.

Mrs. Somogyi finished placing the poultice and was collecting her things to go. She turned to Eszter: "What will you do? It isn't safe for her here anymore."

Eszter shook her head doubtfully. She wouldn't risk confiding in Mrs. Somogyi, even though she was kind to them. After the landlady had gone, she collapsed against the door for a few minutes. She went to her sewing table and thumbed through the meters of heavy fabric. Éva would need a good coat for her journey. She was sound asleep, cheeks flushed from the *pálinka*. Eszter crept close to take her measurements.

When Éva awoke, on the couch, it was black out the windows and she was still wearing the smock she'd worn to get the crackers. The lantern was burning. Her mother appeared, imploring with a bowl of soup. She'd formed the crackers into balls. Éva frowned at the soup.

"Darling, shall I bring you something else to eat?"

Éva didn't respond. She stared at her bloated hand. It throbbed. Her eyes welled up with tears.

"Is it terribly painful?" her mother asked her.

She hid her anguish in the cushion.

When he arrived, György Tóth took one look at Éva's hand and left the house again in a hurry, returning an hour later with a nurse from the city hospital. Under the gas lamp in the kitchen, Éva sat on her mother's lap while the gray-haired nurse examined her fingers.

"All fractured, likely," the nurse said in a dispassionate voice, looking over the thick rims of her eyeglasses at Éva. "Except for your thumb, which appears to be only badly bruised."

The nurse impressed her in her hospital uniform. She had brought along materials for a splint. As the nurse uncurled the fingers to fit them, Éva felt shooting pain and cried out. Her mother whispered in her ear, "Dove, be brave!"

She didn't like to be called anything but Éva and she was already being brave. Her mother should know it. She began to kick and squirm on her lap.

"I can't do my work," the nurse remarked.

"Here," György ordered. "Let me hold her." He took Éva in his arms.

She sat stiffly, forcibly locked up, pitiful tears rolling down.

"She's spirited," the nurse said as she finished taping. "Mind that she keeps the splint on."

*   *   *

György drove the nurse back to the hospital and Eszter put Éva to bed. She was at the sink washing dishes when György returned. She dried her hands in the skirt of her apron and set a place for him.

"What happened?" he asked cautiously.

She swallowed, struggling to compose herself. "We were accosted by Arrow Cross outside the synagogue."

"What?" György looked sternly at her. "What were you thinking going there?"

"I don't know," she admitted, shaking her head remorsefully. "Passover."

Guilt seeped from under Eszter's skin. Perhaps her sudden longing for her parents, the reason she'd ventured to the synagogue, was tied to her own deepening vulnerability. Still, she would never say so, not to György. She couldn't distract him from planning for Éva's escape. This was already under way. She stepped back and rolled up each of his sleeves for him, lingering to hold his large hands in hers, her eyes lifting. "Sit, eat something," she said. "Please."

György looked at the matzoh balls in the bowl.

She seated herself beside him, their knees touching. "Have you written to your sister?"

He nodded. He looked her over as he ate. He set down the spoon, reaching to finger the marks at her neck. "Did they hurt you, too?"

She shook her head, averting his gaze.

They heard Éva cry out from the bedroom. She erupted into screams. They hurried in to find her twisting and turning in the blanket, still asleep. "Bring a damp towel, György, please," Eszter said. She gathered Éva up in her arms, pulling her onto her lap.

György returned. He bent down on one knee, putting the compress to her cheeks. Eszter watched his big hand gently mopping Éva's brow.

Gradually, she quieted. Eszter moved to resettle her on the bed.

"Mama, did the soldiers hurt you?" Éva spoke up.

Eszter glanced fleetingly at György. "They weren't soldiers," György grumbled.

"Oh, Éva," she sighed. Leaning in, peering at her intently in the darkness, she shook her head firmly. "No. Never."

"Well, they hurt me," Éva said, in a small voice.

"I'm sorry," Eszter began, stammering. "I'm sorry my darling. I couldn't help you. I thought he would shoot us."

"Why Mama?"

"Because we're Jews." She buried her nose in Éva's hair and breathed in deeply.

"Is *he* a Jew?" Éva asked.

"Who?" She lifted her head.

"Him," said Éva, lifting her broken hand to gesture at György across the room. They both looked over at him sitting by the window smoking.

"No," Eszter sighed, "he's your father. He loves you."

On Easter Monday, Péter came shyly upstairs to sprinkle Éva with water according to the tradition, and as soon as Éva saw him she slid off the couch and chased him around the house as if nothing had happened. Later on, when they were playing with Péter's leaden soldiers, and she had to use her left hand, Péter asked her if her hand hurt her when she fell down the stairs, and she looked at him blankly. After a minute, she shook her head, acting natural. Péter was so easily fooled.

Strangely, she was in a good humor around Péter, while her face fell still as soon as her mother appeared in the doorway.

"I'll shoot you!" Éva barked, marching her soldier over to Péter's. It was strange to have to use her right hand. The injured fingers of her left hand she cradled in her lap, so that her mother, still looking in, couldn't see she'd taken off the splint again. It bothered her to wear it although it wasn't exactly painful. She'd become an expert at biting off the bandaging. Mama would come across the splint stuffed between the couch cushions.

Éva was adapting, right-handed. She could get herself dressed in the morning, except for buttons, which exhausted her. But it was disorienting to do without her left. There was so much she couldn't imagine ever doing again—like batting the ball, to say nothing of scissoring.

On weekdays, when Péter was at school, Éva hovered while her mother cut fabric at the dining room table. She was madly in love with the even run of the blades, the glitter of sharp edges. She had always impressed Péter with her clever cutouts. She frowned at her mother, who seemed unaware, distracted, suffering from a bad chest cold all of a sudden, despite the warmer weather.

"Mama! I was the scissor master," she shouted in frustration. "Remember how I was the scissor master? You said so!" She felt so sorry for herself.

Her mother was coughing, doubled over into her handkerchief, her face gone red from the pressure. Her eyes were
ringed with sleeplessness. Reaching out, she smoothed Éva's
curls behind her ear and bent down to look her in the face. "Your
fingers will heal, Éva." Her hug was too fierce to be encouraging. She went back to cutting the fabric. "Anyway," she added,
"you'll need to use your right hand for school."

Éva glowered. She stared hatefully at her mute hand in its
newly wrapped splint. Her mother's willingness to see a bright
side felt like betrayal.

Péter came upstairs to play one afternoon, wearing good shoes
and carrying a marvelous leather satchel. It was the start of the
new school year. He was in a proper elementary school now.
He proudly showed off the contents of his satchel—a school
primer along with two pencils, a ruler, and a child's pair of scissors, which Éva promptly grabbed despite his protests. She had
never seen scissors so small and was delighted to find that her
right hand could manipulate them. But there was nothing to cut
since Péter staunchly refused her the primer paper. She looked
around. György's old newspapers were now used for kindling.

Éva stared thoughtfully at Péter. Taking up the scissors, she
climbed up behind him on the bed, perched on her knees. "Your
hair is very shaggy. It'll please your mother to have it trimmed."

"No, it won't," said Péter.

Éva eyed his gold locks keenly. "Please, Péter? It'll make
you look like a kindergarten boy. I promise it will, Péter." She
smiled at him.

"How do you know it will?" he asked.

"Because right now it's too shaggy for a real kindergarten boy." She pressed her hands down on his shoulders and he sat for her.

"Don't hurt me," he cautioned.

"I won't hurt you!" She kissed him on the head the way her mother kissed her when she was being silly. "I would never hurt you, Péter." She began to snip. It felt delicious to see his glossy waves falling. She had to concentrate in order to operate the scissors effectively. Her injured hand kept quivering and lifting involuntarily. She found she could scoop up the hair on the edge of the splint, and then get her right hand to make the cut. Her effort was fueled by a dark fascination with the irreversibility of the act, a tremendous feeling in her.

"Are you done yet?" Péter asked.

"Almost," she told him.

Péter glanced at all the hair on the floor.

"Done!" said Éva, cutting out one last thick tuft. She knew at once that she had done something terrible.

Péter whirled around. "Do I look like a kindergartener now?"

Éva stared, nodding.

Mama's shriek at the sight of Péter was confirming. A strange calm washed over Éva. Her mother marched into the room, collecting the scissors and Péter's satchel. She took Péter home and when she returned she gave Éva a swift spanking.

That evening, when György came, Éva waited for her mother to tell him what she'd done. But her mother didn't mention the haircut. György had brought a bottle of cough syrup and was administering a spoonful to her. "Thank you," she said hoarsely, wiping her lips with a handkerchief. She sat in the chair and he stood over her with the cough syrup bottle and a spoon. He leaned in to kiss her, lingering. Éva noticed that her mother was not wearing the purple or the green dress, just her everyday blouse with the faded cherries. She was struck with sharp remorse. She walked quietly from the room, feeling ashamed, intrusive. She climbed into bed. Light from the doorway shone directly in and she could see some of Péter's hairs still on the blanket. She lay very still, thinking they'd soon come in to say good night to her. She could hear them discussing train schedules as she drifted off.

1947

UNCLE ILIE'S MOTHER ARRIVED IN CRISU by train, with a large steamer trunk and a miniature dachshund puppy she called Carol, after the former Romanian king. Uncle's mother was as tall as Uncle, with the same receding hairline and the same sparkling dark eyes, but somehow her gaze radiated generosity. She bent all the way down to be at eye level when she introduced herself.

"I hope you will call me Bunica," she said, extending her hand.

"I am Anca," she replied, pleased to have a granny.

Buni's skin was silky, loose with age like a pudding, and cool to touch even in summertime. Anca stroked the soft underside of Bunica's arm with the back of her curled hand. By now she was right-handed, except when it came to unconscious caresses.

Buni said how lonely she'd been. For six years now she'd worn widow's black. She lifted the lid of her steamer trunk, releasing a fragrance of herbal sachets, and seemed delighted by Anca's curiosity. On the inside of the trunk lid hung a small mirror with tiny red flowers painted along the edges so that the reflection appeared encircled in garland. Anca had not seen herself in a mirror since she'd arrived in Crisu and spent long moments staring.

The steamer housed Bunica's worldly belongings, fastidiously arranged. One side was for clothing, crisply folded, undergarments at the top. The other side contained personal effects. All the letters that she had ever received were saved in their envelopes and the small stack was packaged with twine. There was also a photograph of Kati and Ilie on their wedding day. The photo amazed Anca. They were so young, a handsome couple. Nothing like they were now. Buni would cluck her tongue, regretfully, tucking the photo back inside her lacquered jewel box. The jewel box had a clever hinge that held the cover open in midair. Besides the wedding photo, she kept her garnet brooch inside the jewel box and her husband's wedding band, which she said she was proud of never having pawned.

Also inside the steamer was all the money Bunica had had in her possession when the monetary reform was carried out by the Communist authorities. No matter how much one had in the bank, the amount was supplanted by the same small sum, which the state issued to everyone. The old money had no value against the new. This was done to depose the former middle and upper classes and to prepare for collectivization.

Uncle's mother often talked nostalgically of her village, and on occasion she steeped herself in melancholy. The only thing that snapped her out of it was Carol. Anca would deposit the puppy in Buni's lap and get the horsehair brush and the plaid ribbon she liked to tie on the dog's tail. The dog was high-strung and untrained. "Spoiled rotten," Auntie criticized. Auntie Kati was infuriated by Carol's frequent yapping and mad dashing around the house as if someone had lit his tail on fire, but Anca delighted in Carol's behavior. With the dog about the house, Anca was no longer the focus of Auntie's complaints. Whenever Uncle joined Auntie in admonishing the dog—with a kick of his foot in the dog's direction—Buni would scream in protest. "I'll tie that mutt's tail around its neck," Uncle said, and Anca put her hands protectively over Carol's velvet ears.

Bunica kept several books at the bottom of her trunk: she called them "romances" but they were actually volumes of Mihai Eminescu's poetry. She also had a magnifying glass in a cracked pigskin case, which Anca was not allowed to play with because Bunica needed it for reading. Uncle's mother had been a bookkeeper before her eyesight failed. She held the magnifying glass up and Anca stared at the large brown pool of Bunica's eye enclosing a shining iris. The eye went this way, then that, down the page.

Bunica blinked, looking over at her. "Maybe you like romance?"

Anca nodded eagerly. Bunica cleared her throat and read the verses aloud. It had been so long since anyone had read to her! Her eyes glistened with tears.

Bunica looked over her rims. "Turn the page for me, darling," she whispered softly. "We'll read another, if you like." Bunica waited patiently on her awkward hand. "Your other hand,

Anca, what happened to it?" Buni often asked this, as if the answer might change.

"I was born this way," Anca replied.

Bunica became Anca's advocate. She pressed for her school enrollment, which Auntie had postponed beyond reason. Over the summer, Bunica sewed the student uniform and, once school began, she defended Anca's unruly hair against Kati's combing. The white elementary school headband was hardly enough to control all of her curls, complained Auntie. Bunica herself was balding and blamed the tight braids her mother had forced on her throughout her childhood.

"A wild ocean of hair is worth something," she declared, looking at Anca fondly. "Someday you can sell it to a wig maker in Bucharest, make yourself a fortune!"

Auntie threw up her hands. Anca glared defiantly at Auntie from the safety of Buni's lap. She begged Bunica to be the one to walk her to the train. Bunica kissed her nose and cheeks. She waved good-bye until her hand turned into a bird and fluttered away. "I longed for you as the dove longs for wheat," Bunica would tell her later, when she returned. "Show me what you learned today." Unlike her schoolteachers, Buni never complained that Anca transposed her letters and wrote words backward, as if inside a mirror.

Bunica had lived all her life in Savarsin, where the Romanian royal family once had a summer palace. But King Michael was forced to abdicate and the palace was turned over to the local Communist party. The royal presence had been good for the village, Bunica explained. The palace, built in the early days of King Carol, employed a large number of people and the village had an up-to-date sewage system and well-stocked shops. Whenever the king had parties, the village women went near the palace to sew, since the light coming out through the windows came from a generator and was brilliant compared to that of an oil lamp. The king didn't worry that the townsfolk might spoil the scenery for his guests.

"Michael was tolerant, magnanimous," Bunica said. Uncle belched rudely whenever she reminisced about the king. Uncle did not share his mother's regard for the royal family, blaming Carol II for "tying Romania's hands" such that the alliance with Germany had become inevitable. But Carol II was not to blame for England's and France's disregard of Romania, argued Buni, her cheeks flushed. Besides, Romania had King Michael to thank for the coup, which had ended Antonescu's reign and the alliance with Hitler. Of course, King Michael received little credit for this bravery, so quick was the Soviet machine in setting up a Communist government. With Soviet tanks surrounding the palace, the young king had had no choice but to abdicate. Bunica always said her heart went out to the queen mother and to King Michael and his new wife, who had been forced to leave Romania, like migrant geese, with only the clothes they were wearing. She always put an end to the debate, calling Uncle an ingrate, for the king's washing and ironing had been the family's livelihood.

Bunica insisted that Anca attend services with her at the Romanian church rather than at the Catholic church with Kati.

Anca preferred the darkly royal atmosphere of Bunica's church anyway. The priest wore a tall crown and on the walls there were icons with gold leaf and grim, childlike oil paintings with the holy figure depicted ten times as large as the crowds of ordinary mortals. At both churches people were solemn, and at Bunica's church most everyone dressed in black, in honor of the dead. The Romanian church felt haunted. Since the war, everyone was mourning someone. There were so many candles and glowing faces. And there were always *cozonac*, sweet, rolls to eat. At home, on the anniversary of her husband's death, Bunica cooked *coliva* with rum-soaked raisins. She and Anca ate bowl after bowl, as it was meant for the needy, the very old, and the very young and Auntie and Uncle, in middle age, did not qualify.

Bunica was a good cook and fond of food. In the summer, she requested that Ilie plant eggplant and celery root in the garden. Late in the year she made sausage from Uncle's nutria, his latest smuggling venture. She claimed the meat was high in protein and good for her heart. Uncle had to call for the butcher because he couldn't bear to slaughter the nutria himself. He sat in the frozen yard drinking wine from a shot glass. He was in a mood for several days afterward and wouldn't touch the sausage, though he did sell the pelts. All furs had value. As for the meat, it was extremely lean; no soap was needed for the washing up afterward. Anca was amazed at how her hands quickly rinsed clean. Pig she would feel on her fingers for days.

Uncle kept his nutria in a brick cage that he had built, complete with a tunnel and a swimming hole—they were water rats, after all. The cage had a wire top that could be lifted up to throw in table scraps. Once, a nutria escaped the cage and scrambled out of the yard. Uncle offered a reward for its return. Villagers cornered the animal in a barn, where it kept trying to burrow into the wall, clawing noisily. It was larger than a rabbit, beady-eyed though nearly blind, with sharp orange teeth. Everyone was too frightened to pick it up and it succeeded in wriggling through a hole in the barn wall, disappearing into the cornfield.

The next day when Uncle was at work and Kati was at the baker's there was a knock at the door. Bunica and Anca were stuffing cabbage for lunch, Romanian-style: bite-sized stuffed cabbages that required skill to roll, as opposed to their bulkier Hungarian counterparts, at which Bunica turned up her nose. Bunica wiped her hands on her apron and Anca went and sat in the pantry, which had been her training and was now her habit whenever someone unexpectedly came calling.

The Gypsy boy Crin stood barefoot on the back step, a cigarette butt tucked behind his ear. He wielded the lost nutria by the tail. He was demanding payment. Anca heard Bunica speaking harshly to him. She poked her head out. "Uncle promised a reward," she reminded her. Bunica glared. She looked fierce, charged with anger, and Anca retreated back inside the pantry, her heart pounding in surprise.

Bunica went outside, the screen door slamming behind her. She dropped a coin into Crin's outstretched hand. "Stinking Gypsy," she said, after he'd deposited the nutria in the cage. "Get out, now. I'll sic the dog on you."

Anca emerged from the pantry on quiet feet. Bunica came back in, her face rapidly draining of hatred, leveling off. She took up the wooden spoon and the freshly mixed bowl of filling.

She spooned it onto the cabbage leaf, rolling it swiftly. Anca set it on the baking sheet.

Anca could never admit that Crin was her friend because he was a worthless Gypsy. Bunica was always saying that different kinds were not meant to mix, look at what fruitlessness it had meant for Ilie and Kati.

But it was everything strange and different about Crin that interested Anca—his brown arms, slick black curls, and eyelashes that looked wet. Crin's family had taken up residency in the abandoned stucco farmhouse on the opposite side of the meadow, making their hearth on the floor inside, burning the old fence posts and furniture. Crin was bold, barefoot, impervious—irresistible to her. One evening, she spied him from the bedroom window stealing Uncle's grapes. She crept outside and tiptoed up behind, poking him in the back. She hissed, "My uncle will shoot you."

Crin stared at her. "You won't tell on me," he said.

She meant to disagree, but her tongue stuck in her throat, meeting his mischievous eyes. He pressed his smiling face close to hers, offering her a grape from between his teeth, and she took it from him, their lips pressing purposefully together for a moment. It was a late September grape, the sweet of it reaching to her toes.

"You are Gypsy, too," said Crin.

She shook her head no.

He pressed his arm against hers, and together they stared at their similar coloring.

Just then, the back door opened and Auntie called out. Crin was gone, up and over the garden wall. She lay awake whispering his name. Crin. A crazy Gypsy name. Elegant, powerfully fragrant: lily. She knew she shouldn't care about him.

The following Christmas a pig was stolen in the village, and when the townspeople smelled the smoking sausage coming from the Gypsy farmhouse suspicion and prejudice were aroused.

That New Year's Eve, Anca was awakened by distant shouting. Bunica was asleep in her bed opposite the stove, but Carol sat alert at the foot of the mattress, his nose to the window. She hushed his whining. Looking out, she saw Auntie on the porch in her nightdress, a coat over her shoulders. She pushed open the door and stepped out into the frigid dawn.

The air was tinged with smoke. She began to cough. Auntie ushered her close and she stood enclosed in Auntie's coat. Soon they were both shivering.

"Auntie, what is it?" she kept asking.

Finally Kati lifted her so that she, too, could see across the frozen field to the burning farmhouse. "They're running the Gypsies out."

Afterward, people in the village, and Bunica at home, talked of how much safer they felt. A month later another pig was stolen. For a long time after, the wind would bring the ash across the field.

1952

BUNICA CONTINUED TO DEDICATE herself to Anca's unruly, chesnut-colored hair. The white headband had been replaced by red ribbons, which Bunica tied atop each ponytail before school. Bunica said that the red suited Anca's coloring and she could thank the Communists. Bunica was always irreverent. She refused to feel threatened by the Stalinist cultural regime, which had by now reached the villages.

Each year, since she'd entered the Communist youth group, Anca was named best athlete for the girls. From a makeshift stage in the school cafeteria, she waved to Buni after receiving her medal. Buni, regal in the audience of grandmothers, didn't hide her pride. Still, she was often reminding, "God is more important than your membership in the Young Pioneers, Anca."

Bunica and Auntie Kati had found a little common ground under the threats of a regime that jailed priests and outlawed baptism. "They might dethrone the king but they will not dethrone the Almighty!" Buni would proclaim, going momentarily red in

the face. Across the room, in grave agreement, Auntie made the
sign of the cross with wet clay on her hands. Going to church
was an act of protest that Bunica never tired of. Anca had liked
to go with her but once she entered school the Communist
indoctrination had begun in earnest. Years of young pioneers
had influence. It was not possible to grow up any other way,
unless you were Gypsy.

That winter, 1952, Buni caught a cold that developed into pneumonia. She lay underneath the goose-feather quilt on Christmas
Eve, a rasping wheeze every time her chest heaved. Auntie was
cooking and Uncle was seated at the table drinking *palinka*,
his cheeks blazing after being out on his motorcycle all day,
searching for penicillin. The hospital wouldn't dispense any
medications without examining Buni, and she wasn't strong
enough to travel.

Anca peeled the damp cloth from Buni's forehead and set
it aside. She had been waiting all day for her to wake up. It was
black outside the windows now.

"Uncle, what time is it?"

Ilie took out his watch. "Four-thirty."

She looked sadly back at Buni. "I'll go to church for her,"
she announced. Carol jumped from her lap and shook himself
as she stood up from the chair.

Auntie Kati paused, setting down the paring knife. "Not
by yourself, Anca. I'll go with you."

"Auntie, there's no need. I know the way."

Uncle looked over. "Let her go. She'll be all right."

Anca pulled on her coat. Auntie Kati stepped forward to button it for her. "Light a candle," she said, pressing a coin into her hand. "Come straight home afterward."

"Yes, Auntie."

They kissed cheeks. Anca looked tentatively at Uncle. He had had the paper open to the same page all afternoon. She went and kissed him, his cheek quivering against hers.

She had never walked the road alone like this, at night. Buni's decline had forced her into independence. The night sky was clear, the first stars cut deep within it. She felt an ominous weight on her shoulders. Her throat burned from breathing in the frigid air. When she reached the church she entered at the back, which was the congregation's custom under Communism.

Inside the sanctuary, everyone was whispering about a truck full of bananas that was parked in the village. The bananas were going to be given out to children for Christmas! Anca had never seen an actual banana before, let alone tasted one. Bananas were exotic. It was an effort for anyone to concentrate on prayer. She tried, for Buni's sake, but her mind wandered, imagining the yellow fruit. After the service, she quickly lit a candle at the alcove of the Virgin, Buni's heroine.

Anca followed the line of people out the back door of the church and down the steps. Everyone was hurrying for the banana line, and she was swept along. She reasoned that the service had been shorter than usual, perhaps because of the bananas. All of the other children were being escorted. People were scurrying, pulling their children along by the arms. She was spurred to action, running like the wind. There was no one her age faster.

The line began in front of the blacksmith's. She claimed her place in the queue, adrenaline coursing through her from the run. There were already several dozen people ahead of her. No one seemed to know when the bananas were to be distributed, although everyone agreed it had to be soon. Otherwise, the bananas would freeze.

Bodies pressed together in the line. As time wore on, people began doubting the bananas and, even though there were just whispers, the doubt spread like brush fire. Fortunately, from the front of the line, it was verified; people could see the boxes in the back of the truck with bananas inside. The wait resumed and people began to debate the bananas' place of origin. Spanish bananas? Israeli bananas? They'd better not be Jew bananas! The mood ebbed again. Anca shut her eyes against the cold. She should be home at Buni's side. Auntie would be so worried.

Several people abandoned the wait, abruptly walking away. Someone muttered that they were the smart ones. Whether it was for bread or for something black market, it was always humiliating to endure. Buni called the bread lines "merciless"; she used to carry around a small folding stool and would seat herself, hands folded on her lap.

At long last, the men authorized to distribute the bananas arrived—a local official and a man Anca knew because he worked at the border with Uncle. They were both smoking cigarettes, in no hurry. All eyes were trained on the burning tips. When the butts were strewn, the queue stirred like a band of starlings. Anca blinked, coming to. Soon the line began to move.

At last, she caught sight of the bananas—beautiful lemony bunches, luminous in the back of the truck. As she drew closer,

the smell of the fruit was piercing and fresh, lacing the icy air.
She was just meters from the truck. Now it was her turn. She
stepped up, reaching out her hands.

"Girly, step aside, you don't get a banana," the official said
sharply.

Anca froze, her ears ringing.

"But she isn't Gypsy," the man who knew Uncle said.

The official peered at her in the darkness. "No?"

Anca recovered her wits and shook her head firmly.

"She's Ilie Balaj's niece," said the border patrol. Now he
looked at her. "Where's your uncle?"

She forced herself to speak up. "At home. Uncle's mother
is very ill."

The official handed her two bananas. She wanted to carry
her bananas through the streets for the world to see but the
Gypsy kids might ambush her since the officials had denied
them. She put one banana in either pocket and raced home,
their soft weight against her thighs.

She pushed open the door.

Uncle saw her first. "Anca, where have you been?"

Auntie rushed up, swallowing tears. "Are you all right, girl?"

Anca nodded, a bit overcome. She wished them a joyful
Christmas and pulled the fruits out of her pockets.

"I heard that there was a truck detained this morning,"
Uncle remarked.

Everyone stared at the bananas and then Bunica, who
was awake and sitting up for the first time all day, asked what
Anca meant by bringing home a pair of rotten cucumbers on
Christmas Eve. Anca and Uncle and Auntie burst into laughter.

"Banana! Banana, Buni," they told her. Light flickered in her tired eyes. They all marveled at the bananas' smooth taut skin. Auntie brought the paring knife and Ilie and Auntie argued about how to peel a banana. They looked on as Anca took one of the bananas in hand and carefully pulled back the peel the way she had seen the official at the truck do. The nude banana was set on a plate and sliced like a cake. They saved the other banana for Christmas morning.

Anca said, "Try it, try it, Buni," and even though she had not had an appetite in days Bunica ate several pieces.

It was their last good time together. Bunica died the day after Christmas. The priest could no longer risk presiding over funerals and she was mourned without so much as a tall candle.

Anca watched in vexation as Auntie Kati cleaned out the steamer trunk just a few days after New Year's. Uncle and Auntie had argued all morning over what to do with Buni's things. Auntie was eager to sell the valuables on the black market and said that Uncle's sentimentality was useless. It was how she endured— with a narrow mind and little tolerance for messy emotion. She was planning to store blankets in the trunk. Uncle had stomped out of the house and disappeared on his motorcycle. Anca hovered in the doorway, looking on as Auntie wrapped the little mirror in brown paper so that it wouldn't break. She did soften enough to ask Anca if there was something of Buni's that she'd like to keep. "The poetry books, maybe? I won't be able to sell them." Anca shook her head no, unwilling to admit her longing to Auntie.

*   *   *

She had grown accustomed to swearing her loyalty to and adoration of Comrade Stalin in school and in Young Pioneers, even though at home everyone complained about the Communists. Stalin's death followed Buni's, in March 1953, and she was expected to honor it as if it were the greatest sadness she had ever known.

On the day of the funeral in Moscow, all the local Pioneers traveled on a chartered bus to Oradea for a commemoration in honor of the great and beloved Comrade. Black cloth draped the stone monuments at the town's entrance. Anca's troop disembarked from the bus and made its way toward the central square, where throngs of youth groups were gathered. The crowds were somber. Someone was speaking through a megaphone about the Comrade's brilliant and loving leadership. The voice paused periodically for the crowd to chant in response. Many of the girls in Anca's class were sobbing uncontrollably. Even her teachers were crying into their handkerchiefs. Auntie had warned her to look impressed, but all the grief-stricken faces put her to shame.

A loudspeaker suspended from a chestnut tree broadcast the funeral procession from Moscow. Mournful orchestral music blared. Sirens began to sound from outlying factories. Her focus was lost in the sea of communist armbands, and her thoughts turned helplessly to Buni. She was gone without a trace, thanks to Auntie. It seemed so unfair. She felt the injustice acutely. Tears started rolling down her cheeks. Was it this way for every one of Stalin's mourners? She glanced around. Was it really someone else, a secret someone, they each cried for? It occurred to her they were all crying for themselves. She wept with abandon, finally joining in at Stalin's funeral.

Uncle Ilie was spending all his time out in the shed, listening to the radio with the volume turned down—Radio Free Europe coming in and out of disturbance. He was convinced that the English, if not the Americans, would intervene on Romania's behalf now that Stalin was out of the picture; the world would not leave Romania defenseless, on the brink of the unknown! Even without Auntie saying it all the time, Anca knew that Uncle was a dreamer. But she didn't mind. He had brought home an English-language primer printed in Russia, which he'd claimed was used for spy training, and encouraged her to study.

Uncle drank heavily the summer after his mother died. If there was no radio reception, he sat on his motorcycle out in the yard, going nowhere, a sweaty bottle of Beaujolais in his hand. It was a capital offense to drive under the influence, so he taught Anca to operate the bike. She was tall enough to manage by now. Sometimes, on a hot evening, he'd insist she go for a ride. "Take Kati with you, good riddance!" Auntie climbed on the back, clutching her around the waist. Uncle started up the motor for them and they set out—not gunning the way he always departed but gradually picking up speed, stirring a breeze, across the field to the burned-out farm. "Let's turn back now," Auntie would say into Anca's ear as they approached.

* * *

A group began to gather every afternoon in front of the black-smith's. Uncle was always at the center of it, reading the news-papers aloud. Whenever Auntie caught Uncle stepping out of the house with the paper under his arm, she'd beg him to keep quiet about the Americans. Finally, Uncle Ilie's public opining led to his interrogation for antigovernment action. They stared out the window as he was driven off in a secret police car early one Saturday. Auntie went down on her knees right there at the window ledge and began praying. Anca joined her, one knee and then the other, clasping her hands together uncertainly. She studied her crooked fingers, which looked almost naturally bent for prayer. They were smaller than the fingers of her right hand. She didn't bite the fingernails the way she did on the right. They were like someone else's fingers, a small child's. She shuddered all over and Auntie nudged her elbows off the windowsill, saying she was too fidgety. Anyway, Uncle was an atheist.

The neighbors had seen the police car and brought over soup at lunchtime. Auntie sat stone silent at the kitchen table. Anca finished her homework and went outside with Carol and called him to fetch the stick, but even Carol was distracted. He scratched at the door to be let back in and then stood on his hind legs looking out the window.

Anca looked up at the clouds. She walked over to the hen-house and scattered a handful of cornmeal. Auntie and Uncle had always been at odds about something, but they'd seemed to reach an ominous impasse since Buni's death. An invisible wall existed between them now. Anca thought of the wedding photograph in Buni's steamer trunk and wondered what had become of it. Uncle could be so selfish, Anca had to admit.

He did only what he felt like doing around the house, often neglecting what Kati asked of him. Like most wives, Auntie did all the cooking, housekeeping, and mending. Uncle had called her paranoid when she'd pleaded with him to stay home from the blacksmith's.

Anca threw grapes at various targets around the wall, which was a game that Uncle forbade but she couldn't resist. Carol at the window was the only witness. Later, she lifted out the big brown hen and let her loose in the yard to gobble up the evidence. The clouds didn't part all day. Just before dark she spotted Uncle coming up the path. She ran into the house to tell Auntie. She felt soaring relief. She tore back out into the yard and flew into Uncle's arms as he came inside the gate. Carol came running, let out.

"Godspeed, Ilie!" Auntie cried out as he came up onto the porch, her eyes searching his face. She cupped a hand on his broad check and kissed him on the mouth. No one seemed more surprised by this show of affection than Auntie herself. She blushed.

Uncle looked at Anca. "Has she been hitting the bottle?"

Anca smiled. They led him inside.

Uncle returned from the interrogation with a packet of cigarettes in his pocket and, just like that, he took up smoking. He never spoke of it, not even to Auntie Kati. She claimed his silence was confirming her worst suspicions. And the cigarettes. She wouldn't allow them in the house. He paced the porch in clouds of smoke.

*   *   *

One night after his interrogation, Uncle happened to notice what Anca was reading. She had devoured the thin contents of the primer he'd given her, memorizing the vocabulary and each of the rudimentary dialogues, and even though there was nothing more to learn from it she often leafed through it. Now he ordered her to throw it into the fire. She looked up at him in alarm.

"There's no point in learning English," he told her gruffly. "We are closed off here, in Romania. It's final now."

She hated to do it, but she didn't dare disobey him. She stared as the flames ate the book.

Uncle had somewhere to go every night now, setting out on his motorcycle like clockwork. "I've got business," he barked the one time Auntie stuck her head out the door to inquire. Auntie fretted out loud that he'd become an informant, and then she fretted further, "If so, at least we should have sugar in the cupboard."

Each evening after he disappeared down the road on his bike, Anca went out to the shed to listen to the radio. It was an escape, traveling the reflections of the ionosphere searching for English-language broadcasts. She was thirteen years old, a top student of French and Russian, and couldn't help being interested in English. She didn't care if there was no point in it! Sometimes she caught the BBC—for as long as ten minutes. Proof of another reality. She felt such promise at the first foreign syllable. The moment swelled with possibility. Other times, the BBC disappeared and would not return over several evenings. Then she felt stricken with an unquenchable yearning, listening anxiously to the shortwave static.

1954

ANCA LOOKED IN THE WINDOW of the pharmacy. The custom apothecary cabinets had been restored to their original purpose: tiny bottles of chemical powders lined the shelves behind tall glass doors. The front glass case displayed toiletries, perfumes, and first aid supplies. Several scales presided on the counter and a pendulum clock hung over the door. Anti-Jewish laws in the 1930s had shut the business down and, for decades, villagers had had to travel to a neighboring town or do without. The reopening of the pharmacy in Crisu looked like progress, but the state had assumed ownership, and not only of the pharmacy but the stationer's and the delicatessen as well. Everyone knew the farms would be next.

The new pharmacist's name was Simona Ursu but people addressed her as Miss Pharmacist. Her auburn hair was braided and coiled on her head and she wore a white coat over her clothes. She was young for her position and there was a rumor that she'd received the post because her father was a party bureaucrat in

Cluj. It could take forever to fill a prescription if she was in a mood, but she was also secretly admired. Anca noticed straight-away that Miss Pharmacist was a lefty. She watched through the window as the pharmacist leaned on the counter, her weight resting on one hip, writing with a fountain pen.

Ever since the pharmacy opened, Anca had walked down the main street on her way home from school. Finally, she decided to go inside. A bell over the door jangled as she entered the shop and she inhaled the chemical scent. A few customers were waiting in line at the counter. She stood self-consciously in the front case studying the hair combs. With Buni gone, she'd recently discovered a series of knots at the nape of her neck.

"Is there something I can help you with?"

Anca came to attention. She pulled her fingers out of her hair. The shop had emptied out and Miss Pharmacist was addressing her from behind the counter. She clicked her heels like a Young Pioneer. "I was admiring the combs," she floundered.

Miss Pharmacist had a pretty, uncomplicated face but a square jaw that often made it look as if she were gritting her teeth. She turned back to her work behind the counter.

"Miss Pharmacist," she stammered, thinking of something else to say, "do you prefer the new pills to the old powders?"

She looked up, appearing a little taken aback. "I don't have any choice in the matter," she said, a bit crossly. "It's nonsense for anyone to complain."

Anca blushed deeply. "I wasn't complaining. I was only wondering what difference the new pills made."

Miss Pharmacist's expression softened and she sighed, shrugging. She said that her training had involved chemistry,

and counting out mass-produced pills hardly felt like pharmacology. "Which isn't to say that an idiot can do it," she added.
With a small knife, she funneled the pills she'd been counting
into a vial. "Also," said Miss Pharmacist, "there are still plenty
of ailments the state doesn't produce pills for and I know the
recipes and I'm allowed to mix the old powders."

"Is it true that penicillin can cure pneumonia?" Anca asked,
willing the conversation to continue.

The pharmacist raised an eyebrow. "You would like to study
pharmacology?"

Or medicine—Anca almost divulged but caught herself
because she didn't want to seem arrogant.

"Penicillin is miraculous," Miss Pharmacist affirmed.

Just then the pharmacy door swung open and the butcher's
wife entered the shop.

The pharmacist looked sidelong at Anca as she hoisted her
book bag, preparing to depart. "You are welcome any time, you
know," she said before turning to her customer.

Anca ran home, overdue. Auntie would demand an expla-
nation, but telling her about Miss Pharmacist was out of the
question. Auntie would spoil it somehow. She would tell Auntie
Kati that she had had after-school obligations. Ever since the
great leader had succumbed, the youth groups were being kept
busy. For the cause of Marx and Lenin, be ready! "We are always
ready!" Anca chanted as she ran breathlessly up the pathway.

Auntie Kati was on the porch, mixing clay, visibly recovered
from the state inspector's unannounced visit earlier in the week.
The inspector had gone from shelf to shelf counting pottery.
He asked Auntie Kati to dispose, then and there, of the cluster

of unglazed irregulars she'd selected out—as if she might have
tried to pass them off for sale! Auntie Kati had been mortified. Nowadays there were quotas she was not to exceed, and
her prices were set by the state. She occasionally talked as if
she was going to quit the potter's wheel and go to work in the
toothpaste factory, but it wasn't possible to take her seriously.
Auntie Kati's work had a transforming effect on her. She made
even the arduous clay mixing look easy.

"I was worried!" Auntie Kati barked as Anca came up the
porch steps. She paused in full motion over the mixing vat. "You
promised me you wouldn't ever be late if I let you walk home
alone." She wiped her hands on her apron.

Anca frowned. "I'm not a child, Auntie!" She was fourteen
now.

"All the more reason," Kati shot back. "They can stop you
on the street. People disappear in broad daylight."

Anca rolled her eyes. Auntie Kati slapped her for her rude-
ness. There was silence.

Kati reached back to untie her apron. "I'll draw the kettle
now that you're here."

"I can brew my own tea," Anca said sullenly.

"Very well," replied Kati, cinching the apron, retying. She
did not look up later when Anca placed a glass of tea beside her.

She liked to visit the pharmacy on Monday or Tuesday, when new
shipments of medication were received, and also on Fridays when
the pendulum clock wound down. Perched atop a step stool, Miss
Pharmacist opened the glass door of the clock and cranked the

works with a small key. The clock hands quivered with resistance at her final turn. Next she would rotate the hands. The slightest tap of her finger set the pendulum swinging.

If there were no customers Miss Pharamacist pulled a stool out for Anca to sit on and Anca looked on as Miss Pharmacist compounded suppositories for the butcher's wife's hemorrhoids.

Simona Ursu was twenty-eight years old, which, she said in her own defense, was not too young, as she had overheard villagers remarking. She was also unmarried. Wasn't it peculiar that she could be both a novice and an old maid at the same time? The pharmacist couldn't help lamenting village life.

"At home, in Cluj, we would go to the theater," she sighed. "I even performed with an amateur company as a student. I also competed at tennis."

"Tennis?" Anca was impressed.

Miss Pharmacist eyed Anca tentatively. She went behind the counter, opened up one of the deep drawers, and took out a tennis ball. "My cousins in France used to send me tennis balls. It's the only one I have left. It's far superior to anything available here." The ball fit easily in the palm of her hand. Anca leaned forward to stroke the ball's brushed fabric. "When there are no customers I sometimes take it out," she admitted. She glanced out the front window but the street was empty. She bounced the ball once on the floor and it jumped right back up to her hand, returning as if it had never left. Anca looked on, delighted. The balls that she knew from the school yard were fashioned out of rags bound and tied together. Uncle had a football, but it was ancient and had lost its form and couldn't be kicked without the leather cracking.

"May I try it out?"

Miss Pharmacist shook her head, saying, "Not here, not in the pharmacy." She slid the ball into the pocket of her pharmacist's coat. She glanced calculatingly over at her workstation. There had been no customers for hours and the routine prescriptions took her only a few minutes. "It won't hurt to lock up for a short while. I have a racquet in the back."

"But it's begun to snow," Anca noted, looking out the window. "Won't it ruin the ball?"

Miss Pharmacist bit her lip, considering. "In the alley," she brightened, "behind the building, the snow doesn't collect."

The ball shot through the air, ricocheting off the wall. Anca swung out with the racquet the way Miss Pharmacist had demonstrated. She had good coordination and took to the motion automatically, but sometimes her left arm swung out spastically of its own accord to bat the ball.

Miss Pharmacist called out, "Are you left-handed?"

Anca stopped abruptly, catching the ball. She was out of breath. She plunged her left hand into her coat pocket.

"Well, you can use a backhand stroke," she suggested. "Hit the ball with the racquet. Otherwise it's a waste of time."

Anca served herself the ball and began again, poised on the balls of her feet, lucid and alert. Tennis was a thrilling discovery. She lunged, making contact, again and again, sweeping the air with the racquet.

Miss Pharmacist stood on the sidelines, encouraging. "You're a natural!" she called out. "Excellent stroke!"

Afterward, they warmed up beside the ceramic stove inside the pharmacy. The snow was steadily falling. The thought that Auntie would be worrying kept creeping into her head, but she ignored it. She was under a spell from the tennis. Miss Pharmacist had lit all the lamps. She handed Anca a cup of elderberry tea, dropping a sugar cube in it. Sweetened tea was already a treat, but a sugar cube dissolving at the bottom was a marvel. Anca stared into the teacup. She had heard about sugar cubes. Uncle had mentioned confiscating boxes of sugar cubes at the border recently.

Miss Pharmacist reached across the counter, taking Anca's curled left hand into her own. She tugged gently at each of the fingers. "Why is it like this? It looks arthritic."

"I was born with it this way." She shrugged self-consciously, adding, "I would have been left-handed, like you."

"It's better to be right-handed," Miss Pharmacist replied. "I never got fives in school."

The pharmacy door swung open. Anca gaped at the sight of Uncle. Ilie seemed equally surprised to see her. His nose was deep red from the cold. Her eyes darted to the wall clock. She jumped up. She'd lost all track of time. She watched Uncle dust the snow from his coat sleeves. She assumed that Auntie was worried and had sent him looking for her, but now she realized that he had come in of his own accord. Apparently, it was not the first time. Anca didn't know Uncle to rely on any sort of medicines. After an awkward moment, he ordered Auntie's headache pills. Miss Pharmacist went about filling the order.

"Your aunt knows where you are?" Uncle asked her.

She shook her head, sliding from the stool.

Miss Pharmacist handed Uncle the parcel. "Your niece is a tennis prodigy," she said brightly.

"Is that so," he said. He looked sidelong at Anca. "I'll give you a ride home."

"Wait, Anca," Miss Pharmacist said brightly, "open up." She reached over the counter to pop a sugar cube in Anca's mouth. "So you won't catch cold on your Uncle's motorcycle!"

"I didn't know sugar was medicinal!" Anca said.

"Don't be so gullible," Uncle told her.

Miss Pharmacist waved as they went out. Anca followed Uncle around the side of the building to where his motorcycle was parked, in the center of the tennis court. She climbed onto the seat behind him, he cranked the motor, and they drove off in the falling snow.

She smacked the tennis ball and hopped backward, perched on her toes, ready for the wall to ricochet it back to her. Here it came and she swung and made contact, and then again. Now the ball went flying at an angle to her left, she turned for the backhand, and with her left hand groping for the racquet instinctively swung with two hands, slicing the ball forcefully back to the wall. "You are going to be a champion, Anca!" Miss Pharmacist popped her head out of the little window at the back of the pharmacy—it was her kitchen window, actually, because she lived in the rear of the shop—watching and shouting encouragement and then disappeared again to see to customers, leaving Anca to herself. She didn't know why it felt so right to hit the ball off the wall. Her left hand was bubbling painfully with heat but she didn't even notice.

"That's twenty minutes, now Anca!" Miss Pharmacist called out to her. "Don't be late or she won't let you visit me." Miss Pharmacist had picked up on the conflict between Anca and Auntie.

Anca stopped and, out of breath, walked over to the window, handing up the racquet and ball. "I won't be, I promise," she said breathlessly. "Thank you for the tennis." She curtsied, then blew a bright kiss and ran off down the alley, out to the street.

It was raining so there could be no tennis, and there were fewer customers. Miss Pharmacist stood behind the counter funneling pills. Anca roamed the store, absently fingering the dense knot at the nape of her neck. It was like a bird's nest had formed inside the thicket of her curls.

"You need to use mineral oil," Miss Pharmacist commented, glancing over at her.

Anca looked up and then realized, pulling her fingers out. "Mineral oil?"

"But your aunt will have to help you. You can't do it yourself."

"I don't want her to know it's knotted. She'll make me cut it."

"I see," said Miss Pharmacist. "Well, in that case, I'd better help you." She began gathering supplies from the drawers. "First you need to wet it down. Use my sink. There's a clean towel on the shelf. You'll have to heat some water first." She beckoned Anca behind the counter, opening up the back door for her. "You can manage it? Make yourself comfortable. Just knock on the door from inside when you're ready and I'll come tease it out for you with the oil."

Miss Pharmacist lived in one room. Her kitchen was at the back, partitioned off by a red-checked curtain. Light from the alley made it possible to see without the need for a lamp. Anca found the kettle, filled it, and lit the stove burner. While she waited for the water to heat she glanced shyly around. The cupboard shelves were surprisingly well stocked with dry goods. There was a sack of flour, like those allotted wholesale to the baker, and there was salt and pepper and the box of sugar cubes. The thought of snitching one distracted her, and she pulled the curtain back and had a look around the main room to resist temptation. Miss Pharmacist had a telephone! It sat on the small writing desk next to a hammer-and-sickle paperweight and an inkwell. There was a dresser with lopsided drawers and on top of the dresser were bars of Turkish soap, bottled perfume like the ones in the glass case out front, and one of the tortoiseshell hair combs. Over her bed she had fashioned a canopy from an embroidered tablecloth; it had a romantic look to it and Anca was awed. She noticed a pair of suspenders hanging from a dresser knob and an ashtray with a cigarette stub in it. She realized, in a flash, that Miss Pharmacist had a boyfriend. She felt a twinge of jealousy.

Once her hair was wet, she knocked cautiously on the door. She could hear the cash register and a few minutes later the bell over the door, the customer departing, and soon Miss Pharmacist appeared carrying a bottle of mineral oil and a packet of gauze. She immediately pulled the light switch in the middle of the room and everything was awash in electric light. "I put the sign out. Forty-five minutes. It should be enough time."

Anca sat in a kitchen chair with the towel on her shoulders and Miss Pharmacist stood over her, working the oil into the matted hair, carefully teasing it out. "You have so much hair, Anca. It's enough for two!" she laughed.

"My grandmother used to help me take care of it," Anca swallowed the lump in her throat. "It never had knots before."

"It just needs a good combing," Miss Pharmacist said. A few seconds later, she added thoughtfully, "If I had been here then, I might have been able to get her penicillin."

Anca looked up inquisitively at Miss Pharmacist. Somehow she knew that Bunica had died from pneumonia. Anca must have spoken of Buni, but she didn't remember doing so. It hurt too much. She wasn't used to talking about herself to anyone. But Miss Pharmacist was not like anyone else. She was often saying so herself. She didn't fit in here in Crisu. Anca felt the same.

"I miss her so much!" she burst out.

Miss Pharmacist looked a little startled. Then the telephone rang. Anca jolted in her seat and Miss Pharmacist pressed a restraining hand to her shoulder. Anca's eyes rolled up, studying Miss Pharmacist's face expectantly. She seemed about to answer the phone, pausing with the comb for a second. She glanced down at Anca, then resumed combing with a pensive brow. At last the phone stopped ringing. The silence echoed around them and Miss Pharmacist said, "I'm sure it was the butcher's wife. She goes to the corner and calls from the phone booth if she comes by for her suppositories and I've put the sign out."

Even though the comb pinched and pulled, it was pleasurable to have someone attending to her, and the mineral oil worked magically. She was so glad to be rid of the knot, which had become a dark secret she kept from Auntie.

Anca was wrapping her damp hair in a Young Pioneer's neck scarf for the walk home, afterward, when the telephone rang again. Miss Pharmacist had gone back out to the shop, leaving Anca to wash the oil out. In Miss Pharmacist's absence she again contemplated the sugar cubes, just one, she thought, it was so cold out. The ring of the phone interrupted her thoughts. She lurched again and hastily gathered up her school bag and went out. It surprised her to see the butcher's wife at the counter talking to Miss Pharmacist. It was someone else calling.

Miss Pharmacist glanced at her.

"The phone is ringing again," she mentioned, and Miss Pharmacist nodded, calling after her, "Good-bye, Anca!"

She stepped out into the cold air. It was clear that Miss Pharmacist had made it up about the butcher's wife on the telephone. She was filled with curiosity as she sprang into her sprint home.

Later that week, when Anca stopped by the pharmacy, she came upon Uncle standing at the counter. His back was to the door. Miss Pharmacist's playful expression sobered when she looked over and saw Anca. Then Uncle turned around and, looking surprised, greeted her abruptly. "You're not in school," he remarked.

"Early dismissal," she replied. "We have exams tomorrow." She stood in the doorway, hesitant.

Uncle nodded at Miss Pharmacist. "Don't be late home," he told Anca as he passed in front of her, leaving without a package. Anca recalled that Auntie had declared the headache medicine useless and had suffered all day long in the darkened pantry with her skull pounding. She looked tentatively at Miss Pharmacist. It was a dry day and she had been hoping to practice tennis.

"Anca, here," Miss Pharmacist said, catching her attention. She had taken the tennis ball out of the drawer. She tossed it lightly over the counter to her. Then she went in back and returned with the racquet.

"No, I can't," said Anca. "I'll be late." She shook her head, confused. "What did my Uncle want?"

Miss Pharmacist said quickly, "I don't discuss my customers."

Anca handed her back the ball.

One day she spotted Uncle's motorcycle parked in the alley behind the pharmacy. All the shops were closed. The situation became clear to her. She was on her way home from Pioneer preparations for May Day, and she paused in the street, her feet feeling heavy. It was as if the breath had been knocked out of her, an effort to turn and walk away.

She stopped visiting the pharmacy. She walked the long way around the village, past the livestock pens and the barn that housed the combine. As the days passed she grew more bereft. On a sunny, tennis-perfect day her heart ached.

*   *   *

Since state ownership, Auntie Kati had to travel by train to fire
her wares in a cooperative kiln. The bimonthly trip took Kati
away from Crisu overnight. She would do several day's shopping
in advance of leaving and prepare all the meals to be eaten in her
absence. All Anca needed to do was lift the pot lids. Auntie Kati
didn't like leaving Anca with Ilie scarcely at home but she had no
option. No choice at all in life—she often complained to Anca.
Even the shape of a vase was now prescribed. She slept on a cot
in the kiln room while she monitored the fires throughout the
night. In the morning, the factory would be humming with the
sound of kick wheels, women throwing toilets in an assembly
line. Auntie Kati called it "a pitiful sight."

With Auntie away, there was no hurry. She played tag in
the school yard until it grew dark. The game broke up when it
started to rain. The back road would be muddy, so she decided
to cut through town. The sky had darkened and the rain was now
falling at a slant. People hurried off the streets. Miss Pharmacist
had the sign out, closed temporarily. Lamplight from the back
window lit the motorcycle so that it gleamed. Without thinking,
Anca ducked into the alley, out of the downpour. She stood very
still and listened. Phantom tennis balls ricocheted off the wall.
She went on tiptoe to Uncle's bike. She could hear a symphony
playing on the radio inside. She pictured Uncle, the mournful
expression that came over him whenever he listened to music.

Anca had seen Ilie start up the bike a thousand times but
had never done it herself. Taking hold of the handlebars, Anca
turned the bike and rolled it out to the street. Straddling the
seat, she struggled to keep her balance while trying to ignite
the motor. The thumb of her left hand was not keeping hold,

the way it managed to whenever she'd driven the bike before. She was having no success and was wary of being seen. She tried one final time. When the motor sputtered out again and refused to crank Anca gave the bike a despairing shove. It toppled onto the road with a dense shudder and clank. She turned on her heel and tore up the street.

What a waste! What had she been intending—a joy ride, like in the summertime? She had wanted to interfere somehow, but now she felt angry with herself for meddling, for caring. She wiped away tears with the back of her hand as she ran. There were more important things in the world—the Russians making a launch for the moon. She stared forlornly up at the March sky.

A light was on inside the house but Kati wasn't due back until the next day. As she came up onto the porch, Anca caught sight of Uncle through the window, asleep at the table, bent over with his head nested heavily in his arms. A shot glass sat on the open newspaper. She glanced instinctively at the shed where he usually parked his motorcycle but of course the spot was vacant.

Uncle and Carol had befriended each other since Buni's death. The dog jumped up with a bark when Anca came in. Uncle roused himself. She went to change into dry clothing. When she came back into the kitchen, she walked over to the stove and peered into Auntie's pots. She tied on one of Auntie's aprons, then sliced the bread. She broke the seal on the last of Buni's eggplant pickle and set out plates, Kati's old folkloric ones. She could not remember the last time she'd sat across the table from Uncle for supper. He was like a distant relative visiting from out of town.

After he'd eaten, Uncle announced that he was going back to the village to fetch his motorcycle.

"It's run dry," he told her. "A leak."

Anca watched from the window as he headed off, throwing the moonlight with his gasoline can. No wonder she hadn't been able to start it! The dog gave several plaintive barks and she shushed him. Hours went by. When Uncle finally returned he was on foot. He came through the door like a raging bull. He strode to the cabinet and without taking off his coat uncorked the *pálinka*. His chest heaved against his coat seams. "She's crazy," he seethed, his jaw twitching with the liquor. "She's cut the branch underneath herself."

A truck trailer had become lost en route to the border and driven down Crisu's main street, flattening the motorcycle. Ilie blamed the pharmacist for putting his bike in the road but she had denied it. He had never mentioned Simona Ursu before, but now he acted like nothing was secret. "She's cracked."

Anca mustered everything to respond as if she couldn't care less. "Perhaps there's a pill she can swallow."

Ilie cursed and muttered until the drink caught up with him. He sat down heavily and stared in front of him.

Anca acted confused. "Why would Miss Pharmacist wreck your motorcycle?"

He eyed her thoughtfully before answering. "She's angry at me because I've ended it."

She had thought it better to seem impartial but now she changed her mind. "Uncle, you don't know whether it was Miss Pharmacist or Gypsies trying to steal the bike." She could tell he was listening, and she barreled on shamelessly. "The Gypsies just abandoned it when they realized it was out of gasoline!"

When Auntie Kati returned from firing her pottery, Uncle and she had a terrible row. He must have confessed to her, because Auntie said atrocious things about Miss Pharmacist and Ilie returned the hurt saying he'd known all along that Kati's womb was a dried-up old sack and now there was proof of it. Anca was at the table doing homework when Uncle strode out of the bedroom. A second later, Kati ran at him throwing cups and plates from the sideboard and calling him a liar. He ducked out of the house, letting the door slam in her face. Then he pedaled off on his new bicycle.

Eventually, Miss Pharmacist's belly swelled for all of Crisu to see. She was the talk of the town again. The pharmacist should have known better! Of all people, she possessed the ways and means to prevent pregnancy. What would her father in Cluj have to say about it? Was she some sort of double agent? In the heat of the gossip Uncle moved out and Auntie Kati became a recluse.

Anca hesitated in front of the pharmacy. There was no reason not to say hello—no exact reason, since the truth about the motorcycle was now beside the point. She pushed open the door, the familiar bell and medicinal odor greeting her. As soon as she saw the pharmacist she regretted entering. Simona Ursu was pale and sallow. She came around the counter to greet

Anca, and Anca looked away from her protruding middle. They kissed cheeks.

"I'm glad to see you," said Miss Pharmacist, her breath stale.

Anca looked nervously around, making excuses. "I was just dropping off Auntie's scissors across the street." She felt helpless, almost panic-stricken, pointing to the clock. "Look, it's wound down!"

Miss Pharmacist took no notice. "Please Anca, you don't hate me?"

Anca shook her head, mortified. She had liked to arrive in time to see the pendulum slowly cease, the weights at their peak. The clock hands would halt, quivering.

Miss Pharmacist began to cry into a handkerchief, and her face looked homely, with reddened eyes. "I can't endure an abortion. I love Ilie and he loves me!" She gripped Anca's arm. "I have to see him," she insisted, "but he's furious. He thinks I put his motorcycle in the middle of the road." She blew her nose. "Will you tell him to come to me, please, Anca?" Miss Pharmacist didn't seem to know that Ilie no longer lived at home. She sobbed again. "I went to the border but he refused to see me!"

"You just said he loves you."

"You're young, Anca, you can't understand." She paused, mopping her eyes, and blew her nose again. "At first I just thought he was spying on me. No one meant for it to happen."

"How could you be so *gullible?*" Anca spat, but her sarcasm barely registered.

Miss Pharmacist was rambling. Uncle wanted her to have the abortion. He had been going to drive her to Salonta for the operation. Out of desperation, she siphoned his gas tank while he slept. "He went home to get the gasoline and while he was gone, I don't know, it was like a miracle when his motorcycle was run down," she said, and for a split second Anca considered claiming responsibility. "Talk to him for me? Tell him to come to me," she begged, squeezing Anca's cold hands in her own moist ones. Her face contorted with anguish. She didn't look like herself. "I have to see him. Please, Anca! I swear I didn't put his motorcycle in the road."

"I told him it was Gypsies," Anca said meekly.

Miss Pharmacist stroked Anca's cheek with the back of her hand, petting her insistently. "I know what you can't resist," she said, going behind the counter and pulling open the drawer. "I'll give you my tennis ball and you'll speak to your uncle."

The ball fit perfectly in the curve of her hand and she surprised herself by maintaining her left hand, bouncing the ball right to left as she walked along the road. She kept near perfect rhythm. Bouncing the tennis ball up the path to the house, Anca regretted not asking for the racquet and the sugar cubes as well. After all, the sugar cubes might have been in Auntie's cupboard if it weren't for Miss Pharmacist because Anca was certain the sugar cubes had come through the border. She was suddenly angry with herself for getting involved all over again. As she neared the gate she tucked the ball out of sight. Auntie was in the yard raking chicken manure. She looked small and hunched in her long coat. Just now, without the ball to distract her, Anca admitted to herself that she had no intention of going to speak to Uncle.

On her way to return the ball on Monday morning, she found the pharmacy closed. She squinted into the dark window. Her breath caught in her throat noticing the clock was still stopped. After school that afternoon, a police car was parked in front of the building. Anca went across to the sharpener's to collect Auntie's scissors and the customers were all discussing the news: Miss Pharmacist was dead. She had prepared a lethal tonic for herself. At the sharpener's, everyone said Anca should go and tell her uncle, but she couldn't, she explained, he was living in the barracks at the customhouse. They looked at her gravely, then someone said, "Soon enough he'll find out."

Anca walked along the road clutching Auntie's scissors. A moist wind was whipping in from the wheat fields. The sun was going down, her shadow on the road in front of her was long and looming. She turned off the road and climbed the remains of a fence, taking cover in the old orchard as rain began to fall. In the years since the fire was set on the Gypsies, the old farmstead had become a dumping ground.

She reached into her coat pocket, taking out the tennis ball, and began bouncing it on the hard ground. In the changing light the ball possessed a ghostly glow. The motion was instinctive, but now it filled her with a sickness. She stopped. The darkness reverberated deafening quiet. She wiped the tears with her sleeve as she roamed the junk heaps.

As she approached an old covered well, an owl from the rafter flew down in front of her, its sharp, accusing face filling her with horror. The beat of its wings. The well had dried up long ago. Anca stared into the dank blackness and after a moment let go of the tennis ball, dropping it down. The ball echoed as it bounced for a few seconds and then it was silent. She bit her lip. "Come back," she called into the dark. "Please come back!" Her heart soaring and sinking all at once in her own disembodied reply.

For a change, Auntie Kati had not waited up. Anca added the parcel paper from the sharpener's to the kindling box. The scissors glistened in the firelight. She lit a lantern and set it on the windowsill. There was no mirror because Auntie had sold the mirror with the painted edges on the black market along with Buni's jewelry, but Anca could see her reflection in the windowpane.

She gathered up her hair, twisting it around her curled fingers, then hacked with the scissors, as if through rope. The hair fell, strewn on the floor. She glanced down at it. Her left hand quivered with memory. There were reams of hair, an ocean. She gritted her teeth and kept snipping. Rain began to stream across the windowpane. Soon, she was transformed. Her eyes jumped out at her the same as the barn owl's. Denying herself her fortune from a Bucaresti wig maker, she swept up the heaps of hair, afterward, throwing it all into the fire.

1957

AS IT TURNED OUT Anca was one of the only girls in her village eligible to earn a higher education. Discrimination against ethnic Hungarians had reached a new height after the uprising in Budapest. Student-led demonstrations calling for the reinstatement of Imre Nagy as prime minister had been crushed by the Soviet military. In 1956, the whole world had looked on as Russian tanks rolled into Hungary. In Romania, it was an opportunity to remove Hungarian teachers and intellectuals from public life and to deny Hungarian students entry to universities. Anca considered herself lucky, since her exam scores were not outstanding.

Her scores would dictate her plan of study—any notion of the sciences was dismissed then and there. She applied to take her diploma in French and Russian and was admitted to Timisoara University. Auntie Kati organized a small celebration in Anca's honor, hoarding ration cards in order to prepare a gulyás. Two of Anca's schoolmates came with their parents. Auntie had said she could invite as many girls as she wanted, but Anca had come up with only two friends. She had become much more popular with the boys, but Auntie would have none of this. It was a nice party, regardless. Zsuzsi's father, a drinker and a bigot, held forth while Auntie and the other women served the gulyás. Anca and her friends drank champagne for the first time. After a surprise of plum dumplings, Anca's schoolmates departed, the girls kissing cheeks emotionally, as they were each headed in different directions, one to technical school and one to teacher's college.

A couple of days before she departed for school, Anca set out with Carol on a strand of rope through the corn and tobacco fields, the shortcut to the border. Preoccupied with the irritating tedium of coaxing Carol, who was not accustomed to being led anywhere, Anca was oblivious to the parched fields and the pitiful crop, the difference that the decade had made on the landscape. The dog could not travel two or three meters without stopping to sniff and mark the surroundings. She decided it would be faster to carry Carol. By the time she reached the line of cars the sun was directly overhead, and her arms were slack with Carol's weight.

Romanian-Hungarian tension was at its highest point since the war, and the border was always a gravely serious place. As she approached the customhouse, Carol, disliking the nearness of the cars and trucks, began yapping in panic. The dog squirmed, nails scratching. It was too much to keep holding him, so she set him down. He began to run back and forth at the end of the tether. A border shepherd took up barking, and Uncle, in the window of the customhouse, noticed them and stepped out.

It had been over a year since she'd last seen him. He had stopped by once at Christmas, with several pairs of women's hosiery, which Anca had been delighted by, despite not wanting to care. Today he was in uniform and carried a clipboard, very official looking. And to think that he had started out raking the no-man's-land! She could muster only ironic feelings for Uncle right now. He had run away—as if the grief were only his— leaving Anca alone with Auntie.

Despite developing cataracts, Carol seemed to recognize Uncle immediately. The dog went wild, wagging his backside, barking stormily. Ilie was eager to avoid a display but his eyes smiled at the dog. He ushered Anca to the back of the custom-house, the dog dancing circles around him.

Anca shouted over Carol's noise. "Auntie says you must have him now that I'm leaving! He's going blind as a mole! He whines at the window and barks at ghosts."

Uncle went down on one knee and reached out for Carol, who scrambled into his arms.

Anca smiled. "I hope he doesn't piss on you." Uncle had put on weight and was grayer than she remembered. He stood with the dog panting, prideful in his arms. Carol licked Uncle's chin and he chuckled.

"Buni would feel betrayed, Carol," Anca scolded playfully.

Uncle looked at her. "Kati is surviving without me?" he asked.

Anca scoffed. "Only Carol misses you." Although it wasn't true.

Uncle had not kissed Anca's cheek in greeting but he did so now. He asked about her plans and was impressed to hear that she was going to university. "I knew you weren't stupid," he teased.

She felt herself warming to him. Uncle didn't take life too seriously.

"Join the Communist League, if you can," he suggested.

She frowned at this. "Uncle, you can't give me any advice."

"I suppose not," he said, "but you'd be stupid not to." He squinted at her. "I almost didn't recognize you with short hair."

She shifted uncomfortably, thinking of Miss Pharmacist.

"Well," Uncle said finally, "tell Kati I will send something."

Money, rather than smuggled goods, Anca wanted to say, but knew better. She wasn't ungrateful, and, anyway, this was not the time or place. Corruption at the border had to be kept silent, if not invisible. Uncle said he would tie Carol up in the shade until his shift ended, then take him back to the guards' quarters with him. "I'm still waiting to be assigned housing," he confessed, "because she won't divorce me." He found someone to drive Anca to the bus stop so that she wouldn't be late returning.

The next morning they were up early. Auntie made sandwiches for the train ride and Anca finished packing. The carriage arrived to drive Anca's luggage to the train station. They sat pressed together on the backseat, unable to speak.

"You are a brave girl," Auntie finally said, her hand cupping Anca's chin as they stood on the platform alongside the train. It was too much praise. Tears escaped. They kissed cheeks. Anca climbed aboard, Auntie shoving the crates up after her. They stared at each other through the window glass as the train pulled away.

*   *   *

Auntie Kati always claimed that, without Uncle, she was nobody in Crisu—never mind that she had lived there all her life. Once Ilie was gone it was only a matter of time before she came under scrutiny. When Anca visited one weekend in her first semester, Auntie looked worn out. She had been stopped on the road a few days earlier by secret police.

"They asked me to sign a paper denouncing Father Csergo! And then when I wouldn't, they gave me a notebook. I was supposed to write in it names of Csergo's associates." They were peeling potatoes beside the stove and Auntie was relating her roadside interrogation in a whisper.

"Somehow they knew I had made the holy wafers. There was a Mass, a few weeks after you left, for Imre Nagy. You know, there is a rumor that they are holding him here in detention, in Romania?" Auntie Kati sighed fretfully. "I thought it was possible they would just forget about me. I am nobody. But a few days later they brought me in for more questioning." She looked up mournfully and blew her nose into a napkin. "You know, it's true what you hear, they do have the white toilet paper in the bathroom next to the interrogation room. It's incredibly soft. I had to try it out."

"Auntie, what did they say?" Anca asked impatiently.

She shook her head again. She went back to peeling potatoes. "It turned personal. They asked me why I didn't divorce Ilie."

Anca looked blank. "It's not their business!"

"Don't be stupid," she said to Anca. "Maybe he's behind it."

Anca shook her head. "Auntie, no. They want Father Csergo, that's all."

"I was so frightened," said Auntie Kati. "They said if I didn't denounce Father Csergo, I'd be punished. I kept imagining being sent to slave on the Danube–Black Sea canal like a criminal, and I couldn't bear it. I finally signed. There was a long list of names before mine. I'm not the only coward." She looked anxiously across the table at Anca and held up a potato, shaking it in Anca's face. "Nothing, not even a potato, looks the way it used to look, before Communism. Do you see how dry the flesh is? And the cabbages now are shriveled with blackened edges." She shook her head, and then she set the potato aside and, elbows on the table, rested her head in her hands.

"Oh, Auntie," Anca said gently.

Soon Auntie Kati received notice from the housing authority in Crisu. The Tóth house had been deemed large enough for two families. Kati was given no choice in the matter even though her name was on the property deed. A horse and cart arrived one afternoon with somebody else's things.

Auntie suspected Mrs. Iordache and her spinster daughter of informing and felt it necessary to refrain from even a small Christmas celebration. Anca had to admit the daughter was a bad egg, the way she picked her nose while cooking and served herself before her mother.

When they had a moment alone in the house, Auntie Kati made a point of showing Anca where she had hidden her Bible.

"Look between the cracks," she whispered.

Anca was on her hands and knees in the pantry, peering between the floorboards. She could just make out the spine of a book. Auntie had even found a rusty nail to hammer so that the board looked like always.

"I didn't want to die without you knowing where it was."

Anca looked at her gravely. She made an excuse to depart earlier than usual and rode the bus out to the border to find Uncle. When he opened up the door, his face softened at the sight of her and he swept her into an embrace. She could smell the liquor on him. "I am destitute over Carol!" he cried. The dog had died only the day before, although he had been sick for months apparently, a tumor. Anca had never seen Uncle cry, even when Buni died. He was halfway through a bottle of vodka, squeezing the tears out of his eyes and wiping his face with his sleeve, then tossing back the drink. He showed her out onto the balcony, where the dog lay frozen in a cardboard box. He had wrapped Carol in a newly purchased bedsheet patterned with forget-me-nots. Gray hair had made him sentimental, Anca thought to herself. She surveyed Uncle's cramped quarters, not much larger than a closet. At least he didn't have to share the space. A small electric Christmas tree glowed on the little kitchen table.

She drank a shot with him. "You should go back home, Uncle," she said, setting down her glass. "She's so alone now, Uncle. She loathes the roommates." She reached for the bottle before he could and corked it. "Auntie needs you, Uncle."

For a long time he said nothing, and then he said, "I did think I might bury Carol in the garden, when I can work the ground."

*   *   *

She was back in Timisoara when the telegram came from Auntie Kati, indicating only a train arrival time. Auntie was not a casual traveler. When she descended to the platform at the station in Timisoara, she appeared a shadow of her old self. She'd lost kilos. Anca rushed forward, a bouquet of violets getting crushed in the embrace. They should find some place to speak, said Kati. She said she planned to leave on the outbound train.

"There's barely time for a cup of tea, Auntie!" Anca protested.

Auntie Kati glanced anxiously around. "Not here, not in the station café."

They rushed out onto the street holding hands and went into a cafeteria, where they ordered sorrel soup—a sure sign of spring. At last they were seated near the window, in the bright sunlight.

Auntie Kati studied her. "You've been out in the sun, not in the library," she remarked. "You look like a gypsy."

"I've been invited onto the tennis team."

Auntie looked skeptical. "Anyway, I'll sew you a visor."

"Gypsies don't carry tennis racquets around with them, Auntie."

"No, I suppose not," Auntie said. She leaned across the table, finished with chatting. "I will be arrested. The Iordache daughter has denounced me."

"What? No, Auntie."

"Several weeks ago," Auntie explained, "I found cigarette ashes in my room. I couldn't bear the Iordache daughter poking around in my things, flicking her ash! I can't sleep at night. Last week, I heard the daughter tiptoeing around. The footsteps went into the pantry.

"I climbed out of bed. I was so frightened. I took the butcher knife down from the peg, the knife we used before the state took our pigs," she said. "I was going to slit her throat if she had uncovered my Bible."

Anca's jaw dropped open.

Auntie Kati looked grim. "She has a long gooseneck from all of her snooping. But she was just stealing pickled peppers, standing there with a fork, eating."

The daughter had gone to the police after Auntie Kati threatened her with the knife. Auntie Kati boldly denied any wrongdoing but secret police officers had raided the house.

"They tore the bed apart searching," remarked Auntie Kati. "Remember I used to keep my Bible under the mattress? Do you think they knew it?"

They found hard currency hidden inside a ceramic vase, illegal money, from the sale of Buni's things. She was not arrested outright but a hearing was scheduled. She had lost no time in making the trip to Timisoara to see Anca. Hard currency was worse than a Bible.

"What does Uncle say?" asked Anca, when Auntie Kati had finished talking.

Auntie shook her head. "I haven't seen him since he came to bury the dog."

Anca shook her head in dismay.

Auntie Kati said, "He asked me about a divorce again. I told him I haven't made up my mind. I don't care if it's been years." She looked around worriedly, then whispered shrilly, "I'm Catholic!" She gathered her bag into her lap, reached in, and took out a parcel. "There isn't time to think, Anca," she said, sliding the package across the table. "Please, keep it safe for me."

Anca wanted nothing to do with Auntie Kati's Bible but she felt obliged to tuck it into her satchel. For Auntie's sake, she would hold on to it.

Kati was jailed for two months in a remote penitentiary. She shared a cell with twenty other women and no bathroom, only a hole in the cement floor. Visitors were permitted once a week. Anca never knew whether Auntie Kati received the soap or the lotion that she sent. She managed the long trip to see Auntie Kati only once, early in the ordeal, and Auntie had made her promise not to come again. So much travel was unnecessary, she claimed: Anca should concentrate on her exams. They had had to shout to be heard in the crowded visitors' hall, and Auntie just gave up trying. She sat stone-faced on the opposite side of the table.

Just a few years ago Auntie had seemed never to age. Except for gray hair, she had looked exactly as she did in her forties when Anca first arrived. Auntie Kati hadn't exactly been young looking then, but by the time she reached sixty she looked well for her age. The village women often remarked on Auntie Kati's trim figure, a result, they said, of never having borne children. Anca didn't even recognize her at the prison gate. Her hair was shorn close to her ears and she was like a skeleton in her clothes. Uncle had tried but failed to have the mother and daughter relocated; the mortal enemies were destined to continue living under one roof. As a result of her imprisonment, Auntie Kati was demoted from pottery to toilet bowls.

One week after her release, in June 1958, the news of former Hungarian prime minister Imre Nagy's secret sentencing and execution was made public. A few days later, Uncle showed up in Timisoara bearing more sad news. Kati had gone about smashing every piece of earthenware in the house—except for a shelf of irregulars. She went to bed complaining of a headache and appeared to have died in her sleep. He didn't tell Anca about the bottle of poison he found until after Kati was laid to rest in the Roman Catholic cemetery; in spite of Communism, it was still the practice in Crisu to bury accordingly.

"At least it was her choice to end it," Uncle said about the poison.

Anca frowned. "Her choice? What choice?"

It was the afternoon following the burial. They had both eaten their fill of the dishes that neighbors had sent over. Uncle was drunk. He was saying he had bribed the prison guards so that Kati was allowed a shower and a clean towel every week. He'd been afraid to visit her. "I just turned around and went home. Couldn't bring myself to line up with the other visitors."

Anca's thoughts drifted. Auntie's Bible was like lead inside her bag. She had hoped to slip it inside the coffin, but the neighbors said the undertaker couldn't be trusted.

"I was too guilty," Uncle was saying. He eyed her unsteadily. "I suppose you know it was me."

Anca stared at him, her ears feeling singed. "Uncle, what are you talking about?"

"I've informed on everyone, so why not?" He had a terrible, ironic tone in his voice.

"You gave them Auntie?"

He poured two shots and handed one to her. "They wanted her anyway. Don't ask me why."

She studied him for another minute. "But you must know why, Uncle?"

His eyes began to fill with tears. He wouldn't look at her. "They screwed me. I screwed myself, that's all." He tossed back the shot and wiped his mouth with the back of his hand. "There was nothing I could do! I had to give them something. So I told them Kati had a Bible under the mattress."

She didn't want to believe it, even though she had heard of family members, husbands and wives, ratting on each other.

He snorted, pausing. "So what? They wouldn't have imprisoned her for it!" He was reaching for the bottle again. "But I can't deny it," he said. "I knew that money was in the house." He pressed his palm to his forehead, wincing. "I never forgave her for selling my mother's things so quickly."

"So you took your revenge?" Anca's heart was hammering inside her. "Wasn't one betrayal enough? With the pharmacist?"

"That wasn't my fault."

"You were under orders there as well?" she spat.

"To report," he said.

"Miss Pharmacist wasn't an 'enemy of the people,'" she said scornfully.

"They wanted her father out, in Cluj, I think. I don't even know. Anyone can be an enemy. They don't explain their motives." He paused, looking morose. "One thing led to the other. Kati should have divorced me! They would have left her alone."

"You're talking nonsense."

"I'm not. Trust me, Anca, there's more to it. You can never know." He reached for one of the neighbor's *pogacsa* and ate grimly, legs wide apart, crumbs falling to the floor.

She looked away from him in disgust and gazed sadly around the room. The absence of Kati's pottery had stripped the place of color. It occurred to her that now there would be no reason to come back to Crisu. Uncle shifted in his seat drunkenly, his eyes brimming. Anca sniffled, then blew her nose. Out of respect for Auntie Kati, she wouldn't steep herself in sentiment. She squared her shoulders, a little haughtily, and asked him, "Are you too far gone to walk me to the station?"

He inhaled deeply, pulling himself together. He pushed his chair back and after a false start heaved himself upright. He took something out of his breast pocket—the wedding picture. "I found it in the drawer in her room."

Anca stared at the photo. She felt that same disorienting feeling she'd felt as a child, looking at Auntie and Uncle on their wedding day. "She looks happy. You both do," she remarked.

Uncle nodded. "She couldn't have a child. That's what changed everything." They exchanged a level glance. "It was before you came."

Anca nodded.

"Too many years had gone by," said Uncle.

* * *

As the train began to move, departing Crisu, Anca turned away from the window and Uncle's complicated face. The landscape soon began to flash past—the toothpaste factory and outlying wheat fields, the river no longer safe to drink from flowing under the trestle. People could be glimpsed in the fields harvesting, men scything and women gathering the stems. The combine, which the town's largest landowner—a sworn enemy of the people—had formerly rented out at the harvest, had been taken over by the Communists and fallen into disrepair. The seeds now had to be separated by hand like in olden times. How Anca had hated that work; Auntie Kati had motivated her to study, saying that if she didn't like the fields she'd better get into university.

Romania was poorer than ever now, thoroughly plundered by the Soviet authority. And although the Russian troops had recently left the country—the newspapers were full of talk of a new national era—Anca had a bitter taste in her mouth. She rested her head back on the seat and bit back more tears. The conductor came and went. She was the only one in the compartment. She glanced down the corridor but the train was empty. She reached into her bag and took out the parcel she had carried all this way. Untying the string, removing the packaging, she looked down at Auntie's old Bible in her lap. Tentatively, she opened the mildewed cover. Several pieces of yellowed parchment were tucked inside.

Carefully unfolding the old papers, she scanned the print. The blood rushed to her head as she realized she had uncovered her Hungarian documents. She stared blankly. It was a shock, this vestige of Éva Farkas. She was two years older than Anca, and a Jew.

She thought of how Auntie had always made a point of her knowing where she had hidden her Bible. She recalled the café in Timisoara last spring with the sorrel soup, Auntie Kati so anxious for her to take the parcel.

Her hands trembled, folding up the papers, quickly tucking them into her bag, out of sight. She closed the Bible, brushing off the dust with the flat of her hand. God had done nothing to discourage Auntie from killing herself. Reaching up, she opened the window and shoved the Bible out. Warm air rushed in, and she dropped back onto the seat, sat crumpled for a moment. She wondered if she shouldn't rid herself of the Hungarian papers as well. She went to reach for them, then checked herself. She couldn't throw her own papers out. Even Auntie Kati had believed the identification worth saving. A little dizzy from the speed of the train, she focused on the distant trees. She'd forgotten about Éva, hadn't she?

II

1958

It was October but the cafeteria in Timisoara was already serving cabbage soup. It would be cabbage or potato from now until springtime. Anca sat with her roommates, but they rarely spoke at meals. The mood in the dining hall was tense, not social. Everyone was preoccupied with the Communist League officer's table in the center of the room. At lunchtime, the table of officers was known for showing off with spoon-fighting antics and outbursts of fraternal slogans and chants meant to intimidate. They had very real power on campus.

That fateful day, in her sophomore year, one of the officers stood up at the table and called out across the hall: "Somogyi Péter!" The officer was Áron Messer, thin, black-haired, a Jew if she wasn't mistaken. He was waving to someone coming through the serving line. "Somogyi Péter!" The surname put first was Hungarian-style. She looked curiously over her shoulder. A tall boy with a head of sandy curls walked toward her with his tray. He wore a white lab coat over his clothes. Her stomach knotted up as he went past.

"Who is he?" she asked one of the other girls.

"The new chemistry lab assistant, accompanying Professor Mihály Fekete."

Fekete was the first academic visitor from Hungary since the unrest. Anca looked on from the distance of her seat. The professor's assistant was making himself comfortable amid the league officers, rolling up his sleeves, taking up the soup spoon. He jerked the curls out of his eyes, and it came to her, her pulse quickening. Could it possibly be her childhood Péter?

The weather was unusually cold, but the science building was one of the few being heated, so she was happy for a reason to loiter. Other students had discovered the heat as well and were seated on the benches doing homework after classes. She took a spot opposite the chemistry laboratory and thumbed through her French worksheets. She hadn't waited long when the lab door opened and the lab assistant stepped out into the hall and walked down the corridor to the men's room. She sat upright, staring after him, restless flickers of recognition emanating. He disappeared around the corner. Péter! She had not thought of him in years.

The door to the laboratory had not swung closed behind him. She had a sharp-angled view into the lab. It was so brightly lit! There were rows and rows of glass cabinets with more glass inside, vials and beakers and jars of different shapes and sizes. Just then, she saw the professor himself, Fekete, who had helped Biró with the invention of the ballpoint pen. The esteemed chemist was a celebrity on campus. He seemed to rear up from behind the glass pane, although he was actually just coming to close the door from inside. She felt unnerved at the sight of him, owl-eyed and scrutinizing, and abruptly collected her books, stuffing them into her bag with her good hand. She hurried off but got only as far as the lift, thinking of Péter.

She stationed herself against the wall opposite the elevator. It was almost dinnertime and the building began to empty out. The elevator went up and down through the center of the building and opened on both sides. Eventually, even Professor Fekete went home, in a fur hat. She caught her breath as he passed, pressing herself into the wall.

Finally, the lift came to rest. Quiet surrounded her, the silence pulsating. Minutes passed and she grew tense. What was she waiting for? Who? Her banished self, the isolated past, was a dense forest. She felt its pull. It was just over her shoulder. She heard the click of a door and footsteps coming down the empty corridor. She swung her bag over her shoulder, trying to appear nonchalant.

He came around the corner and stopped beside her in front of the elevator. After a few seconds he reached to press the button for the lift and she blushed at having forgotten it. The elevator arrived. He slid the door and politely waited for her to step inside.

"*Köszönöm.*" She thanked him

"*Szívesen,*" he replied.

She bolstered herself against the elevator wall, her legs grown weak, as they descended.

"Are you Hungarian?" he asked.

"Well, yes, no, my Auntie is, was." She felt tongue-tied now. She was alert with anticipation, all her senses heightened.

He said, "I am Somogyi Péter, from Szeged," holding out his hand.

"I already know who you are." She reached awkwardly for the handshake.

He must have assumed she was referring to his association with Professor Fekete. He shook the curls out of his eyes and smiled proudly. The elevator halted at ground level. She stepped out, disconcerted yet heedless after standing so near him, on the brink.

"You don't remember me, do you?" she asked him.

They were alone. He looked at her curiously.

Pausing, her tongue welling as if tasting butter, she said at last, "I was called Éva. Farkas Éva."

For a moment he looked dumb, then the blood sprang to his cheeks.

She suddenly felt intense dread. It hit her so forcefully that she turned and charged for the door. He shouted after her to wait, but she flung herself against the heavy door, pushing into the cold evening.

There was no room inside her lungs. She gasped for air as she ran. He was coming right behind her. She sprinted down the stone walk and was halfway across the yard.

"Éva, Éva!"

Something bounced in her gut, hearing him call her name. He was not the slowpoke of olden days, but still she could have given him the slip.

He caught her by the arm. "My God. Is it really you?" He pulled her to a stop.

"Well, maybe it is, maybe it isn't," she panted, laughing nervously. "You wouldn't have known me from the next Hungarian!"

He shook his head in earnest. "I thought you were dead."

She could see her breath in the moonlight. "Well," she said quietly, shrugging, "I'm called Anca nowadays."

"Anca?"

"Anca Balaj. That's what you must call me."

He smiled brightly into her eyes. "It's a miracle." They embraced. He pulled her in tight. She could feel his heat, and her own. Together they walked across the frozen campus. He was much taller than she, which had never been the case as children. She had to stretch her neck to see his face.

"When did you grow?"

He laughed in a man's voice. "After you left, I guess."

He had been a little boy, a bit coddled, with those angelic curls. A silence set in. There was light coming from the dormitory windows. "Will you come to my room so that we can speak more privately?" he asked her. "My roommates are at the dining hall."

She nodded her head. He took her by the hand.

Péter told her what he knew about her mother. Eszter Farkas had been taken to Auschwitz by train, after the ghetto was emptied. Mercifully, she had died en route. Crammed in like a piece of cattle, given nothing to drink. She had been suffering from walking pneumonia. The information had come to Mrs. Somogyi through a survivor.

Anca sat beside him on the bed, her coat unbuttoned, the red muffler loose around her shoulders. She strained to absorb his information. She blinked, looking about the small room. He was boiling water for tea on a portable burner borrowed from the chemistry lab.

Péter didn't know how long it was after she had been smuggled out that the Arrow Cross arrested her mother. He had few details. For a second she wondered if he even told the truth. She studied his profile in the blue light of the gas burner.

"I used to ask for you and Mother scolded me and told me I mustn't." He handed her a cup of tea and sat down with her again. "I remember running through the empty apartment while my mother mopped the floors. There were a few of your books, which Mother said I could keep."

She was desperate to remember—ghostlike images pressing the surface, but nothing definite. She felt a resurgence of apprehension. "You won't tell your mother you met up with me, Péter? It's not safe, even now, if someone found out."

He set down his teacup and rested his hands on her shoulders comfortingly. Close-set eyes skewed the handsome face. "Mother died two years ago." He pulled her toward him and she held on to him, her cheek against his shoulder. She watched the steam rising from the kettle in the darkness.

"Tell me everything you remember about Mama," she whispered.

"She was beautiful, like you," he said. "And young, I think, not much older than we are now." Péter looked at her closely. "Don't you remember her?"

"Not really. It's all a dream."

He cupped her face in his hands. "She fed the pigeons in the courtyard," he said. "Mother disapproved. I would watch from the window. I was terrified of pigeons. I was so cowardly."

"Well, I was jealous of you, anyway," she said. "Because you went to school."

"Then you *do* remember."

"Only now. It just came to me." She blinked back tears. He was six feet tall, with the shoulders of a colt. If it weren't for his name she would not have identified him. She reached impulsively to caress his cheek. He caught her wrist and pressed his lips to the backs of her fingers.

By the time the roommates returned, flooding them in fluorescent light, she was reluctant to leave. Both of the roommates were Romanian, so she and Péter could continue talking freely. Péter teased that she sounded like a peasant. She told him about Crisu and Auntie and Uncle. When the roommates climbed into their beds and the light was switched off again, Péter made room for her on his cot. She lay on her side to conserve space and he moved in close, fitting his knees behind hers.

The next morning she opened her eyes, recollecting, looking around the unfamiliar room. Soon she sensed Péter awake behind her. His body pressed against hers. She turned over and wrapped her arms around him tightly. He was solid, present.

A few days later, on the tennis court, her left hand was resurrected. She had long ago incorporated her left hand into her backhand stroke. Miss Pharmacist had shown her the technique, but sustaining the hand had never been possible for any length of time without pain. Suddenly this changed, and her hand was freed.

She was between sets in a practice match and spontaneously switched the racquet to her left hand. Maybe she sensed the return of strength. She gripped it firmly. She concentrated on the lift of the racquet. It felt too heavy but she didn't let go. She served, hitting the ball into the net. She waited for the painful nerve spasm that would upset her hold and wilt the connection but it never came.

"Was that left-handed?" her teammate asked, returning from the sideline.

Anca nodded, excitedly. "Let me see if I can do it again."

She had no control but she hit the ball over the net. A coursing energy traveled down her left arm from the shoulder, but no pins and needles, no shaking out the hand for relief. She didn't switch back for the volley. She was spastic and groping with her left hand, everything felt mixed-up, but she managed to return the ball. Finally, overexerted, she lost hold. The racquet dropped with a clatter onto the court.

"Enough showing off!" her teammate called out to her. "Let's finish our set."

Anca stood center court, her right hand on her hip, her left hanging loose at her side, the sweat glistening on her face. "I'm finished," she said heavily. She thought she might collapse. "Forfeit." She waved to her teammate and walked off the court, scooping up the racquet.

The varsity showers were the only hot ones on the campus. She tipped her head back, drinking the streaming water. She clenched and unclenched her fingers in disbelief. There was no tremor or pinch or even numbness, as if the nerves had finally let go. The water ran cool and she turned the faucets off left-handed. Perhaps she had ignored it so successfully that she hadn't noticed it quietly gathering strength. She changed into her clothes in a hurry, eager to tell Péter.

He was waiting for her in his room, hunched over a notebook working out an elaborate equation.

She was out of breath from running across the campus. "Péter, look. My hand, it's come back to me!"

"You're freezing," he said squeezing her hand, "You need a pair of gloves."

"Here, I'll show you. May I borrow that pencil?" She pinched the lead between her fingers and pressed the tip to his notebook, bearing down carefully.

"Hey," said Péter, pulling the notebook out from under, "don't write on my work." He stood up. "The water is boiling. Do you want a cup of tea?"

"Sure," she murmured. She stared at the letters she had written in the notebook. They were like a child's. ANCA. She felt no tremor of the nerves.

"What happened to you anyway? I've been trying to remember. You fell down the stairs?"

She hesitated, looking across the room at him. Posssibly he had never known. "I was born this way."

He squinted at her. "Really? I don't think so."

"It's the official story, anyway."

The expression on his face she took for pity. He passed her a cup of tea. She reached out deliberately with her left hand, her fingers pressing against the warm porcelain. Raising the cup to her lips gave her the queer feeling of someone else feeding her.

It was a wonder, her left hand rising from the dead, yet Péter acted nonchalant. He flopped down on the bed, stretching out lengthwise, so that his head was at the pillow. She noticed him looking at the clock on the overhead shelf.

"Come here," he said softly. "Show me what you can do with your cured hand." He took her in his arms. "I've been thinking about you all day," he whispered, pulling her closer. "Look at the woman you've become."

She had never kissed like this before. She tore herself away, out of breath, and inhaled his curls when he bent his head to her breasts. She looked down at him, the fabric of her blouse darkening under his kiss.

When she'd given it thought as a child, she had pictured herself losing her virginity on her wedding night like most brides from Crisu, the sheets hung out as evidence the next morning. But there were plenty of girls in university who shared a bed with a boyfriend.

"It's my first time," Anca confided.

He went to lock the door.

His penis rubbed against her with such expectation that she couldn't easily ignore it. She was impressed by how it rose to meet her fingers. It was taut and responsive as a tennis ball. She might have laughed, except that it did not seem polite with Péter in such earnest. She held tight and kissed deeply, at Péter's urging. When he pressed himself up inside her, she saw its real use. Her legs splayed like the petals of a poppy in the sunshine.

*   *   *

They had only minutes now until his roommates returned from dinner, Péter informed her. She was pulling up her stockings and smoothing down her skirt when the roommates entered. They all greeted each other, Péter sounding odd in Romanian. She seated herself at the edge of the bed. Péter lay stretched out proprietarily behind her, wearing only his boxers and socks, as if he wanted them to know what they'd been doing. She tried to shake off her embarrassment. She made the fist of the Young Pioneers, hailing the boys playfully. One of the roommates studied medicine and the other psychology. She showed them her hand and they gamely debated the cause of its restoration. Of course, she told them she had been born lame, but they hypothesized that the deformity was also a psychic injury. She translated to Péter. He looked smug.

"You are living a lie here," he burst out critically. "We should get married. You should come back to Hungary with me."

"What's he saying?" one of the roommates asked.

She shook her head, unwilling to translate.

At times, she found it hard to trust the doting look that came into his eyes, whispering to her in his bed. "Éva, my Éva!" Péter made her feel so exposed: he was always flinging the blankets back.

"Anca," she insisted, even in the heat of passion. "I'm Anca now."

What if he revealed her secret to someone else? It was not a crime to have hidden during the war, but she had been living under false pretenses ever since, existing as a different person, with documents denying her ethnicity. Even if it wasn't criminal, it could be construed to be. Any secrets could be used against you. The risk was always at the forefront of her mind as she lay spent beside him, listening to her own breathing.

He readily agreed to be discreet outside of the dormitory. It was safer this way for both of them with the political climate on campus. Fekete's presence at the university was too important to risk being undermined even by petty gossip. They sat separately at meals, Péter walking past her on his way to the officers' table. Sometimes he'd reach out quickly, depositing onto her plate the second dinner roll he received from the cafeteria crew since he sat with the officers. She was glad to eat the extra bread, but it was a reminder of the divide between Péter and herself. She watched him out of the corner of her eye as he talked and laughed with Áron Messer, who also spoke Hungarian.

When she questioned Péter's association with one of the Communist League's biggest instigators, he defended Messer. "He's sympathetic to Hungarians," he said.

She shook her head. "That must explain why so many were expelled last spring!"

"There was no other way to get past it," Péter claimed. "They couldn't risk another uprising. The Russians would have driven tanks into Timisoara!" The muscles in his neck tensed.

She could see that it was what he believed. There was no use in arguing. Péter was one of them. He acted ignorant of all the hypocrisy surrounding him. He nagged her about her mediocre marks, rejecting her view that it didn't matter whether she received 5s or 3s since the academic system was corrupt. "Only league members earn fives," she claimed.

They had found a place to meet where there were no roommates, in the basement of the math and science building, spreading out a blanket in a small alcove by the wall behind the boilers. There was a cat that sometimes slept there with them, curled in the corner, keeping its distance. It opened its eyes sometimes while they were making love.

Péter was eager to persuade her to apply for membership to the league, for the security, he said, if nothing else. "I'm certain I can have influence."

She said she wouldn't think of joining, glibly adding, "It's full of Jews."

He looked at her in surprise and with disgust, and, feeling chastised, she reached for him with her awakened hand, but he moved so that her hand slid from him. Anca noticed the cat watching.

"Péter," she said slowly. "The party is a sham and you know it."

"Listen, my *Éva*, the party is more important now than ever, as a *result* of the uprising. People should not have fled. Do you know how many hundreds of thousands paid their way to the West?" Péter was up on one elbow, gesticulating with his other hand, almost wagging a finger at her.

She remembered Auntie talking about the Hungarian exodus after '56.

"Hungary has a future!" he insisted. His rationale was full of the standard jargon, and yet it was also distinctly Hungarian, she realized. He seemed filled with pride of country like no Romanian. "The world knows now the evil of the Soviets. It will be a short period of hard-line rule to break our spirit, but then they will back off, and Communism will flourish, Hungarian-style."

"Isn't it nice you can predict the future," she said flippantly, turning away from him.

"Éva, you know nothing about it," he shot back. "Romania isn't *Hungary*."

"Stop calling me Éva!" she hissed.

The cat jumped up and leaped through the boilers, disappearing. Sorrow threatened to engulf her. She watched him pulling on his clothes. She had been reckless in approaching him. Péter had been Éva's. Still she clung to him. She reached for him now, fervent, and he kissed her forehead.

One Saturday she went with him to lunch at Professor Fekete's, who was staying in university housing not far from campus. He had a housekeeper, who was also an excellent cook. She had prepared several courses for them and uncorked bottles of Bull's Blood wine, which tasted like some of Uncle's merlots. Everyone spoke in Hungarian. There wasn't a proper dining table so they sat in the living room around a large ottoman.

Fekete was not quite so imposing at home, without his lab coat, a pair of slippers on his feet. Tufts of gray sprouted from his ears. Still, Anca was in awe of him. He had studied in Geneva and had lived in Vienna during the war. He called Vienna a sentient city, and admired the museums and theater, yet he insisted Vienna was not west, but central, Central Europe—just like Budapest.

The professor made little of his connection to Biró. He'd been a doctoral student in the lab of the inventor's brother, who developed the ballpoint ink. "Of course, Biró helped my career but I turned away from materials chemistry after earning the degree."

They were eating second helpings of Mari's stuffed cabbage. Mari, the housekeeper, was ethnic Hungarian. She was plump and wore a cook's apron and cap. She had short, boyish hair and high cheekbones. She sat opposite Fekete and he often winked at her. Fekete was not an elitist, Anca decided. The professor seemed to be in love with Mari, despite his wife in Budapest.

Mari crossed herself before taking up her spoon. Péter sniffed, disdainful. Then she whispered a prayer for Imre Nagy.

Fekete sighed, reaching out to finger Mari's earlobe "Everything would have been different in Hungary but for Trianon, I'm afraid."

Péter held up a finger. "Please, just a second, Professor," and got up to put a vinyl recording on the phonograph, turning up the volume on Wagner, in case of listeners behind the walls. They huddled together eating and lamenting the long ago but never forgotten shrinking of Hungary after World War I, the enormous loss it had been to Hungary, two-thirds of its territory, and the unfairness of it for the Hungarian population in Transylvania ever since.

Tears rolled down Mari's round cheeks as she spoke of Erdély. She was crouched at the professor's side, clearing the dirty dishes onto a tray, murmuring, "It is Hungary's sacred land."

Fekete rested his hand on her head momentarily.

Although Anca knew Trianon was the regret of all Hungarians, it was also the past. Auntie Kati had not carried on as if there were something to be done about it. "But Hungary has been on the losing side of two wars by now," Anca couldn't help pointing out. It was a factor the professor was not addressing.

"Romania switched sides during the war!" Fekete laughed in disgust. "What is worse?"

"Being on the wrong side is worse," Anca replied. Professor Fekete was a man of science. He shouldn't concern himself with petty politics—not even politics but patriotism. She looked in bewilderment at the professor's livid face. The conversation had buckled. She didn't dare glance at Péter. "I'm sorry if I've been rude, Professor," she hastened to say. "I didn't mean to offend."

Professor Fekete shook his head. He sat back on the cushion. "On the contrary," he said, looking at the others. "We have been insensitive to the fact that Anca is Romanian, despite how well she speaks." He bowed his head at her and smiled. "I am a guest in your country."

She felt a little ashamed. She'd drunk too much wine. She smiled back at him and sat up straighter in her chair. She glanced at Péter, who had grown quiet. They should turn the music down and openly speak of science.

Mari bustled out to the kitchen, returning with a tray crowded with a silver coffeepot, espresso cups, and a flourless layered torte as a special treat, saying she had been hoarding the sugar rations for weeks. Fekete claimed not to have noticed the dearth of sugar and Mari laughed. "You see, you are sweet enough already, Professor!"

Fekete made much ado over the *Dobos torta,* with its caramelized glaze. "Perfection! But Mari, I am homesick because of your cooking!"

"It would be a privilege to hear you talk about your work, Professor," Anca said, as Mari poured the coffee. The few times that Péter had discussed Fekete's work with her, Anca had been incapable of grasping it. Péter claimed that the professor was a pioneer of a new field of inquiry known as molecular biology.

He turned to her, as if taking her in anew. For a second, she recalled his intimidating face through the window of the laboratory door. She stammered, "Do you make experiments as well as theorize?"

"Of course," he replied. "There is no use in one without the other."

She nodded.

He folded his hands in his lap, eyes fixed on her, a little bloodshot from the wine. "Well, we grow E. coli bacteria and we extract the deoxyribonucleic acid and we analyze it." He paused. "But not here, we cannot do this here in Timișoara. There is no lab for it. Here we are just playing." His lips pursed.

"Professor, this nucleic acid, why is it important? Péter has tried to explain it to me. He describes it as a kind of, source of, omniscience."

"What?" interjected Péter, rolling his eyes at her. "I never said anything like that!"

"Well, but Anca is a literature student," Fekete offered kindly. He cleared his throat. "There is still much to discover but it seems as though the main role of the molecules is the storage of information."

She had no idea what he was talking about. Péter tapped her foot with his toe underneath the table. She shouldn't embarrass him further, with more stupid questions. As the professor continued talking, she gathered the potential of his words, envisioning an intricate blueprint, a code for all existence.

Later, on the walk home, Péter explained that the major discoveries had been made in the West. Several of the instruments needed to do the experiments were not obtainable, even in Budapest, and Fekete had been reduced to an itinerant beggar, visiting eastern bloc universities in his attempt to generate support for molecular research.

Péter reached for her hand as they walked down the cobbled street, and she had to resist her compulsion to break loose and flee. He would not be able to catch her this time. Being with Péter discouraged her. Even Fekete was oppressed. Even science was politicized: the fact of Eastern Europe's isolation in the world was too much to bear! (She would never call it "Central Europe.") It felt utterly personal, like a birth defect.

It came as a secret relief, midterm of the second semester, when Professor Fekete was forced to flee the country. The climate of inquisition returned to the university with the snowdrops on the lawn outside the dormitory. The lauded professor was expelled from the very faculty that had invited him. Fekete and Péter Somogyi were interrogated in the middle of the night and put on a train back to Hungary the next morning. Péter rushed to Anca's dorm room to say good-bye. She swore she wouldn't be able to bear it until he sent a letter yet she was glad, later, that no letters came for her.

Although they had been careful, there were people who knew about her and Péter, so it didn't surprise her when she was finally called in for questioning. But she was hardly alone. Anyone who had taken a course with Fekete was suddenly under suspicion. The officers of the Young Communist League were busily presiding over hearings, secret sessions, and cross-examinations. For individuals accused of anti-Communist activity, there were no appeals upon expulsion.

The interrogations were being conducted in the Foreign Languages library and, as a result, the library was never open, which was the worst crime of all, Anca felt. Inside the library, the officers of the league were seated behind one of the long reading tables. Áron Messer sat at the end, with a ballpoint pen poised gracefully in his hand. She had always felt uncomfortable around him, even before he had befriended Péter. He was an arrogant Jew.

When she was asked to explain the nature of her relationship to Péter Somogyi, she cleared her throat. "It was personal."

For a moment, the chinless senior girl who asked the questions looked blank. "You and Péter Somogyi were *intimately* involved?" She made it sound shocking.

Anca blushed.

"You must have overheard discussion regarding the professor's work?" There seemed to be just this one officer doing the questioning, while the others hovered magisterially.

She shook her head. "Of course not. I'm a student of humanities, anyway. I wouldn't have understood what I was hearing."

"You were present at lunch in the professor's flat on occasion."

She felt a nervous twinge at their knowledge of this but tried to appear unruffled. "Just once."

"Then you must have heard conversation between Péter Somogyi and Mihály Fekete regarding Imre Nagy?"

"Well, they *are* Hungarians," she said flatly. "It's to be expected." She let out a long sigh and crossed her legs under the table. She caught Áron Messer's eye.

He said to her, "You were screwing Péter Somogyi, you must have known he and Fekete were nationalists?" He had spoken out of turn. The others looked at him but he was staring demandingly at her.

She bit the inside of her lip.

"How is it that you know Hungarian?" he demanded.

"My Auntie," she said quietly. She stared down at her two hands. "And what about you?" she shot back, suddenly looking up at him. "You and Péter were friends as well, weren't you?"

He seemed to go white with rage. She strained to hear what he was whispering, now huddled with the others around the table. In just a few minutes, the huddle broke and she was dismissed. Exiting the library, she spotted Mari, Fekete's housekeeper, seated on the bench waiting to be called in. They barely acknowledged each other, which was the only way to behave under the circumstances.

*   *   *

She stayed in Timisoara during the summer to train and compete on the tennis team. A hush fell over the campus in the warm months. Her footsteps echoed beneath the vaulted ceilings of the empty halls. It was a relief to walk the corridors free of scrutiny. Had she been an intellectual, she would not have survived her own interrogation. The best and the brightest students who didn't conform were purged. The summer was an interruption to the rage and injustice. She shared a room with two other girls, teammates, instead of the usual three or four. Except for the expulsion lists that remained tacked to the doors of various buildings, the empty university seemed tranquil, unscathed. At the same time, fewer efforts were made in the janitorial department during the summer and toilets were perpetually backed up, which brought hordes of flies. Sinks were never cleaned and there was no hot water to be had.

In addition to tennis, she had a job in the Modern Languages library, in the basement of the Humanities building where the trials had been held. It was one of the best libraries in which to work not only because of its holdings, but because the majority of the languages faculty had permission to travel and weren't around. In the summer heat the library was airless as a tomb. Oddly, this atmosphere appealed to her and she would open a window only after lunch so that the janitor wouldn't find her suffocated when he came to clean at the end of the day.

Her tasks included shelving the books that had been taken out and never returned to the stacks. Tall piles of books filling several carts were waiting for her at the start of the summer, which explained why it was difficult to find books during the semester. She was also supposed to type new catalog cards, but pounding on the typewriter disturbed the cavernous stillness. The sound was so grating that she neglected the typing altogether and spent most of her time reshelving.

She spent long hours browsing the books, leisurely flipping through pages. One day, standing on a step stool dusting the top shelves in Russian reference with a feather duster, she came across a row of novels in English, an anomaly since there was no department of English at the university. She carried the volumes down. The summer had turned humid, and her brow was moist just from climbing the step stool. She had read *Tom Sawyer, Sister Carrie,* and *Tales of the Grotesque and Arabesque* in Romanian translation. She had never heard of *Frankenstein.* She flipped the book open. The tone was strangely romantic. The promise of confession drew her in. He was divulging someone else's dark secret. She sat down on the floor, yanking her skirt up so that her legs felt the cool stone.

A truly fantastical vision—Victor Frankenstein's science perverted into part man and part abomination—yet she was immediately convinced of its miraculous premise, which reminded her of Fekete's DNA molecules.

She heard the door to the library open and the janitor with his bucket and mop entering. She was glad he came to clean the floors but she hated to put the book away. She set her bookmark, stowed the book on a shelf, and folded up the English–Russian dictionary she'd taken out to assist her reading. It was the only dictionary of English in the library.

On the way home she bought a box of raspberries from a peasant on the street. She slept fitfully in the heat. Exhausted from tennis, only her mind was still awake. She rolled over in bed, listening to the tomcats prowling outside, thinking about *Frankenstein*. How could she not empathize with the odious fiend, his desire to be loved? He never asked to be created. It occurred to her as she lay there staring at the ceiling that Frankenstein's monster could be taken as an expression of Frankenstein's own self. In fact, all the characters were like permutations of each other. She didn't know what it meant, but it felt like a glimpse of the future.

She thought fleetingly of Péter, his happy predictions for Hungary. Here, in Romania, it was a different story. She drew her knees up, cradling herself. Both of her roommates were snorers. Sometimes it lulled her to sleep. She dropped off before dawn and slept through the alarm, until one of her roommates flicked a bath towel at her. She shuffled to the bathroom to douse her face in frigid water and to relieve herself while the flies were still quiet. By midday the buzzing grew so loud she was afraid to enter the restroom.

1961

THE GYMNASIUM IN TICU occupied an old-style, wood frame building set on a barren foothill at the edge of the dusty village. She had been posted at the high school as a teacher of modern languages. At the first faculty meeting the dean introduced Anca to her colleagues. She looked cordially from face to face and was alarmed to come upon Áron Messer seated in the dour semicircle of teachers. He was completely out of place here. He had been Communist League secretary in university!

In a panic she imagined he'd been sent to spy. She was unnerved, feeling his stares. The meeting was adjourned and he was at her elbow before she could blink.

"I'm so pleased to see you, Anca Balaj."

He acted as if they'd shared fond memories. She could see that something about him had changed. He'd lost confidence in himself. She asked, "What are you doing in Ticu, Áron Messer?"

He shrugged. "I've been here a year already." He lowered his voice. "I'm miserably bored and alone."

He asked if he could walk her home. Along the way he showed her a mushroom grove. They had nothing in which to gather the mushrooms. Áron stepped behind a tree to unbutton his shirt, took off his under vest, and fashioned a sling. His shirttails were out and he had not finished rebuttoning. He looked over at her, a serene expression on his slender face. His skin was the same olive color as hers. But there was pent-up energy in him that he couldn't conceal. Beneath the surface he seemed wound, ready to spring.

It was disorienting to see him now and to recall his arrogance, his dictatorial authority during the university trials. He said he'd sworn off politics and claimed to have joined only in order to stay in school.

"I got swept up, it was impossible not to. If I didn't report on others I'd have been suspect. I wasn't the only one, you know."

"Don't make excuses for yourself." She had no patience for this way of thinking; it reminded her of Uncle.

As they walked in the shade of the birches, Áron began to confess to her all the students he had denounced over the years. "I named whoever I believed was anti-Semitic. I figured they were my real enemies. I had no choice: denounce or be suspected myself."

She felt like spitting at him, the Jew, the coward. "Is that why I was called in for questioning?" She stopped, turning to look at him. "I'm anti-Semitic? It's true, after all."

He shook his head. "We had reason to believe Fekete was spying."

"What reason?"

"Communications with invisible ink," he paused. "Possibly with Imre Nagy while he was being held in Snagov."

"You must be joking!" She felt insulted. "Nagy was dead before Fekete arrived! Fekete was a physical chemist!" Her screeching reverberated under the canopy of trees.

He hung his head. "It sounds so ridiculous now. But the housekeeper was a university informant."

Fekete's button-cute housekeeper, Mari: Anca recalled her inciting Fekete's nationalism with her tears. She took a deep breath.

He was buttoning up his shirt, his fingers climbing. "I'm not who I was in university, I promise you, Anca."

His hair was certainly longer. A lock fell across his eyes. The susurrus in the branches soothed her. Finally, they emerged from the wood. Two children were pumping the well on the street corner.

"I'm having to get used to village life again," she remarked.

"The only nice thing about Ticu is the mushrooms," said Áron. Then he added, "Well, maybe now Ticu has two nice things."

She was renting a room, living with an old lady who looked to be one hundred years old. The old lady was picking spearmint outside the little stucco house as they came up the road. Áron was kind to her, introducing himself formally and insisting that she and Anca keep the mushrooms.

She made a soup and brought a portion to school the next day. They shared it in the teachers' room after classes. She'd awakened early to launder Áron's vest and hang it on the drying line before work. He walked her home again at the end of the day in order to collect it. The vest was warm from the sun. He said that no one had washed his clothes for him in a long time, and she told him he was not to get used to it. He pressed the garment to his nose, inhaling.

She would come home after school and the old lady would be waiting to feed her, since the old lady went to bed each night by seven-thirty. After the morning shopping excursion, she generally did not see a soul all day, and she relished Anca's company at dinnertime. She talked obsessively about the changes the war had brought—perhaps racked with guilt for having lived through it all.

Jews had been in Romania for centuries. They'd found shelter from pogroms and easy terms of settlement. They'd prospered. Even in the countryside, in Ticu, this had been the case. Ticu was once a town of many Jews. "Jews kept the shops, all those on Main Street used to be Jewish shops. They were excellent tailors," the old lady told her. The old lady was not a bigot. She was like most of the people Anca knew. Romanians had admired and envied Jews. But they were here first; Romanians were the ones who had been suffering all the while! Life was completely unfair.

"Did you hear they gassed those six million Jews?"

Anca nodded uncertainly. It was twilight and they were drinking tea after the meal.

The old lady sighed. "But maybe it wasn't that many."

Anca didn't reply.

"No one really knows," said the old lady.

It was true; there had been no official acknowledgment of the holocaust. And even when victim statistics were printed they were inconsistent.

Anca had been trained to teach Russian and French, but Russian was no longer compulsory in Romania and the gymnasium in Ticu was dispensing with it. Stefan Siminel, the dean of faculty, wanted to offer English. Áron had been recruited to study it as soon as he'd arrived. The dean was very much for Anca joining Áron in teaching English.

"But I'm not qualified," she protested. "And there isn't a textbook available."

"The two of you will write the textbook," said the dean, energetically. Stefan Siminel could be very persuasive. He was a great fan of the West, and he kept a small magazine photo of President Kennedy in his English-language dictionary. In his late forties, Stefan Siminel was overly friendly at times, affected yet sincere. It was a pleasant surprise to have a boss who was not beleaguered and downtrodden like most academics.

It was true what Stefan Siminel had said: the structures of English were simple enough. In the classroom, speaking was never emphasized beyond the rote dialogues anyway. Anca and Áron spent hours together at the teachers' table writing out spoken exchanges for students to memorize. Áron was clever, the way he could incorporate a subtext in a superficial conversation about the weather. His intelligence was sharp, striking, almost physical. Light burned in his eyes, and it was exciting just to be around him. She found herself longing for him whenever he left the room, even for five minutes to cross-check a word in the dean's English dictionary.

He looked over her shoulder at the dialogue she was writing. "You are foreign. Where is your home?"

"In Ticu," she replied. She hastened to fill in the blanks. "I live with the old lady. He is kind to me."

"'She' is kind," he corrected.

"'She.' Yes, of course," she said. Switching to Romanian, "I don't know why I make that mistake."

"It's a Hungarian speaker's mistake," he replied.

She paused. She supposed it was. She remembered the old Áron, speaking Hungarian with Péter back in university. "How is it you know Hungarian, Áron?"

He shrugged. "I speak a little." His eyes darted away from hers. Then he said, "I hid there, with my sister, during the war."

"In Hungary?"

"Yes, well, Transylvania, but it was the war, and we were inside the partition."

"Where did you hide?" she asked. She was straining to remain nonchalant, as if nothing he said could surprise her. She felt seized with paranoia. It was too great a coincidence.

"We hid in the barn of a pig ranch on the eastern plain, with a couple of others from our village. The rancher's wife fed us what she fed the pigs." He rummaged in another teacher's desk for a cigarette and matches. He opened the window. He turned his head to look at her, exhaling smoke. They had been talking Romanian, but now he used Hungarian, "What about you, Anca Balaj?"

"I told you already." She added, "When you were league secretary."

"I guess I'd forgotten."

She told him crossly, "You shouldn't ever forget."

"Nor should you," he returned heatedly.

The blood was rushing to her cheeks. She found herself making excuses about how late it was and packed up her bag, mindlessly filling it with notebooks and pencils she would not need overnight. Classes were starting the next morning. As she exited the building downstairs, there he was, still looming in the open window, smoking another cigarette. She walked hurriedly out of the school yard.

At breakfast, the old lady remarked that Anca had come home late again the previous evening and Anca explained that she and Áron were cramming for the first day. "I see," said the old lady, spooning up her coffee. "You've found a boyfriend already."

Anca quickly shook her head. "He was a Communist League member in university. Now he scorns it."

The old lady shrugged, wiping up the last drops in her cup with her finger. "So he's a changeling. They are everywhere."

Anca quietly sighed. Áron had told her that after the war he had been eager, grateful to believe in something. Communism had been his lifeline. She washed the breakfast dishes and was preparing to leave when the old lady spoke up. "Wait, Anca, I have something for you on your first day."

She followed the old lady as she shuffled outside into the backyard. "For the new English teachers," the old lady said, reaching up to pluck two plums from one of her trees. She set the plums in Anca's hands and Anca bent to kiss her loose cheeks.

The school yard was alive with children. The youth leaders blew their whistles and the students formed lines by grade level. She joined the other teachers standing alongside the school wall. With the usual slogans, the first-day rally got under way. Stefan Siminel, the dean, made a short speech about the importance of scholarship to the Communist party. Then he listed the new initiatives for the school year, including the introduction of English instruction. The students cheered wildly at this and the dean turned and waved Áron and Anca to the podium. "May I present your English teachers!" Áron looked as embarrassed as she was. Siminel was grinning broadly. She saw him wink at Áron.

Afterward, as they were preparing to lead the students inside, she remembered the plums. She pressed one into Áron's hand.

"From the old lady. She thinks you are my boyfriend."

Áron smiled. "Am I?"

"Well I don't give plums to everybody," she admitted, looking away.

Áron believed he was paying for his sister Sara's immigration to Israel in the posting to godforsaken Ticu but, of course, he'd never know for certain why the league had primed him, then dropped him. It wasn't unheard of, even among the loyal subjects. Maybe he'd shown too much ambition. He readily admitted to having been hungry for authority. Now he had been quietly, perfunctorily, dismissed from action. At first, he had prayed Ticu was a bureaucratic mistake.

"If it weren't for Stefan," he told her, "I wouldn't have survived my first year."

"You're the dean's favorite, I've noticed."

He denied it but she had been surprised to find Áron on such familiar terms with Stefan Siminel. He said that the dean had insisted he dispense with addressing him formally. Clearly, the dean was delighted to have a colleague of Áron's caliber. Áron's degree had been in math and history.

"But his mind is capable of anything," Stefan Siminel had said to Anca, in convincing her to embark with Áron on an English curriculum.

Since then, she had observed the dean's interest in Áron on a regular basis, at the teachers' lunch table or in a faculty meeting. Áron was a natural leader. Even the older teachers in the school respected him. It was easy to become enamored, and she kept telling herself she should never forget the Timisoara Áron. He was an intellectual who had conformed. Anca suspected that Stefan Siminel hid out in the party for his own reasons. But she should not be so critical. Her tennis team status had insulated her. No one was completely innocent.

The dean was intent on his staff's welfare and the teachers at the gymnasium were not unhappily employed despite Socialist wages, except of course for Áron.

"Until your arrival," Stefan Siminel told Anca, "he walked around like his heart was broken."

The dean had taken it upon himself to do what he could to cushion Áron's situation, including securing any American films that touched down in Romania. He would organize a private showing at his dacha. Stefan Siminel was crazy about

Olympian turned Hollywood movie star Johnny Weissmuller. In the summertime, he set up the school's projector in the garden of the dacha and *Tarzan the Ape Man* appeared on the stucco wall after dark. Anca was invited along with Áron now that they were a couple. The dean set out a few chairs for guests, including the neighbors, so that no one would make trouble—since the films were undubbed bootlegs.

Tarzan was a fabulous spectacle. It was impossible not to be impressed by Weissmuller ululating from the jungle treetops. He was a portrait of health and manliness. It was exciting watching him swim faster than alligators, his powerful arms motoring him across the river, and the effortless way he climbed out onto the opposite bank, as if there were no breaking his physical rhythm. He was blond and tanned, sinewy but powerful. And they all knew him to be Romania's native son.

"How does he do it?" one of the neighbors wondered.

"They are trained lions, circus animals," someone replied.

"Yes, but they are still wild animals. They are mauling him!"

"He is Tarzan, he knows how to handle them. Look there, he has stuck it with his hunting knife."

"Quiet down, ladies and gentleman!" the dean called out.

The dean grew his own grapes like Uncle, and the wine was plentiful and fruity. He had uncorked about a dozen bottles. It was a small celebration. No one needed to be at work the next day, and the bugs weren't out. Occasionally, the dean's father stayed out at the dacha with his birds. That evening he sat very close to the wall and a pigeon that went around on his shoulder was silhouetted at the edge of the flickering movie screen.

As the film rolled Anca curled up under a blanket with
Áron. They laughed quietly as Jane tried to teach Tarzan to speak
English. He might be clever, but it wasn't possible to domesticate
him. The jungle was part of Tarzan and he couldn't escape it.
Between reels, the dean vaunted Weissmuller's swimming career;
he'd never lost a race! Someone wondered aloud about whether
or not he was really born in Timisoara. Before the debate could
start up the dean set the film rolling again. Anca noticed that she
was the only woman still watching. The others had called Jane
idiotic, preferring Tarzan when he was still single, and wandered
back to the bonfire during the break to slice the dean's cheeses
and salamis and peppers for sandwiches after the movie. Anca
hoped they wouldn't hold it against her for not helping.

Tarzan and Jane were swimming together underwater. This
was before the Americans began censoring their films. Jane was
completely naked. At first, Tarzan is just playfully chasing Jane
around the bottom of the lagoon. The swim slowly becomes a
synchronized dance. Jane holds fast to Tarzan's shoulders, her
arms sliding down his muscular legs until she holds his ankles.
He glides through the depths of the water, pulling her—Tarzan,
then Jane, turning a somersault.

The scene was mesmerizing. When it ended, the audience
let out an audible sigh. Stefan clapped his hands together. There
were tears in his eyes. "Beautiful!" he cried.

Afterward, when all the neighbors had gone and Stefan was
packing up the projector, which he left locked in his car overnight, he and Áron debated Weissmuller's birthplace, whether it
was Serbia or Timisoara, Romania. No one's facts were verifiable
but the dean claimed Tarzan was Banat German.

Anca shook her head. "He looks Hungarian to me."

"I don't even care," said Áron. "I just wish I could swim like that."

"Well you'd have to actually go in the water first, Áron," she teased. He was notorious for sitting on the Ticu riverbank all summer long. She would never feel sorry for Áron the way the dean did. He had got what he deserved and it had changed him for the better.

"No. Seriously," the dean said earnestly, looking at them in the garden torchlight, "think what you could do if you could swim like that."

In unison, they whispered, "The Danube."

Stefan Siminel had managed to obtain hunting privileges for Áron and a few other faculty members. That autumn, after she had been in Ticu already one year, Anca accompanied Áron on a hunting trip over a long weekend, in the Carpathians. They boarded the train for Cluj early in the morning. She had no interest in hunting, but just the same it was a pleasure to be departing Ticu. Fog rolled over the meadows and outlying foothills, stripped for mining. Workers' housing—cement barracks—lined the distant landscape. A shepherd could be seen moving his small herd beneath the enormous pipes that ran up to the mine.

For a few moments of fun they pretended they were leaving forever. They were both obsessed with the gossip that trickled in from outside, reports heard around the country, instant legends, of people escaping in hot air balloons, swimming the Danube, digging tunnels, even repairing the engine

of an abandoned Nazi fighter plane and flying out without ever
before having flown.

Áron remarked that the train was passing the village where
he was born. She sat up.

"Áron, I had no idea your village was so near Ticu."

"Of course," he said. "They want to rub my nose in it."

She didn't have a reply. Out the window she caught sight
of the thatched rooftops beyond the thin forest. "Don't you ever
go back there, to visit?" she asked.

He shook his head. "Of course not." He added, "I was very
young when we left."

In Cluj they ate their sandwiches while waiting for the mountain train. She recalled that Simona Ursu had been from
Cluj. It was a beautiful city, in the foothills of the western
Carpathians. She stared moodily out the window as their
train finally departed. Snowflakes began to pelt the windows.
As the train gained momentum the falling snow became a
dizzying vortex. Beside her, Áron was hunched over a trail
map, preoccupied.

The long, narrow car became crowded and noisy with
activity. Several large groups had boarded—party members.
Hunting was an elite pastime. Áron saw someone he used to
know and jumped up to shake hands. He was quickly drawn
into a circle of hunters. They were all dressed in dark green and
several were wearing felt fedoras decorated with distinguishing
hunting pins made out of animal hair or feathers or wild boar
bristles. She watched Áron drink from a flask that was being

passed around. He talked boisterously, his lips glistening. In the army, he had been a top archer and orienteer and apparently something of an expert in making arrowheads. He had taken out the case he kept his bow and arrows in and the other hunters were inspecting his arrowheads and talking about whether it was ethical to tip them with Aconitum.

They disembarked the train at a small outpost and followed the groups walking to the hunting chalet. The snow had stopped falling. Trees grew thick on either side of the carriage road. There was a store for provisions in one of the lodge's wooden outbuildings and several village women sold smoked cheese and meat and apples along the road. The chalet itself was a sprawling structure with a steep shingled roof. A stone chimney was puffing smoke.

The sun had come out to take the chill off the cold afternoon. Áron went inside to obtain the permit while she packed away their purchases in the rucksack. The chalet was a busy place. Hunters talked in small groups and inspected one another's weapons. A professional photographer was taking hunting party pictures. An impressive rack of antlers was mounted over the double doors.

Áron emerged, striding back across the road to her. "Look," he said, showing her the bottle of vodka he had bought from another hunter. "We'll have something to celebrate the hunt." From the depths of one of the side pockets in his pack, he unearthed a silver-plated flask. By the engraving she could see it was a Communist League trinket, and she told herself she wouldn't drink out of it. He uncorked the bottle and carefully filled the flask.

*   *   *

Áron had a hunting knife like Tarzan's. He spent a long time sharpening it on a sliver of whetstone, beside the fire, after they had made camp. She was plucking the feathers from the little woodcocks he had bagged. There was a new animation in him ever since shooting his bow earlier. She had been behind him on the trail and he had come into view for her just as he was pulling back and sighting. She didn't even see the arrow flying through the air—just a flurry in the brush, and then stillness, and Áron bounding off to retrieve whatever it was.

She gathered up the small plucked birds. The bones would be hair-thin, like a rodent's. Áron's concentration was still fixed on the glinting blade of his hunting knife. He seemed to not know she was there.

"Here," she said, nudging him with the birds in her hands, interrupting his reverie. "Surely it's sharp enough by now."

He carefully trimmed and gutted the birds, the fire snapping with the burning entrails. "I'll go and clean them," he said and set out for the stream. It was black outside the sphere of firelight. Her eyes followed him into the darkness. She called out, "How can you see where you're going?"

He called back, "I see better in the dark, like an owl!"

While she roasted the pair on a spit over the bright coals Áron collected more firewood, dragging up dead limbs of felled trees, chopping the wood with a small hatchet. He was invigorated and, something else, uninhibited, unrestrained. All night long she stayed warm in his body heat.

*   *   *

It was still dark out.

"Whoever wakes early finds gold," he whispered in Hungarian. There was no time to waste. No brewing coffee, even urinating would have to wait since it would leave a scent. She laced her boots and followed him out of the tent. The temperature had dropped overnight and the sun was barely above the horizon. Áron was treading carefully but quickly and she didn't want to be left behind. Within a few kilometers of walking they began to see the split-wedge tracks of deer on the frosty ground. She climbed stiffly up the rock face after him, leaving the tracks behind. Now they were walking along the ridge, on an outcropping about twenty meters high. They had a distant view of the stream edge below them. Áron pointed to the pair of roe deer drinking. The young bucks disappeared from view only to reemerge a few seconds later within range, and Áron took aim. The deer looked straight up at him and he sent the arrow flying. The buck leaped upward, shot through its lungs. Both deer bounded off but the struck deer balked, its chest thrusting, and began to stagger. Its neck was craned, its chest heaved. The deer took a few more awkward steps, shuffling on its forelegs, and then collapsed. Áron flew down the steep ridge after it. He pulled the arrow, which was trapped between the ribs. He kneeled beside the fallen deer, reaching to stroke its long neck. Then, turning to look up at her on the ridgetop, he cupped a hand, calling, "Go fetch the flask, please, Anca!"

*   *   *

After a shot of vodka Áron went to work suspending the deer from a branch with a length of rope to finish bleeding out. He tore the animal end to end with his knife. Steam clouded up in the cold air. He removed the rump, which he cut right away into steaks, and then he carefully removed the loins. She made her way back to their camp returning with tea and sandwiches and the metal box they'd rented from the hostel, but Áron didn't stop to eat. He had removed the ribs and now was severing the front hams and the stew meat. Various piles of meat and innards lay strewn. His face was glistening with sweat. His hands and the front of his jersey were drenched in blood. She rinsed the meat and packaged it in the box, covered over with ice from the stream edge. She had never cared for venison, not even the sausage, but she understood that they would be able to sell a portion of the meat. By the time it was done there were buzzards in the trees. Oddly, the deer was mostly skin and bones. The meat weighed a third of what the deer had weighed.

She unbuttoned Áron's shirt for him and helped him slip out of it. His hands and forearms were coated in bloody grime. He went to where he could straddle the stream and plunged his arms into the water and began vigorously rubbing them clean. She scrubbed his shirt for him. They passed a sliver of soap back and forth. The sun was high now. It must have been close to noon. They had not seen another soul since setting out from the chalet.

Áron had left one of the steaks unpacked. They salted it and cooked it. In the drippings he cooked birch pulp. They also brewed tea, which was needed after the vodka.

"Delicious," Áron kept saying, savoring the venison.

He had sliced the meat thinly and sprinkled it with pepper. The birch pulp was crunchy and somehow sweetened the meat.

"We could live off venison," he said. "Smoke it for the winter and find a cave to hibernate in. We wouldn't need to swim the Danube."

She smiled. She was hungry and it was tasty. After eating, they rested in the sleeping bags.

"The only place I've ever felt at home is in the woods," Áron said.

"A Romanian Tarzan," she suggested playfully.

"Well, but the myth is ancient, no?" he said. "Romulus and Remus raised by a wolf."

"Yes," she murmured, thinking of it. She reached out, caressing his face, his new whiskers. He caught her by the wrist and gently bit her on the knuckles, his eyes flashing darkly. She pulled him in, her hands in his hair. He suckled her breasts. She closed her eyes as he moved down her body, spreading apart her legs and lapping with his tongue.

They were falling asleep, afterward, when they heard the cracking of branches and twigs and a crunching of leaves.

"What is it?" she whispered.

"I don't know," he said, getting up.

He called out a greeting but there was no reply. The footfalls were loud, coming closer. From where they lay in their sleeping bags, they couldn't see beyond the rock outcropping. In front of them the fire was still going strong. They felt the ground shudder. A brown bear lumbered into view, swinging its massive head. Áron threw another log onto the fire, building up a barrier between them and the bear. The animal stepped out of the way of the commotion in the fire, glancing across the flames at them with amber eyes.

They crouched underneath the ridge cropping. The bear was after the aluminum meat box, turning it over onto its side, nosing it along the rock.

"I meant to secure it in the tree," Áron lamented.

Anca was too frightened to speak. She watched the brown mass clawing the aluminum box and grumbling, its huge arms pelting the box along the ridge rock. Behind the bear, Áron's white shirt was flapping in the sun.

"He's a rogue bear if he's that hungry," whispered Áron. "Did you know the game warden feeds the bears that the party shoots? Raises them like cows—I was talking to some hunters on the train." He paused, anxiously watching the bear ten meters away. "He's going to break it open."

The bear's shoulders were immense. It bared its teeth as it gnawed the lock. Then it reared up and with a sweep of its forepaw sent the box tumbling down the slope and barreled down after it.

Áron leaped out of the shelter, grabbing up his bow.

At the bottom of the slope the lock on the box had popped and all the carefully packed meat had spilled out. The bear was busy devouring the contents. It was against the law to shoot at it (bear permits were reserved for party elite) and the arrows Áron shot around it didn't deter it. The bear did not leave until everything was gone. They watched it lumber off finally through the trees.

The box was busted and they would have to pay for it. It seemed like such a waste. Áron's face was drained of color. He was furious with himself. As the evening encroached a dark mood set in. He sat beside the fire, drinking vodka.

"There's something I have to tell you, Anca." He turned to look remorsefully at her across the flames.

"What is it, darling?"

He paused. "I know about you. I know you hid like I did. In Timisoara. Péter Somogyi told me."

She felt her blood surge.

Áron went on, "I should have said something sooner. Excuse me."

She lunged away from him as he reached for her. She was afraid of the pitch darkness, but she stumbled off into it. She could hear the stream and made her way down. She crouched at the edge and cupped the frigid water and drank, gasping for breath at the chilling shock of it. She felt tricked, humiliated. Soon she heard him approaching. Now he stood beside her—his long legs.

She paused, looking up at Áron. "Is it in my file in Timisoara?"

"No. I interrogated him in private. I promise I never recorded it. I never would have." He crouched down beside her. "We're like twins, Anca."

"Yes, I know," she said uneasily. "I've known." She stared at the hand he was extending. He pulled her up and she stood facing him. He dried her cheeks with his shirtsleeve.

They hiked out the next day and boarded the return train to Cluj and then the train to Ticu. She had dozed off for a while after departing Cluj. Now it almost felt as if she were waking from a dream. Beside her, Áron was busy preparing the coming week's lessons. She sat up on the seat, rubbing her eyes.

The countryside began to look familiar. "There is your village," she said, her fingertip touching the cold window. The distant thatched roofs flashing past.

He nodded without lifting his eyes.

"You must have gone back there, after hiding?"

Now he looked at her. His whiskers had begun to grow in on his chin. She loved his crooked lips. "It took us months to get home," he finally said. He had bought a packet of cigarettes at the chalet after paying for the broken meat box. He took one from his breast pocket, reaching up to crack the window. "I remember we began finding mushrooms to eat. Sara said it was a sign we were near." He sighed, looking beyond Anca out the window, and she caught the reflections flying by in his eyes. "Our house looked the same as ever. Right away I recognized the curtains in the windows. Mother's curtains! I kept shouting it." He fell silent.

"Don't tell me," she said. "It's too painful. I shouldn't have asked."

He shook his head. "But I want to tell you," he insisted. He sat up straight against the seat back and put the cigarette between his lips, his hands cupping the lit match. He blew out a vital stream of smoke. "I remember Sara knocked on the door, but a stranger answered. It was the same rug on the floor, our table and chairs, our pots and pans. But I kept looking at the curtains. For a long time we sat outside just staring at the house."

"What sort of curtains were they?" she asked quietly.

"Blue." He smiled sadly. "She was a seamstress. She'd sewed them herself."

She reached for his blood-tinted hand and he grasped hers, clutching tightly, together staving off the emotion. The train pulled into the little station at Ticu and they disembarked with their packs. It was evening. The air was perfectly still. Her eyes cast about the shadowed buildings. She kissed Áron good night and started up the road that led to the old lady's house. Strangely, it felt as if she'd never left.

1967

HER BREASTS WERE SWOLLEN like balls of sheep cheese, and now she was four weeks late. Soon it would be too cold to take their clothes off outdoors. She finished braiding the tall grass, tied the ends, and slipped the necklace over Áron's head. After six years together she was surprised to feel so hungry for him, out of her mind with desire. But it was another effect of pregnancy. She held on to him, cresting, shutting her eyes, the beauty of being flashing its bright light.

They lay on their backs in the meadow and watched the movement of clouds through the birches. The expanse of sky slowly sobered her. Abortion, as well as birth control, was illegal now, under Ceauşescu. She usually bought pills smuggled from Hungary, but it hadn't been possible with the recent crackdowns. The old lady's herbal tincture had had no effect. She thought of getting back in touch with Uncle Ilie. He might find her the money for an illegal abortion, if she told him the father was a Jew. She was ashamed for even thinking of it. Tears filled her eyes.

"Are you crying, Anca? Don't. It'll be all right."

She shook her head. "No, it won't, Áron. It's wrong. A child. Now."

"I know I should feel that way, but I don't," said Áron. He whispered urgently, "It's *our* child!"

She rolled away, turning her back to him. "What future will it have here, Áron?" She couldn't stop crying. "Nothing. No dreams. It's not possible!"

He came close, whispering in her ear. "You don't know, Anca. He may be the next table tennis champion!"

She smiled through her tears and took the handkerchief he was offering. The sport was extremely popular ever since Ceauşescu's visit to China. Over the summer, the dean had set up a Ping-Pong table in the garden out at his dacha and Anca discovered she had a talent for it.

She gave birth to a boy on the midwife's floor just before dawn, May 1. She shredded a rag, grinding it between her teeth every time the pain came, but he was born quickly. The midwife, a Russian, with pale blue eyes and graying curls, held the baby up for her and she gasped at the hole in his face.

The midwife shrugged. "There's an operation, if it's necessary, but you'll have to travel to Bucharest."

The midwife cleaned and swaddled the baby and then she told Áron he could come in. He had passed the hours in the midwife's kitchen, which she shared with two other people who were apparently used to fathers sitting in wait because they'd acted as if Áron weren't even there. The midwife set the baby in Áron's arms, saying, "Severe cleft palate. He will be difficult to feed."

From where she now lay on the recovery cot, Anca could see the bewilderment on Áron's face. He looked down at the baby, then over at her. She smiled as he came toward her with the swaddled infant in his arms. He leaned in to kiss her cheek, and sat down carefully beside her on the rickety cot.

The midwife's bed was behind the curtain that enclosed them, and they could hear her climbing under the covers after being up all night. She had turned off the light. Outside it was overcast for the workers' holiday. The room was in shadow. They peered at the baby, whose eyes were open. He was dark-haired with dark pink skin.

"He's as beautiful as any baby," Áron whispered, and gently, with his forefinger, traced the curved brow and sweet, retroussé nose and little pointed chin.

"So delicate," she murmured.

"Oh," said Áron, "before I forget." He carefully reached into his pocket, taking out the cap the old lady had been knitting. "She brought it by last night and said we should put it on him right away."

Anca took the cap and carefully fit it over the baby's small head.

She tried to put him to her breast. Her breast was swollen almost larger than his head, the nipple a stiff brown spout, but he was unable to latch on. The reflex was there but not the mechanism, his underjaw failing to find leverage. Soon he was frustrated, yelping like an angry pup, and finally crying with fervor. Áron took him, at last patting him to sleep on his shoulder. She stared at her glistening nipples leaking the early milk. A feeling of horror. It was such a relief when he quieted.

"It can be surgically corrected," she whispered, shifting her gaze to the curtain. "She told me."

Behind the curtain the midwife was snoring.

The old lady visited Anca at the midwife's the next day. She had brought sorrel soup. She recounted the events of the holiday, which had gone by without Anca noticing. Anca was tired from the night of frustrated nursing, too tired even for the soup.

"I wonder, will you circumcise?" asked the old lady. She added, "I heard it can cause infection."

Anca looked at her baby asleep in the old lady's arms, the garish cleft. She reached out for him.

The old lady leaned forward, relinquishing the bundle in her arms. "Anyway, Jewish blood is through the mother," she said, sniffing.

Soon he began to cry from hunger. Her breasts were full and hard as wood. He would close the underside of his mouth on her but couldn't suckle. She was spraying all over him. It was a horrific, chaotic effort. The midwife convinced her that some milk went down his throat and he did act as if he'd tasted something, or else he was tired out from trying, because he settled down again. "Take him home," the midwife encouraged, "Maybe he wants to be at home." But when they took the baby back to their rooms in the old lady's house he still wasn't thriving. She was meant to feed him every few hours, but nursing him was an illogical operation. Her breasts ached with all the milk she produced for him. The midwife had given her a special feeding bottle. She squeezed her milk into the bottle, but the milk was slow to run down of its own. They discovered that if Áron kissed her while she expressed the milk the flow increased. So they kissed over the milk bottle, the child staring up at them blindly.

He was just like other babies, and yet he was an aberration. She felt as if she could see straight into his head through the hole in his face. Out of desperation, she sent a telegram to Ilie in Oradea, explaining the predicament. Stefan Siminel, the dean, took up a collection on their behalf. Their newest colleague, hired for Anca's leave, covered Áron's courses while they traveled together to the pediatric surgical hospital in Bucharest. Áron was calling him Zalman, after his father, a blatantly Jewish name, to which she silently objected. She was wrought with anguish and fatigue. He was tiny, skeletal. To calm herself, she doted on his long, princely fingers and his silken curls, his large puppy ears like Áron's.

Aboard the train it was hard to wake him. He made very little noise now. "He conserves his energy," Áron remarked anxiously. He held a shawl around her while she tried in vain to feed the starving child. Any of the peasant women in the coach could have told them he wasn't going to make it.

By the time they reached Bucharest she was exhaused and had developed a fever. Áron telephoned for an ambulance. On a bench outside the station she sat with the bundle in her arms while Áron paced the sidewalk. She looked down at the baby

through the haze of her fever. He had such pretty hands. She
bent to kiss the world's tiniest fingertips.

The doctors in Bucharest told them the baby was too weak
to endure anesthesia, so there would be no operation. He died
within a few hours. The hospital wasn't as crowded as usual, so
they were offered a bed, where they huddled together with the
baby. She could see his fragile heart slowing down, his small
chest heaving for breath and finally ceasing.

She was given penicillin for mastitis of the breast: it was
truly a miracle drug. She slept deeply. Several times she began
to wake up. She saw Áron's face and asked for the baby and he
had to tell her all over again that Zalman was dead, gone, his
corpse already in special transit back to Ticu.

Their return trip was overnight, partly a local route. Passengers
got on and off in the darkness. Sometimes the car was crowded
and sometimes it was empty. Áron drank from a bottle of vodka
he'd purchased from a peasant outside the Bucharest station. It
was a chilly night and they pressed together in the seat. In front
of them someone was snoring. The train banged over the tracks
and she felt it in her womb. She looked up at Áron, who was
wide awake. He pulled her closer. He began to roll down her
stockings and she didn't even think to protest when he undid
his belt, although the midwife had said she should wait several
weeks. She was young and strong, even after the infection. He
leaned over her, pushing himself in, and she braced herself
against the seat. It was painful and painless both. It was open
and raw. She could not make it stop. If only it would kill her!

She bit into her lip to keep from crying out. She felt the painful letdown and her shirtfront was soaked in her baby's milk.

There was a Lada parked outside the old lady's house. Uncle was standing in the door. He had arrived the previous day. The old lady had shared the news that Áron sent from Bucharest and allowed Ilie to stay overnight. Anca was touched that he'd come at all. He looked well, tanned and surprisingly fit. He was living in Oradea and had a girlfriend. "A Gypsy," he said with ironic pride. He shook hands with Áron and the old lady ushered them inside. She had spread out a tablecloth and set out glasses and a bottle of *tuica*. Áron of course had been drinking all night. After two shots he turned green in the face and excused himself for the outhouse—so Uncle always thought of him as soft, mistakenly.

Uncle Ilie couldn't understand why Áron and she weren't married—for the subsidies. When she replied that two people who loved each other didn't require marriage, which was Áron's claim, he told her she was an idiot. He rubbed his stubbly face. "The doctors might have helped you in Bucharest if you'd been married."

She was furious with him for saying this but there was no energy left for a fight. It had been so long since she'd seen him, and already she couldn't wait to be rid of him. He was telling her to move to Oradea. She should come with or without Áron. She had forgotten what a bully he could be. When she mentioned she had begun competing in table tennis, Uncle pressed, "The national team is in Oradea!"

He stayed long enough to drive them to collect the corpse. On the way to the cemetery, Áron argued with Uncle over which road to take. She looked on from the backseat as Uncle's arms flailed, knowing-it-all, and Áron's face grew blotchy from his restraint. Beside her, on the seat, the wooden box was still cold from the morgue, despite the warm day.

They buried the baby in the children's cemetery near the riverbank. Uncle wired money when he returned to Oradea to pay for an engraving but, as it turned out, she needed the money to bribe the midwife. She never told Áron that they had conceived on the Bucaresti return train. She had been visiting the midwife for bleeding and then the bleeding just stopped and her nipples began to tingle. The midwife confirmed the pregnancy, with eyebrows raised. She washed her hands at the kitchen sink and came back into the room while Anca was dressing.

"It's risky," she confirmed. "But you are strong from the antibiotics. You can manage, I think."

"But I can't, I don't want to," Anca confided.

The midwife looked her over. "Have you brought envelope money?"

Anca nodded. Then, during the procedure, the midwife accidentally nicked the uterus. She was contrite and returned the money. Anca ended up having to have a hysterectomy. She traveled to the city for the operation, Áron at her side, knowing nothing of why she wouldn't stop bleeding.

It was a lonely recovery. She was tormented by dreams of her baby's malformed face. In a way, her guilt precluded regret. It was a wet, purple chasm halting her. She still loved Áron, but their life together seemed doomed.

*   *   *

One year later, early in the morning, she stood staring at the blank marker. Áron had refused to visit the gravesite with her. "I'm not going to act religious with you," he'd said.

The earth had resettled and grass was growing over the grave. She had been sorry not to afford the engraving, but now she felt glad her baby remained nameless. Zalman? Áron had named him after a ghost. She set down the violets she had gathered and took out of her pocket the handkerchief the old lady had sewn for her when the baby died. She wiped away her tears, then hurried home to help with preparations for Workers' Day.

Áron had received another letter from his sister Sara. He sat at the old lady's table drinking tea, his eyes darting across the page. Recently, he had begun talking about emigration. Israel was still paying Romania for its Jews. For once there was an advantage to being a Jew. "We deserve a home," Áron had said. He'd turned into a Zionist seemingly overnight. It seemed to be exactly what his survival required, just as Communism once had been.

"You were born here," she had reminded him. "This is your home."

He had exploded. "I was not born here! I was born in a house with curtains!"

She did not want to fight with him today. The parade was to begin at noon. The old lady was going in and out, putting the jars of compote out on a table in front of the house. The house had a couple of plum trees in the backyard, so the old lady made dumplings with fresh plums for August 23, Independence Day, and compote for Workers' Day. Her compote was lovely, so sweet after all the winter apples.

Áron hesitated, folding up his sister's letter. She handed him a serving of dumplings but he declined it. He looked grim.

"Áron what is it?"

"I can't bear it here, not since Zalman," he confessed in a painful whisper. He cried out thoughtlessly, "I should have left with my sister!"

She ate the dumplings herself. Áron sat brooding on the opposite side of the table. The old lady came back inside the house, excited about the holiday in a way that irked Anca. The old lady busied about the kitchen. Then she spied the Gypsy peddler going by in the street and hurried back outside after him.

Anca pushed the empty bowl away with her fingers. Áron reached for her hand. "Let's emigrate together."

"Together? How? We're not married."

Áron shrugged. "We'll get married."

"I'll have to expose myself officially." She paused. "They'll arrest me for fraudulent papers before Israel ever hears of me! Do you think they'll let me choose—Israel or prison?"

"Yes, I do, in fact. Romania is profiting, Anca." He looked at her crossly.

They hushed up as the old lady came back inside with a braid of wild leeks and a ball of wool from the Gypsy. Anca tried to take an interest in her prizes. Áron said he had lessons to prepare and got up to go over to the school. "But it's the holiday," the old lady pointed out. She studied the two of them. She had shown a great deal of concern ever since the baby. She kindly said she would not need any help in serving compote to the local youth groups. Anca should get some fresh air, along with Áron.

Anca followed Áron out of the house. There was nowhere to talk that was private. Their bed was in the old lady's back hallway. They had made love in the open meadows. Sometimes they heard the heated cries of others in the tall grass. It was hard to tell the lovers from the cats in the summertime.

They headed down the footpath toward the school, speaking in English, which was their habit when out in public. "I think you have fear," he stammered. "Fear. That is all."

"Of course," she replied. "Of course. Perhaps."

"We waste time here. This life is waste." He sounded so impassioned in his rudimentary English. She smiled to herself. The streets were crowded with Workers' Day celebrants. Youth groups were passing out flags and hard candy. Anca joined a line. Áron tugged her sleeve like a little boy. "Anca, I am going."

"Wait," she said. She unwrapped the candy and cracked it between her teeth and slipped half between Áron's lips. The candy tasted of real sugar, not honey. May 1 was a major holiday in all the Communist countries. Every town with an outlying factory staged a parade. May 1 was also the day when the strand by the river opened. She always got her first sunburn of the year.

The parade had started. They stood on the corner under one of the sickly walnut trees that lined the road. One day in the previous autumn the youth groups had been called upon to pin small brown paper balls to the limbs to look like the fruit the tree never bore of its own. There was a rumor that Ceauşescu was traveling the bountiful Romanian countryside and that his cavalcade might roll through Ticu.

Stefan Siminel waved to them as he strode by with the other town leaders.

She watched the miners' float roll by and the youth groups falling in behind. Then came the gymnasium sports teams. All the Ping-Pong girls saluted her when they passed and she leaned in and kissed Paula, team captain, on the cheek.

"Áron," she said, turning to him, groping for the correct English. "Maybe. It's not such pity."

He retorted with, "How can you say it? Of Zalman?"

She persuaded him to walk to the river with her so she could go swimming. There were lots of people picnicking on the grassy bank. A large block of ice in a metal vat kept beer bottles cool. Anca didn't liked beer, but there was also cola, meant for the children, which she drank.

They watched the sausages cooking, clouds wafting from the barbecue. This was a Romanian specialty, *mici*—sausage meat served on a thin round of bread called *franzela,* and with mustard. Delicious. Folk music played on outdoor speakers suspended from the walnut trees. There was a rich, springtime feeling. She lay in the sunshine shivering in her bikini while Áron badgered her about Israel. He had no patience for the Pioneers in uniform walking up and down the bank selling flags. Anca fished inside her purse for a coin and pressed it into the girl's hand, and then she waved the Romanian flag in Áron's face. "You never know who is watching," she scolded him.

He whispered in her ear. "Come with me to Israel."

She rolled over, pressing a finger to his lips.

*   *   *

She asked him to wait before initiating an official inquiry to emigrate. Once he applied, he would come under intense scrutiny. He could lose his job. Thank goodness they weren't married.

She conducted herself as if these were their last days together.

"You two are trying for another child," the old lady remarked one morning at breakfast.

Anca smiled sadly. "In fact, we are splitting up." She hesitated. "Áron is going to apply for Israel."

The old lady looked impressed. "If I was a Jew, that's what I would do, too." She was standing at the sink so that Anca couldn't see that she was eating plum compote. It had been a meager harvest the previous year and the old lady had become stingy.

If one could leave, one should, Anca knew this, and yet she also knew she would not go with him. Áron was a changeling, like the old lady had once said. He was busy reading pamphlets and Zionist literature, reincarnating once more. He claimed he felt alive for the first time since the baby's death. He traveled to the barbershop in the next town and came home shorn, gaunt and pale. In private, she wept. It pained her to witness his conversion, but it proved she was not his twin. She quarreled with him over nothing important in order to avoid talking about emigration. Silence grew between them, making it easier to let go, in the end.

Following Áron's emigration in 1970, Stefan Siminel's father was arrested and thrown into prison for keeping pigeons, since pigeons could be trained to carry secret messages. This victimization was apparently aimed at punishing the dean, who had supported Áron's application and shielded him from subsequent harassment. Somehow, the impact of Áron's departure was displaced for Anca in the old pigeon man, Stefan's father. Stefan and Anca became inseparable, consoling each other. They played endless games of Ping-Pong out at the dacha. The dean was the only one who could still give her a game.

Stefan's father was released from prison finally. She was practically living in the Siminel house by this time, sleeping on a fold-out cot in the dining room, but the old man seemed not to notice her whatsoever. He sat in a chair in the kitchen, leaning on a cane. His shoulders were curled and his chin rested on his chest. He did not speak. Before the arrest she used to see him tending his birds out on the balcony. He was someone she had believed was happy, despite everything.

Stefan's father died within the year. She never heard from Áron. Possibly his letters were confiscated. At first, she thought of killing herself. Just as her father, jumping in front of a train. That was what one did with a broken heart. Something very real, as the muscle itself, had been severed.

The old lady was all for Anca marrying the dean. She had known the old Mrs. Siminel, who was a saint to have put up with a pigeon-head husband.

"Does it matter that we aren't lovers?"

The old lady shook her head soundly. "Separate beds!"

Stefan kissed her, very drunk, on their wedding night, calling her "Áron's mistress" and "Áron's dolly." In the little back bedroom of the dacha, he divulged his feelings for Áron. "You are not the only one who was in love with him," he whispered urgently.

She lay back on the pillow. She had also drunk too much. It was the only way, she'd realized. She reached over, stroking him in his underwear. "Pretend I'm Áron?"

He pulled out his limp penis with a sigh. "It can't be fooled, believe me, I've tried." He took her in his arms awkwardly. "I'm sorry."

She didn't know why she felt like crying. She'd had no expectation. The dean, she knew, could make her life easier. She could do the same for his. Marriage would put an end to rumors about him.

They honeymooned at the Black Sea. It was a popular destination for Eastern Europeans. So many languages spoken. On the beach, she heard people using English, new lovers, across borders, and she longed for Áron.

Stefan Siminel pressed Anca to enter table tennis competition. He designed a rigorous training program for her. Her teaching load had to be reduced to accommodate the Ping-Pong, so he found her translation work on the side with a film distribution company. The reels would come through the post and she would sit in a chair with a paddle and bat the Ping-Pong ball off the wall incessantly, making excuses that she was waiting for the films, but of course she was still hoping to hear from Áron.

Even after she was married, she'd walk to the old lady's house to see if any letters had arrived there for her. The old lady had fallen into a depression as a result of her plum trees getting chopped to clear the way for more miners' housing. She had not been able to attend the wedding. She was frail. Anca had brought pictures to show the old lady finally. She knocked on the door, then walked around to the back since the old lady was hard of hearing.

Letting herself in, she found the old lady slumped over the kitchen table. She occasionally fell asleep at the table after dinner, but it was morning, the dinner dishes had not been cleared away. A fly was buzzing in the room, several flies. The old lady didn't stir. Anca stepped closer to her chair. She peered curiously over her. The old lady's eyes were open in a ghoulish stare. She would have to report the death. First, she walked quietly past her into the pantry to retrieve the last two jars of plum compote.

1975

PING-PONG WAS HER ZIONISM. She had always been quick, with strong reflexes, and, of course, she could serve with either hand. Over time, she developed an arsenal of strokes and spins that had advanced her in top-flight competition. Her ranking qualified her for the national team in the Masters Division and she and Stefan moved to Oradea so that she could train full time. Stefan's good connections had led to his own involvement in the sport, first as her manager and then as regional director. He wore a Western-style necktie and had put on several kilos from taking his meals at the Black Falcon, the hotel where they lived.

The building was an architectural gem in Oradea's city center. It had a stained-glass arcade interior and old world elegance and was not too much in disrepair, except for weak plumbing and a malfunctioning lift. The view from their front windows was of the church tower opposite the avenue. She looked straight into the face of the moon on the astronomer's clock. For some reason she often drew the curtain on it.

She had been in Oradea several months before she got up the nerve to contact Uncle Ilie. She invited him to visit her at the hotel.

"Uncle! You look well." She smiled at him and went on tiptoe to kiss cheeks.

His complexion was ruddy from the sun. "It's all the bicycle riding," he replied. The years seemed to have softened him. He linked his arm in hers as she showed him in. They silently agreed not to talk about the past. Stefan shook Ilie's hand and then returned to his easy chair, watching Olympic gymnastics on television, while Anca made coffee.

Uncle still had his Gypsy girlfriend. He showed off a photo he carried around of Irini. She was striking, carefully groomed, with arching eyebrows. Her hair was pinned up in braided coils. She was looking over her shoulder, wearing a low-cut dress. Uncle had brought along a few of the *Playboy* magazines he was trafficking. Anca leafed curiously through the magazines while Uncle sipped the espresso and looked favorably around the hotel suite.

"You have more room than you need, it seems. I could sleep on a cot, over by the window. You wouldn't even know I was there."

She smiled idly, without looking up from the magazine. "I'm surprised you and Irini don't live together by now."

"I can't live with Irini," he said. "She's in business."

Anca glanced up.

Uncle nodded. "Irini's a professional."

"A prostitute?"

Ilie said matter-of-factly. "It suits me. No strings."

She was too astonished to reply at first. She curled her loose hair behind her ears. He had been going to a prostitute all these years? "Aren't you getting a little old for it?" she asked cautiously.

"It's not what you think," said Uncle. "Irini and I are good friends by now. She knows all my secrets. She takes good care of me."

"But you pay her," Anca said.

"In goods, usually. She'll take the magazines." He craned his neck, saying, "You don't want the 'literature,' Stefan?"

Stefan Siminel turned his attention from the television for a second and looked placidly at the magazines. "Oh, no thanks."

Ilie shrugged. He collected the *Playboys*. He looked out the window at the clock tower and then back at Anca, one hand rubbing his stubbly chin. "You judge me too harshly," he said to her.

Her heart ached with conflicted emotion. She stood up to kiss him good-bye. He made plans to come to her next tournament. She closed the door behind him, glancing back across the room at Stefan's large head, silhouetted against the television screen. Uncle was right; who was she to judge?

Minutes later, the horrible squeal of car brakes down on the avenue brought her to the open window and she looked out just as the Lada struck Uncle on his bicycle. He was pitched from the seat. He went over the handlebars and flew through the air, prostrate, a big man in worker's overalls. Then he hit the street.

She had to take the stairs, four flights, because the lift wasn't working. He lay sprawled facedown on the pavement, his arms still stretched to either side. A few people were gathered. Traffic had resumed, moving slowly around him.

Irini's address was printed on the back of her photograph—a business card, apparently. Anca sent her a telegram. They met at the morgue, greeting each other formally. She was dressed in a hooded wool coat and now she removed the hood and fixed Anca with liquid black eyes. "Where is he? I've brought herbs for the coffin." Her hair was pinned up the way it was in her photograph, and the ebony curls on her head glistened under the fluorescent light.

Together they wept over Uncle's broken body. He was disfigured, almost unrecognizable with his face grotesquely smashed.

Irini's eyes fluttered over his corpse. "You will bury him in Oradea?"

Anca shook her head. "Crisu. With his mother." She added, "And his wife."

After twenty minutes the custodian returned. Irini solemnly kissed Uncle's forehead and Anca was compelled to do the same. He was cold and hard as rock. The custodian ushered them out. They went to the restroom and blew their noses and, standing at the sink, looked each other over in the mirror. Irini radiated appeal. Curiously, she reminded Anca of Buni, with her sparkling eyes and her pride. Irini was rewrapping her scarf and fitting her hands into her gloves.

"You're all alone now," she said sympathetically. "I know he was your only family."

Anca shrugged it off. "I'm married."

Irini opened her purse with her gloved fingers and removed a small silver flask. She unscrewed it and offered it to Anca, who shook her head, politely declining. Irini brought the flask to her lips. She pressed the back of her hand to her mouth, swallowing. Then she said, "You have my address, if you ever need someone."

Anca looked at her in surprise.

Irini offered her the flask again and she took it shyly and drank.

One year later Stefan Siminel disappeared. At a large invitational event in Berlin he took his opportunity. The last Anca ever saw of the husband she never slept with, he was taping up her wrist and discussing strategy before her match, like always. She was going up against a top-ranked German. About halfway through the match, she returned an unpredictable lob with a chop stroke and heard Coach call out encouragingly, but nothing from Stefan, which was out of the ordinary since Stefan and Coach were often echoing each other on the sidelines, in a competition of their own.

She would replay the events in Berlin obsessively and always maintain that Stefan had given her no warning of what he must have been planning for weeks and weeks. It was not as if loyal party members never defected; these were often the people with the ways and means.

As a result of his defection, Anca's passport was confiscated for one year. Afterward, she was approved to travel only for domestic tournaments. Her chances for advancement in table tennis were drastically compromised. Local Securitate followed her and she grew paranoid. Worst of all, she found herself at Coach's mercy. If he asked her to throw a match, she would have no choice but to oblige him. Up until now, Stefan's influence had kept her from this corruption.

It was a hopeless season. Resisting her competitive impulse at the table felt suicidal, and she was reduced to rationalizing that at least Coach was not prescribing drugs like the German coaches, and at least her best was unadulterated. She was ashamed of herself for inviting Coach to the dacha, but she was desperate to gain his favor so that she could stop playing crooked. It was only a few months after Stefan's escape and she couldn't help thinking how the wooden bed frame had never known such riot.

"You can't ask me to do this again," she pleaded with him.

He was flopped sideways across the bed. "What? The fix? Forget about it. Look, you're lucky you're playing in Masters competition. The Olympic level is far worse for players like you."

Coach was always telling her she played too defensively. She was at the time ranked number four in the Romanian competition, had fought her way to this position, and knew she couldn't hold out forever. She had come to the sport late. By now there were training camps for kids in grade school.

She sat up at the edge of the bed, pushing the pins back into her hair. "I've never been able to go against my instinct," she said frankly. "I hate myself when I lose."

"Don't cross me, there's too much at stake," he snapped. "Listen, they want to promote a national model and you're not it. You lose to the Hungarian whore so that your teammate plays her in the finals. It's simple enough for you."

He made it sound political, out of his hands, but she still felt his insults. She began to get up and he rolled over, grabbing her by the wrist, pulling her back down with him. "You want to play in the tournament?"

She nodded, "Yes, of course. I've been training so hard." She felt a knot in her gut, locked inside his hairy grip.

"Be a good girl, then," he said, climbing on top of her again, and he kept on like that. "Be a good girl," in her ear. She shut her eyes to make him disappear.

She trained twice as hard that week, half hoping he would relent after seeing how much she wanted to win. She bested the number one Romanian player with a slice from ten feet the day before the tournament. Coach had been watching, leaned against the wall with his orangutan arms crossed. Later, he knocked on her door at the hotel and she went ahead and let him in. He was gone before it was light out, driving in his Fiat back to the gym, since Oradea was hosting the tournament. It was to be an all-day event with Masters competition scheduled last. Her match wouldn't take place until late in the afternoon. The time passed slowly. Up until the moment of play she toyed with letting go of the match. She should just do what he said and not have to sleep with him again.

Anca shook hands with her opponent and took her place at the table, picking up her paddle. She had won the serve. The game got under way and within seconds any notion of throwing the match vanished from her consciousness. Her game simply refused manipulation. She knew only one thing: the tiny ball. Everything else was reflex. She was at the height of her playing, with spiderlike agility, terrific speed, and an incredible reach for someone her size. The Hungarian couldn't return Anca's left-handed serve. She won easily. Any other outcome would have been unfair. Even Coach could see this. She'd had no choice! He said nothing to her as she came off the court, but she shivered inwardly at the fire in his eye. She raised the water bottle to her lips.

That night, after the tournament, she was waiting in the dim hallway for the hotel lift, which appeared to be working, when she was ambushed from behind. Her assailant grabbed her, immobilizing her in a headlock, and hit her repeatedly in the face. She saw red. The weapon was a Ping-Pong paddle, she realized, before losing consciousness. Romanian paddles were red on one side, blue on the other. The red side was the spin side with pimpled rubber that tore open her skin.

Guests must have come and gone from the hotel suites all evening. She'd never know if anyone saw her, crumpled in a heap in the corner of the hall. The lights were often out in the hotel passageways. It was a chambermaid who found her early the next morning. She woke up inside an ambulance.

A day passed before she could open her eyes against the swelling and take in the hospital room, crowded with beds. It was clear the hospital wasn't under any special orders regarding her care despite her national team status. On either side of her, gynecological and nose and throat exams were under way. An orderly moved between the tables mopping the floor. She reached out for a nurse going past with a tray, but she couldn't move her jaw to speak and the nurse ignored her. By the time a doctor examined her she was numb from the pain. On a scratch pad that the doctor offered she begged for a tranquilizer. He promised to bring her something and then he never returned. Later, the nurse with the tray came to clean and bandage her. The doctor had left the scratch pad behind and she wrote a note saying that the doctor hadn't sent the medicine he'd promised, holding the pad up in the nurse's face. The nurse glanced haughtily over her nose at what Anca had written.

"You have envelope money?"

Anca shook her head sadly. She would have to pay for pain relief. The nurse finished bandaging the jaw and began packing up the supplies on her tray. She glanced at Anca once more, taking pity. "There is aspirin. I can give you aspirin until the doctor comes back?"

"Please," Anca whispered.

Coach showed up at the hospital at the end of the week. He stood at the foot of her bed, stocky, tight-lipped. She stared at his thick hairy forearms. He wore a new Rolex watch like a Russian. Suddenly she knew that it was Coach who had attacked her. The realization gripped her and she cringed visibly, recalling the rapid blows of the racquet. Her head began to throb again.

"It's unfortunate," Coach said, "but you won't be able to stay on the team."

She tried to reply with fervor but it was too difficult to speak. She sounded meek when she said, "I'm going to demand a police investigation."

Coach folded his arms across his chest. "The police? Don't waste your time."

She knew he was right. She groped for the scratch pad and whipped it across the room like lightning, but he ducked out of the way. It hurt to cry. He would have kicked her off the team after Stefan disappeared if she hadn't slept with him. But she'd still have her face.

Her jaw was broken, she'd lost two teeth. There was no one to take care of her. She decided to telegram Irini. She came and collected her directly. Irini did not believe in hospitals. She told the nurse who questioned her, "I am Anca's older sister." She bundled Anca up in a blanket and took her home to her ground-floor flat in the old section of the city. There were three tall windows in Irini's front room and perpetual bed linen airing out over the sills.

Irini pushed the sofa beside the ceramic stove and made up a bed for Anca. The taxi ride from the hospital had worn her out. She lay with her head on the pillows, watching Irini in the kitchen boiling medicinal herbs for poultices. Vaporous clouds wafted from the stovetop, and Irini's curls were tight corkscrews from standing over the pot stirring the rags.

"Here I am, darling," Irini said, coming back into the room with the soaked bandaging. Seating herself on a footstool at

Anca's side, Irini leaned in to place the warm poultices. Perfume emanated from her cleavage. "You'll need to heal patiently," Irini was saying, her silver bracelets jangling. "Otherwise, you'll scar. Scars show on skin like ours." She smiled openly, momentarily revealing gold teeth at the back of her mouth. She dried her hands in the skirt of her apron. "You can stay here with me until you're healed, Anca."

She felt such relief but she glanced around the room uncertainly. "I don't want to impose, Irini."

"No, no," insisted Irini. "I have my business in the back. There's another room, behind the kitchen."

Irini had several long-standing clients she saw regularly. She went in and out through the double doors during the day. As soon as she departed Anca began anticipating her return. She lay on the couch, mummified in the wrappings, with only the pigeons on the roof for distraction. She felt driven mad by them, their infernal ceaselessness.

Every evening after work, Irini cooked eggs and garlic toast. She had a little black and white television set in the kitchen and they watched while they ate supper, or else they played cards. Irini loved to gamble—coins, sunflower seeds, licorice. She drank *tuica* out of an espresso cup.

Irini was talking about her clients one evening, reaching across the table for her tobacco pouch and cigarette roller. She had a tortoiseshell holder for the cigarette. She fit the rolled cigarette into the holder and lit it over the candle. She exhaled and fanned the smoke with her hand. "They all wish I was a man. So I give them what they wish."

Anca was caught off guard, sitting up against the pillows, her face shiny with a medicinal ointment. She couldn't help feeling curious. "What do you mean, Irini?"

Irini shrugged. She smoothed the lapels on her robe and inhaled her cigarette. "It isn't hard for me to act like a man." Irini laughed at Anca's stunned expression, her gold teeth glinting. "I don't have a cock if that's what you're thinking. If I did, I'd frighten them all away!" She paused, setting down the cigarette. "Everyone has two sides to them, Anca." She reached over to a plate of pickles and eyed Anca while she chomped.

Then she said, "Ilie once told me your papers were fake."

Anca was startled. "What?"

Irini looked at her curiously, nodding. "Securitate were blackmailing him over the forged papers," she continued. "It had gone on for years, apparently. You must have known?"

Anca swallowed hard.

"Of course. Why do you think he informed?"

She shook her head, still speechless.

"It was a bargain with the devil." Irini sighed and looked grim, saying, "They stole souls, that's what they did to us."

Anca said quietly, "I never knew." Her head was spinning. She remembered how Uncle had changed, after his interrogation in '53. She never guessed it had anything to do with her. But of course.

Irini leaned in, licking her fingers and snuffing the flame. Then she struck a match and lit the candle again. She was forever doing this, relighting candles in honor of the dead. "He would have hated to see you this way," she murmured.

Anca's eyes filled with tears. She reached for her wine-
glass. Irini had healed her surface injuries but she couldn't fix
her crooked face.

"Anca," Irini said gently, reaching to pour more wine. "Listen to me. There is a cosmetic surgeon and dentist in Bucharest.
Simon Markowitz is his name." She indicated all the work he'd
done for her, opening her mouth wide. She said, "I know him
personally."

Anca had no money for the work that would be needed.
Benefits of membership on a professional sports team had
always been separate from her socialist earnings. "I haven't the
envelope money, Irini."

"Well, then, you will do what I did and pretend to be the
dentist's wife. I can arrange it with him, if you'd like." She said
that Anca should use a hot pepper with the dentist. "Beforehand,
smear it like lipstick. You've seen me do it, whenever the bell
rings at three o'clock?"

"Yes, but—" Anca stammered. "I wondered why you did it."

"It sparks the old man's dick," she said, adding, "And
numbs my taste buds." Irini waved her cigarette in the air,
sitting back. "You play games with the dentist. You sit at the
piano. He might want to blindfold you. But he is gentle, weak,
there's no worry." She was smiling with amusement at Anca's
stunned reaction. "Don't act so prim. You are man enough for
him, I think."

In September 1978, Anca went to meet Simon Markowitz, the
dentist. She had not been to the capital since the last national

tournament, before the earthquake of the previous spring. Large areas of historic buildings in the center of the city had been destroyed. The landscape was a wasteland. The dentist lived in a small flat on the city outskirts, in a monstrous cement block amid several kilometers of identical housing. It was a long tram ride from the main railway station and arriving, finally, at the correct door seemed an accomplishment.

Markowitz opened the door in a flourish, looking at her expectantly. The dentist was elderly but spry and still handsome, a snowball of hair on his head. He ushered her in and they sat at the kitchen table. How happy he was to have heard from Irini. "I am a lonely man. I like a little companionship. You are pretty, with long legs, like my wife Ursula, may she rest in peace."

He had a gentle manner, was soft spoken and educated in his expression. He made her a cup of coffee in his kitchen and hovered in the doorway watching her drink it. In the parlor behind him stood a mahogany piano. The dentist had occupied a privileged place in Bucharest society. His wife had been an acclaimed concert pianist, a principal at the national music conservatory. Markowitz was dentist to influential party members. He and Ursula had vacationed at one of those resorts for party elite on the Black Sea. Among the framed photographs on top of the piano there was a shot of them looking glamorous in bathing suits. Toothaches had earned him an excellent living.

He held up a mirror. She was unaccustomed to seeing herself since the beating. Despite how well the cuts had healed her jaw was crooked. The reflection depressed her. She opened up her mouth for him and he pulled back the lower lip to expose the purplish hole. She shuddered.

He discussed with her the business arrangement. He would wire the jaw immediately and, once the occlusion was repaired, he would take the impression for the bridge. He reached across the little table and took her hand in his. "You will stay here, with me, as Ursula, afterward?"

"For how long?" she asked.

"One year, maybe two. Depending on the anesthesia . . ."

"I see," she blinked.

He helped her out of her shoes and into a women's pair of velvet slippers. Then he showed her to the piano stool and said, "Play me something." She knew from Irini what this meant. He took the cover off a record player and placed the needle on a vinyl recording of Czech piano masterpieces. It was difficult not to love this old romantic music. She had never been modest and didn't mind undressing in front of him. He was kindly smoothing and folding her skirt and shirt, setting the clothing aside. Once she was fully naked except for the velvet slippers, and settled on the stool again, he asked her to put her hands on the keys, "just like you are performing." She set her fingers awkwardly on the piano. "You won't move your hands until the music ends." Her fingertips moistened with sweat. He stood behind her. She could feel him gazing down across her body. She was suddenly chilled by the thought of him attempting to have his way with her. He must have noticed the goose bumps on her shoulders because the next thing she knew he was unfurling a merino shawl, draping it graciously around her.

He reached down to fondle her breasts with feathery fingers while he hummed under his breath. She heard him undoing his belt and braced herself while he rubbed fervently against her. In a few seconds he was satisfied. It required almost nothing of her, she realized.

Although his wife's name was Ursula, he called Anca "little dove," or "Dovey." What was so strange about this? Over time, sitting naked at the piano became routine. She would stare at Ursula's thin, doe-eyed face in the photographs. Ursula had died of tuberculosis years earlier. The dentist had never packed up her things—she had been a clotheshorse—and Anca was to wear whatever she pleased.

Filing down the teeth in order to fit the bridge would send shivers to the nerve endings in her mouth many years afterward, whenever she recalled it. A nurse strapped Anca into the hospital chair. Markowitz snapped his fingers at the nurse and she rushed to his order. A novocaine injection blocked a portion of the pain, but she was undone by the sounds, the dull pressure of the scraping. At times there was searing heat. She gasped and gagged and had to sit upright for relief until the vibrations dissipated and she could swallow. Markowitz looked at her reassuringly over his surgical mask.

As a young Jew during the war, Markowitz had been sent to a work camp. He was spared from toil because he wore glasses. His old, childhood pair of glasses, the ones that saved his life, were stored in a pig leather case in his top desk drawer. Once, he showed them to Anca.

"I was appointed to records clerk, keeping the camp

inventory—because of these glasses." Markowitz could talk about himself ceaselessly but he had never confessed his past. She cringed to be hearing it. "Of course, I was still useful when the war was over and everyone was sent home. People would come to me about their husbands and sons." He paused, scrutinizing her. She felt as if he were looking straight through her, but he was only studying her jaw. "I took whatever they were willing to pay." His voice snapped. "I got rich this way." He reached out and cupped her bandaged chin tenderly in his hand. "Some of us Jews weren't gassed, so we became good Communists." He paused. "And you, Dovey? What is your history?"

She shook her head, adding, out of the side of her mouth, "I was never a good Communist."

The nurse from the hospital came to the flat each morning to change her dressing and to administer an antibiotic gargle. She had to sip it up through a straw. For weeks she could eat only soup. Eventually the bandaging was removed. After several more weeks, Markowitz removed the stitching. He held up the mirror for her to see herself but she pushed it away.

The dentist looked at her appraisingly, then set the hand mirror down on the table and kissed her forehead. "A beautiful girl should admire herself," he said.

In a short while she heard him leaving the house. She reached for the mirror. There was just a little bruising remaining under the skin. Her lower right canine and first molar had been replaced with gold, which shone disturbingly if she opened her mouth too wide. The dentist had otherwise restored the symmetry of her face. Relief washed over her.

Soon, the dentist paid for her to have her hair dyed. "You are even more Ursula," he said, when she emerged from the hairdresser's a redhead. "Let's celebrate." They went to the National Museum café. This was when they could still order champagne and eat smoked rabbit and caviar in the restaurants. Markowitz knew his way around Bucharest and had an urbane confidence that impressed Anca. She slipped her arm through his and learned to walk in high heels, glancing sidelong at herself in the shop windows.

When she'd come to Bucharest to get her teeth fixed she never intended to stay. But she felt indebted to the dentist for having salvaged her face. He was not a sex freak, instead an avid companion. Once he took her to see the national symphony perform in the new Palace of the Parliament, erected after the earthquake. The Ceaușescus themselves were said to be in the audience. She was hoping to get a look at the Mother of the Nation, Elena Ceaușescu, who recently had made herself director of Bucharest's Central Institute of Chemical Research, masquerading as a world-renowned scientist despite having flunked high school. Of course, from the balcony they could see only the backs of their heads—impenetrable silhouettes. Markowitz whispered that it was not even them but paid look-alikes.

*   *   *

She had never known a Markowitz before the dentist, so it seemed incredible that there could be two, but the 1980s took on Gothic distortion that she no longer questioned. At this point, there was nothing she couldn't get used to.

The dentist's second cousin, also called Simon, was editor in chief at the Sentinel, one of the few publishers in Romania publishing literary translation. Once she had decided to stay in Bucharest, the dentist arranged a job interview.

She dressed up in Ursula's clothing and put on lipstick. Her red hair in the mirror no longer startled her. Her jaw was practically as good as new—two small scars that were gradually disappearing. She'd never be able to tolerate cold drinks or ice cream. She wrapped Ursula's silk scarf around her neck, laced her Spanish leather boots, and walked down since the elevator was out.

The Sentinel occupied several offices in Casa Scanteii, a towering marble edifice built by the Russians to house the Russian University in Romania. It was an imposing building. The official Communist party newspaper and the publisher Kriterion were also quartered there.

The editor in chief had two secretaries, neither of whom seemed to like the look of her. She stood awkwardly waiting in their office, nowhere to hang her coat, glancing now and then at the thickly padded Bordeaux leather door that led to the editor's personal office.

"Come in, come in," the editor said, waving her forward impatiently, as soon as he opened the door.

She sensed immediately the distortion. He was a younger, less handsome version of the first Markowitz. Ironically, the editor was balding while his elderly cousin had enough hair for two. The editor was also short and swarthy, whereas the dentist was long-limbed and genteel. Still, their faces were similar, with small sharp eyes and bushy brows, what she considered a Jew's nose, thin, dark lips, and a handsome chin.

He took her by the arm as she entered his office. "Sit down," he said, pulling out the chair for her. He went behind his massive desk and appraised her from a distance. "You have four languages, my cousin says. That's impressive," he remarked. "Are you Hungarian?"

She shook her head no, hastening to hand over identification.

"I wouldn't hold it against you, you know," he said lightly, batting his eyes as he took the papers from her.

"My aunt was Hungarian, from Crisu," she offered.

He nodded. "My cousin says you have some translation experience, with film? Anything major?"

She hoped to impress him, so she said, "Not really"— nonchalantly—"only *Tarzan*."

He looked up. "With Johnny Weissmuller?"

"Of course," she said confidently. "In my opinion, there's no other Tarzan."

He smiled, protesting mildly. "But the Sentinel is a literary and academic publisher. Maybe it's not a good fit for someone like you?"

She took it as a challenge. "Someone like me?" She sat up straighter, flashing her eyes.

He smiled again, clarifying, "From outside the academy."

"Well, but I was a gymnasium teacher of English before I did script translation."

"English?"

She saw she could win him over. She leaned toward him and crossed her legs. "Yes, in Ticu. For years."

"My cousin didn't mention it."

She had told the dentist almost nothing of her past and he didn't ask. She stared in front of her, swinging her leg. She felt him studying her.

"Please, take off your coat," he said, getting up to be of assistance. "The secretary should have seen to it." As he helped her out of it she shivered, feeling exposed, his fingers grazing the back of her neck. She retied her scarf and curled her hair behind her ears nervously. Something about him, his insolent air of authority, appealed to her, or was it just the job she wanted?

"English is the language of diplomacy nowadays," Markowitz the editor was saying. "It has replaced French."

He opened up a drawer and took out a short translation test, directing her to a writing desk on the other side of the room. She assumed she'd be left alone for a few minutes but the editor in chief came behind her chair to read over her shoulder and she had the queerest sensation—of sitting at Ursula's piano.

As soon as she was finished writing he corrected the test in front of her, marking her errors with a red pen. He had pulled up a chair beside hers to do the editing. When he was done he set the pen down and took off his reading glasses, folding them and setting them on the desk. He turned to her with an odd smile on his thin lips. "So you are a lover of books and literature?"

His question surprised her. "Yes, of course!"

"Would you like to see my library?"

She felt compelled to accept the invitation. With his hand at the small of her back, the editor led her into a small, sunken room with a vaulted ceiling to accommodate the bookshelves. Immediately, he slipped his arms around her from behind.

"You're Jewish, aren't you?" He kissed her neck. "It takes one to know one," he said.

She lifted her chin. "I already showed you my papers," she reminded him. She was used to the dentist, who had never questioned her directly. She didn't know what to make of this boldness.

He pulled away the scarf. "Relax," he whispered. "Admire the titles."

The sun was setting by the time she exited the building, stepping gingerly out into the winter day. The view from the steps of the building was panoramic. A grand cobblestone boulevard led up to the plaza, where the huge Lenin monument cast an even huger shadow. The sun's rays at Lenin's back turned the white marble pink.

She paused to wrap Ursula's silk around her sore shoulders. She had let him bind her wrists, with her arms over her head, like a pig at the butcher's. What did it mean to be the lover of Markowitz? Was she a masochist or only an opportunist? She was without answer, her body still ringing from his roughness.

As time went on, she lived more and more a double life. She spent the day at the Sentinel, in the editor's office, as his personal pupil. The radiators were pumping, the lighting was good. Despite the discomfort she sometimes felt, sitting at the desk after a session in his library, she couldn't complain. Markowitz was a talented wordsmith and grammarian, in seven languages. As a translator, she had much to learn from him. He lectured her on the fine line between fidelity and transparency, ideals she was supposed to strive for in translating. "Translations, like women, can be faithful or beautiful, but not both at the same time," the editor was fond of quoting.

The process of translation combined metaphrasing and paraphrasing, and often she struggled to strike the right balance. He criticized the calques and loan words she employed and kept telling her to go back to the source. The problem, for Anca, was not that she didn't understand the source language well enough. And it wasn't that she was not a good enough writer in the target language. The crux of it was that she didn't really possess a native tongue. She was more of a clever parrot, but there was a point of fluency, of receptive language, that she never quite achieved, even in Romanian. It was a source of insecurity that she had once been conscious of but no one else seemed to notice, that is, before Markowitz. He had put his finger on something, a raw nerve. "You are too idiomatic," he would tell her, characterizing her as the text itself, "too transparent." A nasty, cocksure tone in his voice. "You simply aren't faithful enough."

She went home to cook the dentist's lunch each day and returned in the afternoon if there were no power shutoffs planned. Like all other Bucharest residents, the dentist was entitled to only a single 40-watt bulb. Never mind that household electricity

added up to nothing compared to that of the mines and aluminum factories, kept lit up like stars in the night and producing
at zero efficiency. If the lights were turned out, Ceauşescu
believed, people would have more sex, increasing the population, which was at risk compared to Gypsies. The editor liked
to joke about this and developed a bizarre habit of turning the
lamp at her desk on and off to indicate his impatience for her
to follow him into the library. He was sometimes in the mood
several times a day.

"Bring the rug," he told her, and he would take the pencil
out of her hand and toss it aside to hasten her.

The rug he kept rolled up under his desk. He always left
it to her to fetch it and unfurl it at his feet.

During a shutoff, it was agreed she would stay home and assist
the dentist, since it was dark early in the winter. She developed a
secret longing for the shutoffs. Like all the other longings in her
life she was only vaguely aware of it. At home with the dentist,
she lit the lantern and climbed into bed with her translations,
pulling up the quilt. Markowitz whistle-snored beside her, taking
his afternoon nap. She gazed over at him. He was nearly twenty
years older than she was. He demanded so little, and over the
years they had grown close. It didn't seem to bother him that
she slept with his cousin; he must have intended it from the
introduction. He was content to watch her trying on Ursula's
clothes and to take his pleasure behind her at the piano.

In 1984, the Sentinel planned the translation of a book
of regional folktales into English. This was exciting news. It

suggested that they were not completely myopic in Ceauşescu's Romania. It was the first literary classic to be projected in a year. The manuscripts circulated at an editorial meeting. Long after the editor in chief had adjourned the meeting, Anca stayed at the table reading.

Once upon a time there lived a princess who possessed exceptional vision. She could see inside a mountain. To her, the stars were balls of fire, nothing was lost to her, and no one could hide from her.

As she read, she remembered. The words resonated with a familiar tone and rhythm, her mother's voice, she realized, straining to listen. All at once, the table, her chair, the floor under her feet seemed to drop away. Here on the page in front of her was a trace.

Markowitz had plans to assign the work to a different translator and scoffed at her requests for it. "It requires native Hungarian," he said flatly.

She wouldn't deny what she had told him of her linguistic background but she felt haunted by the Hungarian folktale, shaken, possessed. It took her back to a forgotten life, a distant abstraction, beyond a forest of murk. It was real, a source, but she couldn't have it, had rid herself of it, like Miss Pharmacist's tennis ball at the bottom of the well. She could still hear it bouncing. She grew frustrated, regretful.

At home with the dentist, she started leaving Ursula's belongings strewn all over the bedroom floor. She had always been neat and tidy, so it was distressing, this unraveling. The dentist abhorred her underwear on the floor, and yet she made a point of it, tossing it across the room every evening while he sat in bed waiting for her.

"Dove, don't do it. Don't fling the panties," he said, pre-empting, as she was rolling down her stockings one night. No sooner had she stepped out of them than she turned and threw them at him. They slid from his face and he jumped in the bed, looking mortified, as if she'd thrown a hot ember, and she felt so ashamed.

She was under duress, smoking cigarettes in the house despite what the dentist said about tarnishing the gold.

"I don't know why this child's tale means so much to you. But I don't like it with you so anxious." He was looking for something to eat in the kitchen, a little forlornly.

She stamped out the cigarette on the balcony and went inside to wash her hands and tie on an apron. She couldn't confide in the dentist, though she trusted him. Her mother was the most personal secret of all. She had grown up thinking that if she spoke of her she'd cease to exist.

She ushered Markowitz to a seat at the little table and began cracking eggs over the skillet. She stared thoughtfully at the eggs as they took shape in the sizzling grease.

"Aren't you eating, too?" he asked as she set down his plate.

"No, darling." She always punctured the yokes for him, knowing he was too genteel for it. He was busy tucking his napkin into his collar. She stabbed the yellow with a swift flourish.

Later, when Markowitz was sleeping, she carried the lantern into the closet laden with Ursula's clothing and stood on a hatbox to unearth the small duffel bag she had brought with her when she'd first arrived in Bucharest. Inside, beneath the familiar clothing that she had never unpacked, she found her old French notebook. She stood under the flickering lamp, studying the Hungarian identification papers that she'd hidden inside. As if they could tell her something she didn't already know.

"The work requires an authenticity you don't have," Markowitz the editor insisted when she kept pleading, "in any language." He slapped her ass fondly.

"Please, Simon," she carried on. "The story has special meaning for me. Let me try it."

"Forget about it," he barked. "Who do you think you are?"

She paused, feeling hurt. She rolled over, holding her wrists out to him. He looked her over lasciviously. "A Gypsy whore, that's who you are," he said.

"Untie me, Simon."

He ignored her, smiling snidely. "Change your tone. I'm your lord and master."

"Forget the nonsense," she said, angrily pulling at the knot in the scarf with her teeth. "I've had enough of this role!" She bared her lip for several seconds, untying herself.

"My cousin does nice work," he remarked.

She tossed the scarf away. She had torn the silk. There were red marks on her wrists where the bond had burned the skin. Sometimes her fingers fell asleep. It was like having two left hands. The pins and needles faded. She was aware of a throbbing in her temples. She glanced over at him and did a double take. His back was turned, retrieving her scarf. He had more hair on his thick buttocks than on his head. From the back he looked just like Coach. She shook her head to clear it.

"What am I doing here—with you?" She sat up and began reaching for her clothes. He pulled her back down. She had never yet resisted him. Now he wasn't going to allow it. He was thirty or forty kilos heavier than her, and not a weakling like his cousin. She clawed him and tried to knee him. He turned her over roughly and pinned her chest to the floor with his bulk. Grabbing the scarf he tied her hands behind her back. He took hold of her buttocks, rudely pulling them apart. She began to scream. He shoved her face to the floor and she was silenced, her teeth against the tile, fearing injury. Pain seared through her as he thrust. The library door was bolted from inside, sealing them into the vault. Marvelous books surrounded her, ceiling to floor.

She never went back to the Sentinel. A year and a half later Markowitz the editor was ousted, reportedly in part for the folktale book. He'd insisted on including Polish versions and had been accused of sympathizing with Solidarity. Later they learned that he'd gone underground and had gotten out, to Yugoslavia. Translation work was drying up rapidly as the country deteriorated, even translation from the Russian, which had been a mainstay: computer manuals, appliance instructions, auto-manufacturing guides. It was the clearest mark of their isolation when there was nothing to translate.

Everywhere the quality of life grew desperate. In Bucharest, they were the least hungry. Staples—bread, milk, sugar—were not rationed in the capital when the rationing began. But soon enough they would all be starving from lack of nourishment on Ceauşescu's national scientific diet. Ceauşescu crept deep inside the homes, the kitchens, and stomachs. The country had become a monster's reflecting pool. There were routine heat and hot water shutoffs now. The cafés served watery coffee and patrons kept their coats on. The lines at the shops grew hopeless. Romanian television and newspapers had been reduced to emanating propaganda and programs for Ceauşescu, and they watched television as parody, despite how hateful it left them feeling.

By the mideighties Ceauşescu was demolishing the oldest, most architecturally significant neighborhoods in Bucharest to make way for the hideous, cement Boulevard of the Victory of Socialism complex and the cubical fortress the House of the People. That same winter, Bucharest's unlit and unplowed streets were thick with ice and the dentist slipped and broke several ribs. Cancer was detected on the scan.

The prognosis wasn't good. The dentist's mood was irrevocably darkened even though he was tolerating chemotherapy. He stopped going in to work but sometimes saw private patients at home, conducting examinations at the kitchen table and making referrals. She began to assist him whenever he had to make a housecall. Markowitz maintained a thriving practice in postmortem extractions. A mouth full of fillings had cash value, from which the dentist subtracted about 20 percent, depending on inflation. He was sentimental only when it came to his wife.

A private car pulled up outside, and Anca escorted him down through the building, carrying his medical bag. They went one night to the home of Steinmetz. There had been a disagreement over the extraction prior to their arrival. The young widow didn't want the dentist there, but Steinmetz had shown them in.

"It is the practical thing to do, isn't it Doctor Markowitz? He was my son."

Markowitz nodded gravely. The dentist charmed people. He always brought red carnations from the cemetery. He wore his white coat and sanitary gloves and a mask. Anca also put on a mask. The procedure seemed almost like a sacred ritual.

With a mechanical winch that he carried in his bag, Markowitz opened the jaw of the corpse. Once the corpse's mouth was cranked, it was Anca's job to count the valuable teeth and direct his clamp. Using a needle-nose pliers, Markowitz uprooted the teeth. He was skilled at it.

"For such a young corpse there is so much gold, it is worth it for you," he told the elder Steinmetz.

Steinmentz would have been routine, in an hour complete, but as they were leaving the flat the young widow rushed at them from the kitchen, cursing and hitting with her plump fists. "Nazis!" she cried. Anca was horrified. Markowitz went white. The elder Steinmetz struck the widow with the back of his hand, and they ducked out, descending in silence inside the lift. The taxi was still waiting. On the way home, in the darkness of the backseat, Simon reached for Anca's hand and squeezed. "I'm a Jewish dentist, Dove!"

She responded adamantly, knowing her duty: "Yes, my darling!"

Eventually the cancer rendered him too weak to leave the house, especially once the lift had stopped permanently working.

"Consign me to hospital, my dove, I don't want to be a burden."

She refused. "The least I can do is take care of you, Simon," she told him. She was brushing his hair for him, perched on her knees on the mattress beside him.

"There is a therapeutic lamp at the hospital, in the obstetrics ward," he said thoughtfully. "For treating jaundice." His eyes were cloudy from illness. "Maybe they will rent it to me?"

She went by tram to the hospital the next day. The obstetrics ward was disorderly and destitute. The walls were stained with blood and the floors looked as though they'd never been mopped. A young woman was lying on a cot near the window, moaning. Anca waited conspicuously in the hallway for the doctor, Ursula's pocketbook slung over one shoulder. The doctor had just entered the room and, listening through his stethoscope, was leaned over the protruding belly of the woman on the cot. The young woman reared up, wailing, and the assisting nurse hushed her.

Anca swallowed nervously. She had no desire to wait any longer, since it looked as if the birth was pending, but perhaps she misjudged. The doctor had turned from the grimacing woman and was walking away. She seized the opportunity to introduce herself and convey her purpose. The doctor showed her the lamp. They agreed on a price. He looked approvingly at the dollar bills she was handing him and she noticed his gold canine. He disassembled the bulb and wrapped it in paper to protect it.

Behind them all the while on the cot the young mother was in agony. Her gown had come undone and Anca glimpsed the contraction of her giant belly. "Please," Anca said, groping inside the pocketbook for the leftover bills, "give her something for the pain." She pressed the money into his hand. The doctor glanced back over his shoulder, as if it were something he'd forgotten.

Back at the apartment afterward, the dentist seemed so pleased. "This light is new technology!"

Nevertheless, Markowitz's health worsened. He was withering away. Some days he had more dignity to preserve than others. He preferred to spit his toothpaste into the sink rather than into the cup she would hold under his chin in the morning, but this meant getting him to the bathroom. He could barely walk; she would stand in front of him and he would lean against her, holding her shoulders, which were the same height as his since he had shrunk. She shuffled slowly into the bathroom with Markowitz behind her, holding on to her waist. Every moment was an eternal struggle. It would be lunchtime before he was washed and dressed. At night, she had to diaper him. He never protested or complained, except when she tried to take off his glasses so that he could sleep. He was always sensitive about his glasses.

He grew confused, asking her who she was.

"I am Ursula." She climbed carefully onto the mattress beside him, and he caressed her legs in their silk stockings. There was exactly one pair of Ursula's stockings that she never tore, onionskins in her drawer.

Markowitz was dying. There was little morphine to be had, even with his money. He could not find comfort in any position, and they were both weary from sleeplessness. At the same time, the Berlin Wall was coming down. They heard on the radio news that the Hungarians were going across their border with Austria. Meanwhile, Romanians stayed quiet mice—all the lions having fled already.

From Markowitz's flat, she looked down on the streets below and would stand at the window in dull moments. She noticed people talking on corners. Later, she learned from the neighbors that there had been a rally in front of the House of the People. Ceauşescu had been booed off his balcony. The neighbors believed the hecklers were Securitate, that Ceauşescu's own henchmen had betrayed him. It was not so surprising.

All of Bucharest was awake that Christmas Eve. The next morning, as the world soon found out, Nicolae and Elena Ceauşescu were executed. Anca and Markowitz stared wide-eyed at the television broadcast showing their corpses. At first, they thought it must be their look-alikes. They were so afraid to believe! The revolution spirited a few last, lucid days and Markowitz ate the soups she spoon-fed him, and they talked about how the piano could be dismantled if she wished to sell it.

"When I'm gone, little dove, go out and find someone. You're still young. Fall in love, make a home," he encouraged. She held him tenderly in her arms, crying and stroking his hair, which was undiminished to the last.

A letter from Stefan Siminel arrived in Bucharest a few weeks after Simon Markowitz's death. It was remarkable for having reached her at all, as it had been forwarded several times.

Her former husband, the dean, was living in Paris and had
returned to teaching. His letter was an apology for whatever
consequences she had suffered as a result of his defection. He
wanted to make it up to her and offered to help her emigrate,
now that the Iron Curtain was dissolving. At the same time, he
wished her to know that he was homosexual. The fact of the
matter was not news to her but nevertheless she was surprised
by this confession. He wrote of how he had lived so long with
his secret, how wonderful it was to be free.

She sat at the table in Markowitz's tiny kitchen reread-
ing Stefan's letter. The apartment was on the top floor and yet
she felt like she was suffocating. Everyone in Bucharest was
suffocating. She stared out the window. She should join him
in Paris, yet something held her back—her own secret, finally.

III

1990

AT FIFTY, she is returning.

She crosses the border with hundreds of American dollars taped to her skin under her clothing and a carefully wrapped gold nugget inserted between her legs. She also carries her Hungarian identification papers, which bear the name her mother gave her.

The first thing she notices about the Hungarian side is its smooth road. The refugee bus clears the border crossing and then it is as if they are skating on ice. Outside, a cold wind sweeps the plain. Szeged's rooftops come into view beyond the birch forest. She tries telling herself that she is returning home, but the idea falls flat against a harder truth: she will be a stranger here. She looks around the jam-packed bus at her fellow Romanians.

In the refugee detention camp on Szeged's outskirts, she canvasses the Hungarian officials. All the mustaches make it difficult to tell one camp official from the next. Wrapping a threadbare shawl around her shoulders she dusts her reflection with her thumbs in a cracked compact mirror, biting her lips to color them.

"Please, sir. These are my papers. By birth I am a Hungarian citizen. I was just a small child when I left, but now I've come back. I am Éva Farkas—" She chokes on the words, cutting herself off, realizing that this is the same codger she pleaded with the previous day. He teased that if she wanted housing she first had to learn to smile for him.

Now he winks at her. "It'll cost you."

"I am Hungarian," she says, in frustration, and thrusts out her bosom.

"Twenty dollars," he declares, "or else you wait your turn like the Romanians."

Her cheeks burn. "I am worthy. I have a university degree . . ." She is getting nowhere, but she can't see herself offering this mustache any favors. She takes out forints, insisting she doesn't have dollars.

He eyes her as she hands him the money. "Shall I look under your skirt?"

"Right here, now?" she sasses back, tossing her head like a horse. "Aren't you on duty?"

He smirks, rifling through the housing lists on his clipboard. "Josika Street," he tells her, finally. "Seventy-two Josika Street."

"It's a decent neighborhood, I trust?"

He shrugs. "Near the synagogue."

She rewraps her shawl and stalks off, her hips burning from nights on the Red Cross cot. She is too old to reclaim herself!

Why has she come? What is it she is hoping for? She scans the
crowded tent and sighs. She *should* learn to smile. The dentist
used to say so, too, but she has never gotten used to her gold teeth.
Wistfully, she thinks of Simon Markowitz. It was the dentist's
cash she took, as well as the one nugget that was left after the
morphine was paid for. He'd made a point of telling her which of
his own teeth were valuable, if she wanted to extract them, but
when he died she couldn't bring herself to unzip his black bag.

The apartment house at 72 Josika Street is a crumbling, fin de
siècle wedding cake. Whimsical tracery on the eroding facade
has been blackened by car exhaust and the majolica rooftop is
unrecognizable, soiled by pigeons. Her landlord, István Géza, is
a tall man with a tanned, chiseled face and closely cropped gray
hair. She shakes his hand and follows him inside the building.
He explains that the apartment house was built with European
reconstruction money after the flooding of the Tisza in 1879.
She admits to knowing nothing of the city's history.

"Sure," he says, unlocking the door to the courtyard,
"Szeged received international assistance to rebuild after the
disaster. Sections of the ring boulevard are named for the cities
that provided help: Paris, Rome, Berlin, Brussels." He adds,
showing her in, "The Moscow section was named in forty-five."

He moves energetically through the courtyard entryway,
shooing the cats away from the garbage bins and closing the left-
open lids. In the courtyard an unruly rose garden is in full bloom.
Some of the roses are pink and fresh as a calf's tongue. Some
are bloodred. And there are lemony first buds. The brilliant

blossoms contrast with the peeling paint and general disrepair of the stucco.

"After the war," says the landlord, "well, most of the residents were gone. The state council took over the property. Now I am trying to revitalize it." Pausing in the vestibule, he finds the mailbox key on the large key ring chained to his belt and opens her mailbox, removing the junk mail that has accumulated. "You see," he says, looking down at her, "in the old system, there was none of this paper in the box. It's a different world now." He frees the mailbox key from the ring and hands it over to her. "You've come from Romania?"

She nods. "Erdély," she tells him, using the Hungarian word for Transylvania, the region of Romania that was once part of Hungary.

His shrewd expression softens and he smiles down at her, indulgently, showing large teeth. "Come," he says. "My mother will want to meet you."

They go up the stairs to the mezzanine level. The landlord's mother still lives in the building, in the apartment the landlord grew up in. He knocks on the door, taking out his keys again, and lets himself in.

Mrs. Géza comes from the kitchen, a large woman in her seventies, an apron around her waist. "Oh, it's you István!"

She stands awkwardly inside the door, but the landlord ushers her forward. "Mama," says István Géza. "Our new tenant. Miss Éva Farkas." He adds, "She has come from Erdély!"

Mrs. Géza's wrinkled face lights up fawningly. "Our sacred land," she murmurs, her hand fluttering to her breast. "Welcome, dear."

Éva hastens to add, "Well, but most recently I lived in Bucharest."

Mrs. Géza brings out a bottle of *palinka* and three shot glasses. "Sit down, please," she encourages, indicating the couch. They all drink a shot to Transylvania. After a moment, the land-lord abandons her to his mother while he goes out to duplicate her apartment key. Mrs. Géza, in her apron, perches on the round ottoman, her thick arms folded across her chest. She asks how much a kilo of flour costs in Romania and then, pausing, she asks her if she is neat and tidy. She appears to have grown suspicious in the absence of her son. "We can't have dirt in the building," Mrs. Géza is saying, her eyes averting. "There are never rats here, like in some of the houses."

Éva sighs. The apartment house is well located, near the center. She will have to suffer the Gézas. She glances furtively around the spacious apartment. So much room! They don't say another word to each other. Fortunately, Mrs. Géza is in the middle of cooking tomorrow's lunch and once the rush from the *palinka* fades she remembers her pots and gets up to stir them.

The apartment is a replica of Mrs. Géza's, freshly painted. The furnishings are typical bland Communist-era design and poor quality but she isn't fussy. For a long time after the landlord leaves her alone, she wanders the apartment, pausing in the doorways of the rooms, going onto the balls of her feet with arms crossed tightly around her, containing herself. She breathes in the tall ceilings, the window light. Her first evening in her new home, she occupies herself rearranging the furniture—pushing the bulky desk and empty bookcase across the parquet floor. She is barefoot, wearing only her slip. Her arms and legs are still lean and muscular from years of competitive athletics. Her curls have sprung from their pins, her brow is moist with sweat. She chants under her breath, her own name—Éva Farkas—getting used to the sound of it.

To her, Szeged might as well be Vienna, with its well-stocked shops, its obvious industry. She takes to window shopping, a national pastime, particularly in the evening when the shops are closed and there is no temptation. Crowds gather in front of the windows of the Centrum department store. There are imports for sale here, Western imports flowing into the country as through a broken dam.

She wanders the crowded shopping streets, afloat in her anonymity amid the bra-wearing women and all the mustaches and sideburns. Throughout the city there are new street signs reflecting the post-Communist moment at hand. The new street signs are posted beside the old (marked through with an official red diagonal). Marx Square is now Mars Square although no one calls it that.

She is lured under the white awnings of Marx Square by the cut flowers—yellow pompom dahlia and bright zinnia bunched with crimson cockscomb. It is now August, the end of the harvest—sweet tomatoes, eggplant, squash, dried garlic, honeycomb, nuts, and legumes. Small hills of melons are sprawled beside the booths and, everywhere she looks, there are sacks of peppers. The air is pungent with aroma—fermenting fruit, manure, deep-fried food, espresso, and diesel fuel from buses roaring in and out of the adjacent bus terminal.

She can't help feeling lost under the spectacle of so much to buy, dismayed at the way people cock their heads at her accented Hungarian. Peasants occupy the long tables near the entrance while private vendors rent the stalls at the center of the market. The private produce bursts with pride like nothing in Romania, miracles of irrigation.

"One banana? Impossible!" The vendor clucks his tongue.

Even though the bananas are expensive, she persists. It has been lifetimes since her last banana. He is the only vendor with bananas, so she knows she is at his mercy, bending over the bin, inhaling their intoxicating, foreign sweetness. "But you sell them by weight," she reasons, "so it is all the same to you. I'm just one person. I don't need two. Please, I would like one banana."

He is swarthy, a Serb, younger than she is, a silver wedding band on his hand and a pencil tucked behind his ear.

"They are bunched," he insists, looking over her to the next customer.

"But they are random, these bunches," she presses.

"I sell three-bunch or four-bunch," he barks.

While he fills another customer's order she scans the bananas. Once he's made change and closed the cashbox with a flick of his finger, she gets his attention again, pointing, "Look, just two bananas there!" She reaches for the lone pair.

His chin juts out, challengingly. "You want them?"

"I would like to buy one of these."

He shakes his head, irritated. "You're wasting my time."

"Excuse me," she says quietly, meaningfully. "For me, it's an extravagance. I can't afford more than one. I've come from Transylvania." She pauses, a little disgusted with herself.

To her chagrin he is unmoved. Not everyone is a nationalist. "There is a peasant from Transylvania who sells my single bananas for me." He gestures back toward the entrance.

She has seen them, although she didn't know what she was looking at. "They are black, rotted, your peasant's."

"I sell the golden bananas, in bunches," he retorts, folding his arms across his thick chest.

"You are too proud to be a good capitalist," she tells him. And too stupid, she thinks unkindly. She looks fetchingly down at his crotch. "You have the golden banana, I can see that."

It takes him a second, but now a perverse glint flashes in his black eyes. They stare at each other. Without another word she snaps apart the banana pair.

"In the truck I will show you how I ripen my bananas?" he suggests.

She laughs, handing him the banana to be weighed. "No, thanks, I'm busy today."

"Really," he says, dropping the coins into her hand. "The truck has refrigeration!"

Refrigeration? She is impressed. "Maybe next time." She waves.

Gypsy sellers line the exit way with their wares displayed at their feet in duffels, open garbage bags, or those giant nylon luggage bags made in China—in case they have to close shop quickly, clear out. There are also Transylvanian peasants selling embroidery and other folk trinkets, whom the police tend to treat more gently, as long as they stay near the exit. They have all come to Szeged for the day, by bus from Romania.

Purposefully, she does not make eye contact. The Gypsy wants a dollar for the plastic shopping bag, an American dollar, as if she can see under her skirt. Yet the red and white Coca-Cola insignia printed on the plastic is irresistible, beyond compare, even to a banana. It exerts a magnetic pull. She can't explain this disorienting feeling. She is rapidly coming up for air after Communism.

It's true that the handle of her net bag is worn thin and will eventually snap and need repairing. The plastic bag is so shiny and sleek but also strong. It can be folded and unobtrusively slipped inside her pocket. She carefully extracts the money from her hosiery and pushes a slim green American dollar rolled like a cigarette into the seller's hand.

The woman clasps her fingers and speaks to her in Romanian. "Anca! It has to be you. You don't recognize me!"

She looks up. "Irini!" The realization comes like the vacuum rush of air from a departing train. They embrace fiercely.

"You would have walked right past me!" Irini laughs.

"You've stopped putting the ink in your hair!"

Irini was never a large woman but she had been curvaceous, full-figured. She has shrunk, shriveled, her swan's neck now loose like a turkey's. Not only has she let her hair go white, she has stopped waxing her mustache. It is Irini's femininity that has been absorbed in the sunken flesh, the spider lines. Come to think of it, Irini has grown into an old man!

Irini clutches her, looking her in the face. Her dark eyes still sparkle. "Where can we go for a coffee? There must be a *büfé*?"

"Yes, I just passed it. Can you take a break? Let's have a drink."

Irini packs up, stuffing the plastic bags she is selling into a giant suitcase and zippering it. She can't recall ever seeing Irini in slacks before. They each take a strap and tote the suitcase to the beer stalls in the dead center of the market.

"How long has it been?"

"A decade," Irini insists.

"So long?"

They are sipping beers at the standing tables under a sun umbrella. She takes out the banana she bought and insists on splitting it with Irini.

Irini marvels, "You never see bananas in Romania."

"You ought to look into smuggling them here. The vendor has no competitor." It is a bright, sunny day but in the shade of the canvas umbrella it feels cool. They huddle close together, catching up. Irini is now retired. All her old clients are dead, except for one who moved to Germany. They reminisce a little about Uncle Ilie.

"It's almost fifteen years he's been dead," remarks Irini.

Éva sighs in disbelief. "He would have liked to see Nicolae and Elena's heads on TV."

Irini chuckles. She asks to see Anca's dental work and she acquiesces, quickly pulling down her lip to reveal her gold teeth.

Their conversation is interrupted by Irini's cough. It comes over her suddenly, as if she can't clear her throat.

"I recognized you immediately," Irini says, catching her breath. "You look just the same, Anca."

"No, you're being kind, I'm an old woman myself."

"No, never, you are mature, in full bloom!" She pauses, negotiating the urge to cough. "But you would have walked right by me if it weren't for Coca-Cola."

Éva looks on disconcertedly as Irini breaks into more coughing. She still wears all those bracelets, but there is dirt under her fingernails.

"You haven't told me what you're doing here in Szeged?" Irini asks, composing herself.

"Well, I've just arrived." She pauses, hesitant. "I was born here, actually, and so I've returned, to stay." She adds, "For the opportunity. I can reestablish citizenship."

"Really? You're Hungarian?"

"And Jew," she says, and her tongue feels thick.

Irini laughs. "No! I always thought Gypsy blood, like me." They stare at each other for a bright second, then burst into laughter. By now they have each drunk a shot, alongside the glass of beer. Irini is caressing Éva's cheek.

"You haven't changed, Anca," she says dotingly. "Except for your teeth, which are very nice, by the way."

Éva looks around the beer stalls.

"You can't be seen talking to me?" Irini asks, and she starts up coughing again.

"No, no, it's not that. It's true I'm not used to speaking

Romanian here," she admits. Lowering her voice, "Romanian is just one notch above Gypsy, you know."

Irini chuckles. "And what about being a Jew?" she asks pointedly. "How bad is it?"

She shrugs. "I wouldn't know. All the Jews are gone, just like in Romania."

"Never mind," Irini says. "The new mayor of Bucharest is a Gypsy, you wait and see, it's going to be Crin Halaicui!"

"Crin? I once knew a Crin."

They drink up. Irini announces that she has to catch the one o'clock bus back to Romania.

"But why can't you stay?" she protests. "Just one night? I have an enormous place. Fresh paint."

Irini shakes her head. "No, no thanks. I can't ever sleep in a strange bed." She doesn't come to Szeged often, and can't be pinned down to a future meeting.

"Irini, take good care of yourself!" she calls out plaintively.

Irini drags her nylon bag up the steps of the bus, disappearing for a few minutes behind the muddied windows. Just as the bus is departing, she sees an arm poking out an open window at the back, all the bracelets dancing, her hand flapping. The bus rumbles past, but she stands glued to the spot, awash in the leaded fumes and her own disorientation. Finally she shakes herself and heads out to the avenue swinging the Coca-Cola bag.

The streetlights in Hungary are always working. She hurries across in front of the idling cars and hops safely onto the sidewalk as the light turns. The sound of the surging traffic is

deafening and with a shiver she retreats down a sleepy side-
street. Quiet descends within a few meters. Across the street
she sees a cat sleeping on a doorstep. The street is otherwise
empty of life—parked cars, a red telephone booth at the corner.

On the next block the synagogue appears. She cranes her
neck, taking in the magnificent building, a colossal relic. The
wave rises up inside her. She stops short on the sidewalk. The
grand synagogue occupies an entire neighborhood block and
is situated in the shade of several towering yews. Even though
she knew it was nearby, she didn't expect to recognize it. The
resinous fragrance of evergreen needles reaches her as she cautiously approaches the gate. The blood pulses in her ears. Again,
the muscles in her legs stiffen and she can go no farther. It is a
vivid memory flashing. Or is it just a trick of her imagination?
The trees now reach the heavens.

She turns, looking anxiously up and down the block, but
she seems to be the only person alive today. Her skin under her
clothes feels moist with sweat. Clasping her hands over her breast,
she presses hard against the burning bone and squeezes her eyes
shut, clutching her groceries to her. Maybe it is only a menopausal
heat wave. Soon she feels the phantom passing, her senses returning. She darts off the sidewalk as if it were hot coals, crossing,
her boot heels irritably clacking along the sidewalk.

Inside the building on Josika Street, she goes quickly up the
stairs to her new apartment. The first thing she notices when she
hangs up her coat is that her apron is not on the chair where she
left it. As she looks around for it, the empty dish drain catches

her eye. Glancing around the kitchen, she sees that the dish towel she wrung earlier and left to dry over the edge of the sink now hangs from a hook. Her suspicion mounts. She opens up the pantry and finds that the shelves have been reorganized. She uncovers her apron crisply folded inside the cupboard drawer. A coiled spring snaps inside her. She yanks out the apron and pulls it on, rapidly tying the strings at her back with just one hand, an old, compensatory habit.

Across the mezzanine she knocks. Mrs. Géza opens the door and she curses her with her best peasant vulgarity. For a moment, Mrs. Géza acts completely taken aback. Then she puffs out her chest.

"My son is renting that apartment to you," she defends. "He is letting you stay there."

"Mrs. Géza, I will set a trap for you, like for a rat."

Mrs. Géza sniffs, indignant. She steals a nervous glance. "But I was just helping you!" She lifts her chin, eyeing her with disapproval. "Your rag was dripping water all over the kitchen floor, you know."

"A trap! A trap that'll sever your rat's neck."

"Good God!" Mrs. Géza exclaims and hurriedly shuts the door.

She walks back across the mezzanine. Shutting the door behind her, she leans against it for a minute, her fury simmering. She draws herself a bath, indulging in all the hot water that comes charging out of the pipe. She lies back in the long tub, exhaling deeply, and eventually dozes off. By the time she awakes the water has gone cold. Sitting up in the tub, reorienting, the water sloshes around her. She climbs out and wraps herself in Ursula's old robe.

That night she cannot sleep because of the crying. Somewhere in the building someone wails inconsolably. Only one window faces the courtyard. She gets out of bed and walks through the unfamiliar rooms into the kitchen, where she has left the window open a crack and the crying is distinctly louder. She nudges the window farther. A sleepy, end of summer breeze is blowing. Are the cries a child's? The courtyard acoustics make it difficult to locate. She stands listening. It is a middle-aged couple next door, she remembers István Géza telling her, and on the other side of the mezzanine, besides Mrs. Géza, is a family with grown children, the Fehérs.

The glow of a light emanates from the courtyard. She slips her feet into *papucs,* unlocks the door, and steps outside. She looks over the railing. Downstairs there appears to be another apartment. The darkness frames the bright light coming through a doorway and tiny kitchen window, its curtain blowing out. There is no movement inside the apartment, just the wailing. She clutches the fabric of her robe, wrapping it tighter. Soon it subsides. Quiet returns and she looks upward and away, to the open sky.

She is washing her hair at the end of the week, on her knees, leaned over the tub using the shower attachment. The water rushes over her ears for a long while subsuming her in the liquid heat. While she is wrapping her head in a towel afterward, she hears something scrape the floor outside the bathroom door. She opens the door into the hallway to investigate and the door bangs up against something. She peers around it and finds István Géza on a stepladder, unscrewing the overhead bulb. He gazes down at her with an amused, proprietary look on his face.

"My mother noticed the bulb was out. But it's not. I guess you don't ever turn the light on!" He shrugs. "I didn't know you were home."

She slowly finds her words. "István Géza, do you think I am an idiot from Romania? You are not the housing council. It is a new system now. I pay you for privacy!"

He is still smiling down at her, but his lips thin as she continues.

"It's not even true!" she screeches at him, cracking. "I'm not from Transylvania. I was born here, a nasty Jew." Yanking the towel from her head, she whirls it up into a proper whip. She is skilled at this wicked, flicking of a bath towel from long-ago locker room roughhousing. István Géza climbs hastily down the stepladder, packs up, and ducks out. She slams the door behind him.

Why has she come here? She asks herself this, even though she's promised herself she would stop asking. When she looks around her beloved new flat, it is both familiar and unfamiliar. On the streets it is the same way. She is a foreigner in a foreign land and yet she feels, oddly, at home. Proprietary herself. She's not sure why. She goes in to fill the kettle. She buys sugar cubes nowadays; they are available at Julius Meinl,

the Austrian grocery chain, just a few blocks away. She takes
three cubes out of the box, dropping them into her glass one
after the other.

Early the next morning István Géza is knocking. She opens
the door to the landlord wielding a large TV. He speaks to her
over the top of it. "My mother wants you to have her old set."

She doesn't hesitate, holds the door open while he carries
it into her flat.

"Where shall I put it, on the desk?"

"Rather on the bookcase!" she calls after him. "Thank you!"

It appears he is making amends for violating her privacy,
but she will always be mistrustful of the landlord. He does not
turn up again except to collect rent on the first of the month
like a good capitalist. As for Mrs. Géza, she and Éva exchange
words about the weather and the rising cost of things when out
sweeping the mezzanine. It is Mrs. Géza who tells Éva about
the neighbors while out watering her geraniums.

The Fehérs are divorced but live together again now that
they are pensioners. One of their sons is a meteorologist, the
other is delinquent. Mrs. Géza nods her head at Béla Barát when
he steps outside in boxer shorts and *papucs* to smoke a cigarette.

"His wife doesn't allow him to smoke inside," Mrs. Géza
remarks under her breath.

She has many types of geranium besides the vibrant red.
She has promised Éva a cutting of the lemon-scented one,
but it seems to have slipped her mind. The cigarette smoke
floats across to them. When he has gone back inside, Mrs.

Géza looks over. "You see how he has just strewn the butt, there, smoldering beside the doormat? It's his revenge. His wife is an obsessive housekeeper," she explains. "Several times each day she hangs out washrags and shakes a feather duster over the railing. Do you know she owns a special comb for straightening rug fringe?"

Éva has seen Mrs. Barát through the open door, on her hands and knees, intently combing. She would have thought Mrs. Géza approved.

"Who lives downstairs?" she asks.

Mrs. Géza plucks a leaf and holds it to her nose. "Sas," she says finally.

"I heard a child one night."

"She has two. The boy is an albino."

Éva draws a wide arc with the broom she's been holding idle. In her mind, she can still hear him crying.

"There have been all kinds in this apartment house," Mrs. Géza sighs with obvious disdain. "The state didn't discriminate. Now maybe it will change."

Éva doesn't know what to say, but this is the way it is with every bigot and, besides, she's right. She's wrong, but she's right. Éva leans back against the railing, looking sideways down at the courtyard, the late blooming roses. The lemon buds have opened and the blossom is the color of bananas.

"When we first came, it was mainly Jews," says Mrs. Géza. We didn't mind them. They were clean. There was even a Jewish custodian, living downstairs." She eyes Éva cautiously. "You noticed the bullet holes in the stairwell?"

Éva shakes her head.

"One morning, very early, they rounded up the Jewish residents. Barefoot, wearing pajamas, still half asleep. I remember István was a baby and I was up nursing. They shot some of them inside the stairwell, to muffle the sound. Whoever didn't look lively enough for the ghetto, I suppose."

"But you stayed, with your family," says Éva, critically.

Mrs. Géza eyes her. "István said you are a Jew." She pauses. "I thought you'd want to know about the bullet holes." Without another word, she sets down the watering can and goes inside, closing the door behind her.

Éva reaches out and pinches a leaf from the geranium. She inhales it, walking back across the mezzanine. Pausing in front of the Baráts' door with her dustpan, she sweeps up the offending cigarette butt.

She has just fallen asleep when she hears him.

"No, no, Mama!"

She hurries outside. Again, it is completely dark on the mezzanine. Over the railing, she sees the boy standing outside the flat's open door, in the rectangle of light.

"What's happened, child? What's wrong?"

He looks blindly up into the darkness.

The new, automatic light flicks on in the stairwell but goes off again before she even gets to the bottom. She emerges in the courtyard. He is wearing only his underpants. His skin is ghostly white. He turns around hearing her approach, fear in his eyes.

"Relax, it's all right," she says tenderly. He is bleeding from the nose, she can see in the door light. "You're hurt. What's

happened?" Unwittingly, she is speaking in Romanian, adding
to his fright. He recoils when she reaches out her hand.

A shadow rears up from inside the flat, silhouetted in the
open doorway: his mother, Ágnes Sas. Éva has seen her name
on the mailbox. She kicks open the door with her foot. She
barks out at the boy, "Levente, get in here," and he stumbles
obediently back to her. She turns sideways to shove the door
closed and Éva notices the belt in her hand.

Levente. It is a hero's name. A knot in her stomach now.
She goes back upstairs, her fingers trailing along the stucco in
the stairwell, feeling for the pockmarks.

As the first Soviet bloc member to try out Western parliamentary
democracy, Hungary will soon hold multiparty parliamentary
elections. These are the first free post-Communist elections,
and political debates are being televised. With her dinner
plate propped on her knees, Éva stares at the flickering TV
screen hoping to absorb something. Whenever a local candidate speaks, a subtitle with the candidate's name flashes. Her
stomach lurches when she reads Péter Somogyi and she comes
to attention, staring at the screen. The picture scrolls and she
bangs the side of the television set to freeze it.

His title is "doctor" now, and he is vying for a local seat in
MDF, the Democratic Forum party. He is extremely tall. His
hair is thin but still curly. She watches intently, absorbing his
familiar face and manner in disbelief, not hearing a word he is
saying. She is preoccupied deciphering the boy inside the heavy
jowls. It's him, she's certain it is him. The broadcast ends and

her surroundings, the painted walls, the high ceiling, restore composure. She is frozen in place, glued to the cushion, blinking her eyes. He lives in Budapest even though he is campaigning for a local seat, so she doesn't have to worry about bumping into him on the street. But in the ensuing days she catches sight of Péter Somogyi's photograph on political posters around town—looking serious, wearing a Western suit and tie. Political posters are a new phenomenon, as is graffiti. Many people stop and look at the billboards and the occasional epithets painted over them, so she is not a freak gaping after Péter on the walls around town. Once she spies him with a mustache drawn on.

Prompted by the reappearance of Péter, she goes in search of the building where she and her mother had lived with the Somogyis, only to find that the entire neighborhood was razed for block housing. The past has passed, people say impatiently, dismissively. All of Hungary is busy looking forward, not back.

After the election is over she is almost sorry for the white-washing of the newsboards. Péter had envisioned this future, in a way. Hungary had been known as the "happiest barracks" of the eastern bloc. She is not yet a recognized citizen so she doesn't vote, but she would not have voted for Péter's party.

As it turns out MDF wins the election using overtly nationalistic themes in its campaign. She halfheartedly considers tracking Péter down, sending a telegram to him in Budapest. She tries to compose the telegram in her head but is at a loss for words. She imagines him kissing her ruefully on the forehead.

*   *   *

From her kitchen window she watches the boy playing with his train on the courtyard bricks. He is much too thin. His hair is milkweed blowing in the breeze. He wears thick, soda-bottle eyeglasses that strap on. She realizes that without his eyeglasses he could have had no idea of her that night in the courtyard.

The roses remind her of her childhood but, in fact, she never knew this street or this neighborhood, except for the synagogue. She asks herself, going down the stairs and back out into the bright sunshine in the courtyard, who is going to care for the roses if she doesn't? None of the neighbors can be bothered. They are all busily seizing opportunity in the downfall of the old system, coming and going in a hurry.

She removes the spent blooms and trims some of the canes. She observes the boy out of the corner of her eye, ten meters off, crouched on bony haunches on his apartment stoop.

"Where is your train traveling to?" she asks.

He pauses, looking over at her, taking her in for the first time. "To Kecskemét," he replies.

"Is it a passenger train?"

He nods, studying her. After a minute, he asks, "*Néni,* what are you doing?"

She wasn't expecting to be called "auntie" and hesitates before replying. "I am thinning the bush for winter." She carefully makes a pile of the clippings but can't avoid getting pricked. She notices he is still watching. "Bring the dustpan and broom for *Néni,* please?" she asks him.

He walks listlessly over to the toolshed. He holds the dustpan while she sweeps up the rose clippings. She studies the scabs and bruises on his pigmentless skin, his skinny arms and legs.

"I am your new neighbor," she says to him, squatting down so that she can look into his eyes. She holds out her hand.

He stares for a second and his hand lifts in slow motion, the filthy gray fingernails bitten to the quick. She shakes his hand gently but firmly.

It's not easy for her to find a job, and she considers herself lucky when, after six weeks, she is hired by the new Best Western hotel in Szeged. The foreign management doesn't frown at the sound of her Hungarian since she also speaks English. As gift shop clerk at the Best Western, she sells a small selection of maps, foreign newspapers and magazines, souvenirs, bottled water, folkloric linens and ceramic (not nearly as nice as the sort that Auntie made), cigarettes, and snacks

She sells British and American chocolate and Life Savers candy. Snickers is her favorite, the peanuts. Sometimes she has it for lunch instead of soup. One of the chambermaids, who buys Mars, says that the American chocolate is inferior to the British. Éva is not complaining, not after Romanian chocolate. Nothing in Romania was sweet. It was a notoriously putrid task to lick a postage stamp.

After her first paycheck, which will not go very far in this new economy, she develops a sideline. She's noticed the American hotel guests hankering for English news; their lives are important and yet they speak no other languages. The gift shop is always sold out of the *International Herald Tribune* because the distribution from Budapest is spotty and all the hotel guests read it. Once they've read it, they cast it aside, leaving it behind in the dining room or guest rooms. Éva collects for resale the discarded English newspapers from the rooms—providing the maid, the chocolate connoisseur, a cut of the profits. If it is all that's available until the next delivery, guests will pay full price. It is already days old by the time it arrives in Szeged but it doesn't seem to matter.

"I am starving for news," says the American guest, happy to pay in dollars. One dollar bill, so small and flimsy, as if it were worthless. She will get rich!

It is different with *Time* magazine. The hotel gets only one or two issues every few weeks. Sometimes she doesn't put it out, hoards it until she's read it herself. She smuggles *Time* home and sets out a chair for herself on the mezzanine in the waning sunshine and drinks a cup of espresso. She has had nothing to eat since her Snickers but supper can wait. She is in the center of the world for the first time in her life. Since the dismantling of the Iron Curtain, everyone is taking notice and she is fascinated by the coverage. She reads about the recent elections. *Time*'s distillation is odd, oblique, and she is stunned by how distant it all seems in English.

The boy appears on the mezzanine with the laundry basket. She watches him taking the clothes off the line. The clothes have been up for days. She waves to him and he lets go of the clothes-pin and waves back. After a minute, she walks across to him.

"When you are finished with your work here, will you pay me a visit? I live just there," she points. "I have fresh bread. I'll butter a slice for you."

He carries the laundry basket in both arms and sets it down beside the chair she has set out for him. Just then, one of the cats from downstairs turns up. The boy tries to shoo it with a kick but she stops him. "The tabby is visiting me, too."

The cats in the building live behind the dumpster, filthy, aloof. Of the litter born in the corner of the courtyard not long before she moved in, this tabby is the friendly one. Late in the afternoon, he has been coming upstairs for a handout. She brings a saucer of milk. "There are city cats and country cats, I've noticed, and the city cat is more feral," says Éva, tentatively stroking the cat as it laps the milk. Levente sniffles and licks his cut lip so that it shines with butter.

The violence downstairs occurs following the biweekly payday at the university where Ágnes Sas is janitor. She is drunk by the time she gathers the children. Once the haze lifts, she loses her temper. The little girl, Marika, with tiny hoops in her ears, is Ágnes's spitting image and can do no wrong. But fault can always be found in Levente. She beat him once in broad daylight in the middle of the courtyard—no one stopped her—first yanking off his eyeglasses. It was before Éva started work at the hotel and was home in the day. She had watched anxiously from her kitchen window, telling herself she wasn't the only one home in the building. Then it was over and they disappeared inside their flat.

She's moved from being disgusted with her neighbors for their tolerance of Ágnes's abuse to blaming herself. She complained to István Géza. He acted annoyed. The situation was not news to him. "What can I do about it? Hers is still a council flat!" Éva won't go near the police. Everyone is afraid of the police. So the solution isn't just over the garden gate. She imagines the only remedy is something crazy, like poisoning

Ágnes with bad pickles or pushing her off the mezzanine when
she is upstairs hanging laundry on the pulley line. Ágnes is the
only one who can leave her laundry out overnight without fear
of anyone stealing it.

"Levente," she says cautiously, looking up from the cat.
Levente is a proud name; it's almost a mockery to call him by
it. "Why does your mother whip you?"

After a long moment, he says, "I don't finish my soup."

"You don't finish your soup?"

He swings a leg under the chair. "I don't sit up straight at
the table."

"She shouldn't whip you." She pauses. "I can hear you at
night sometimes."

"When I wet the bed," he says quietly, frowning.

She puts a hand on his knee.

He barely blinks, his eyes so far away behind those lenses.

In September, Mrs. Géza suffers a heart attack while sitting in front of her new TV and dies before István discovers
her. Everyone in the apartment house gathers outside as the
paramedics carry her out on a stretcher, the sheet drawn over
her. István follows, sobbing, distraught. At the stair, Béla
Barát offers support and István embraces him fiercely. By
the end of the following week, István is already sprucing up
his mother's place. The council flats at 72 Josika are slowly
being privatized and István Géza is buying them up one by
one. Éva overhears Mrs. Fehér and Mrs. Barát talking in the

vestibule. István has taped a name, Martin Tierny, to his mother's old mailbox.

"An American. He will make a killing in the rent."

"I guess little István has been successful refurbishing and selling used refrigerators and ovens."

"Do you know he builds his inventory by reading the obituaries? His mother once told me, God rest her."

Éva thinks perhaps the American will be a good customer. Her news resale business is growing. English is all the rage, so it's not just foreigners who want her papers. Now she sells the English-language news on the steps outside the university before work in the morning.

She is sharing a Snickers bar with Levente in the courtyard when the American arrives. He has a good, clear voice—Éva strains to listen—but how strange is the echo of English in the stairwell! She glances up curiously as Martin Tierny emerges on the mezzanine. His hair is a wild mop. He wears delicate eyeglasses with thin wire frames. István Géza leads the way with one of the suitcases, smiling with his large horse teeth.

They go inside at Mrs. Géza's, closing the door behind them, and the courtyard falls silent. She closes up the latest issue of *Time*.

"You have another new neighbor," she says to Levente.

He puckers his lips, whistling for his train engine. She notices that he has reopened a scab on his arm, fresh red beads. She doesn't know what provokes his mother, but gathers it is his ghostly skin and the *srác* who deposited that weak seed in her. He is a cute child, despite his ghostly tone, but his manner is weak, pitiable. He is too much a victim. Was this how she looked to Auntie and Uncle? But she had been escaping, surviving. And it was her mother who saved her.

From where she stands on the mezzanine, overlooking the interior courtyard of 72 Josika Street, Éva can see that the bicycle is a small banana-seat model made by Csepel, the premier Hungarian manufacturer—now in a partnership with the American company Schwinn. The long flat box it came in, with the Csepel logo and a drawing of a bicycle printed on it, has been cast aside.

The American Martin Tierny sits cross-legged amid a sea of shiny bicycle parts. He wears canvas short pants, a wool pullover in need of darning, and shockingly filthy tennis shoes. His unkempt dress perplexes her. If he weren't American she might be disgusted by him. Rather, she is fascinated. She has begun to wonder how old he is, having noticed the dove gray in his sideburns.

He has been studying the bicycle's assembly all morning, his head bent over the printed directions. He presses an index finger to the nose bridge of his glasses, flipping back and forth in a Hungarian–English dictionary, a pocket edition. The Best Western hotel gift shop stocks the same dictionary—at a shameful markup. But it's a decent dictionary, not really for tourists. Éva keeps a copy behind the counter and it comes in handy.

She is not the only nosy neighbor this morning. The apartment house is unusually lively, with continual laundry hanging and errand running. The American appears not to notice. Éva relaxes, leaning against the mezzanine rail in the sunshine. She pulls a leaf from the lemon-scented geranium that she lifted brazenly from Mrs. Géza's stoop after her death. She inhales the fragrance. Downstairs, Levente has just stepped out of his apartment door. He makes his way across the courtyard, stopping first at the chess table, but Mr. Fehér shoos him.

He slowly circles Martin Tierny. The American is saying something to him, gesturing animatedly, about the bike. Levente cocks his head, frowning at the bicycle parts on the ground. He crouches down and picks up the bicycle's handlebar joint. He holds it to the neck of the frame that the American grasps in his hands. The American responds enthusiastically. He seems delighted to finally be driving in screws. Later, when the Csepel finally stands complete, the American lets the boy try out the bicycle. Levente's feet barely reach the pedals. The American guides him on the bicycle along the perimeter of the courtyard. The pensioners look up from the chessboard and, opposite, Mrs. Fehér leans over the mezzanine just as Éva is doing.

"You have a new friend," Éva says to Levente, later, when she goes downstairs to retrieve the cast-off bicycle box. "The American!"

He looks confused.

"You were an expert on the bicycle," she continues.

He takes focus, nudging his eyeglasses. "You saw me, *Néni?*"

Éva gestures upward, at the mezzanine. "Everyone saw you, Levente!"

"That man with the bicycle is a foreigner," he says importantly.

"Yes, American," she replies.

"American? Are you sure, *Néni*?"

"Yes, sure," she smiles.

He follows her up the stairs, in the languid, silent way of his. She has never seen him run or kick a ball. As they are going up, they meet Mrs. Fehér coming down. Mrs. Fehér halts when she sees Éva carrying the box. Éva nods at her politely, pleased to have secured the box first. She drags the prized cardboard along the mezzanine and into her flat.

"What will you do with the box?" the boy asks her. He is standing in the doorway.

She isn't certain. She says, "There is always something." She sets out a chair for him beside the door and warms a cup of milk and butters a slice of bread.

The American has come to Szeged with an organization called Teach for a New Democracy. There was an article in the local paper. Martin Tierny is posted at József Attila University, but he doesn't earn a regular salary. He is a subsidized employee, in the program to retrain teachers of Russian now that the study of Russian is finally no longer compulsory in Hungary.

Éva feels no sympathy for these Russian teachers. Each country struck a different deal with the Soviets. Hungary instituted Russian. The Russian teachers are actually receiving state aid for their retraining. Whenever she sells the English newspapers and magazines outside the university, she sees them buying single American cigarettes, espresso and *kifli* from the *büfé*.

They are a somber, melancholy bunch, depressed at having to reinvent themselves, and she has no patience for it.

The American Martin Tierny coasts into the university yard on his bicycle, a leather briefcase swinging. It's an undignified mode of transport but he seems oblivious. He parks the bike and calls out "Hi!" to the Russian teachers as he goes up the steps. He doesn't notice her, standing against the stucco wall. They have yet to formally meet. Once he held the door open for her when she was exiting the apartment building and another time she came across him in the vestibule struggling to get his mail out of the box. She showed him how the metal door opened out, not in.

Is Martin Tierny searching? She wonders. Americans who stay at the Best Western are all searching for their roots. They are the sausage-faced descendants of those who fled in '56, others are Jews, grown children of survivors, a few are simply tourists on a sweep of the new Europe, detouring in provincial Szeged on a whim.

The American hotel guests are prosperous, full of entitlement, and quite willing to fall in love with Hungary. Éva circles landmarks on the old city maps in the gift shop. The maps are sold at a 200 percent markup. There are half a dozen points of interest, including churches, the Turkish bathhouse, museums, and the department store. In response to guests' requests she also circles the synagogue.

The best thing about Americans is that they are not Germans. Éva is at her best in service to Americans. She is mesmerized by American friendliness, the American desire to be liked, a translucent surface. English drowns out other conversations in the lobby. Unrelated guests become fast friends. They talk across tables in the hotel restaurant. Everyone listens to the Americans and the Americans are high-spirited—so pleased that the hotel staff understands them! Even the gift shop clerk speaks a little English.

"Do. You. Sell. Aspirin?"

"But of course," replies Éva, reaching inside the case for a newly arrived product, Tylenol.

The woman's face lights up. Tylenol costs the equivalent of two dollars. She hands over the Hungarian bills without pause. "Tylenol is not exactly aspirin," the woman says, "but it's better than nothing. I have a headache," she divulges.

"It's unfortunate," consoles Éva.

"Do you also sell mineral water? You know, water to drink?" She looks around.

Éva takes a bottle from the shelf.

The woman scrutinizes the imprinted label and shakes her head, impatient. "Oh, no, not this. This is that sulfur water, no thank you." Her skirt lining rustles against the pressure of her ample backside as she walks out of the store. Éva's eyes follow her as she crosses the lobby to where her husband waits, a Nikon camera slung around his neck. They are the Kleins.

With certain items, particularly folk craft souvenirs, state-owned products, Éva will sometimes readjust the price and pocket the difference. She generally does not try this with Germans, who are always suspicious, but Americans are the opposite, behaving as if they cannot read numbers, as if they have no cares about the cost.

Still, she can't bring herself to overcharge for Tylenol. She spends long moments gazing into the glass case at the small, opaque vials that came in recently. The Tylenol is bottled in Frankfurt. She can read the German print on the bottle. Tylenol does not aggravate stomach or intestine. She reaches into the glass case, rearranging the row of plastic vials to accommodate for the one sold. She glances at the door then slides a second vial off the shelf into her hand. She goes behind the door to slip the pill bottle into her coat pocket. Inventory is tight on imports and she may be questioned. But it can't be helped.

She cuts through the cemetery on her way home, a quiet respite between busy avenues. She stops here and there to collect candles. She doesn't like to be seen stealing candles—can't bear the hardened stares from the old widows—but the cemetery has emptied out since All Souls'. She wears the dentist's wife's slightly moth-eaten shawl around her head and shoulders. Tonight, in the children's part, she takes a moment to relight a votive with Best Western matches. She isn't sure what has prompted her. The tiny grave is unmarked.

He is speeding along the darkening pathway on his bicycle. The bike swerves, narrowly missing her, the rear tire furiously spitting gravel. He brakes to a halt and she jumps aside.

"Sorry!" he blurts. "Pardón," he adds, "pardón!" Just then he recognizes her. "Oh, you're my neighbor, aren't you?"

She looks at him in shock. "Stupid shit American!" But he can't understand Hungarian. She turns away and walks off. "I'm sorry!" he calls after her.

After a minute, she hears him pedaling away in another direction. She looks over her shoulder as he goes. He will be struck and killed by a car! She imagines the police detective circling his body as it lies on the street. He is a different variety of foreigner, even Levente has seen this much. An American? The detective will pry open the mouth, noting straight white teeth.

Éva rewraps her shawl and leaves through the cemetery gate. Along the boulevard, the electric streetlamps glow—a marvel to make her way bathed in light.

Inside the vestibule on Josika Street, she notices that he is already home, his bicycle left unlocked again. She lingers in the roses; the fading blossoms are redolent despite the cool evening. She plucks one and tucks it behind her ear. She goes slowly up the stairs, her fingers absently gliding along the wall. Emerging on the mezzanine, she glances in the direction of his door and catches him standing at his kitchen window, looking out at her. She hurries on to her door, the cat at her heels.

She shouldn't be opening up for the tabby because István Géza, who came inside the last time he was by to collect the rent, found the cat asleep on the couch and now forbids it. He claims Éva owes him three thousand forints for torn upholstery. But since then she has the bicycle box protecting the back of the couch. She can't very well turn the cat away when it is there, waiting on her doorstep.

She tosses the pill bottle down on the floor and the cat eagerly begins to bat it from one end of the flat to the other. She looks on in amusement. Then she takes off her coat and draws herself a bath. A little later—standing in front of the steamed bathroom mirror, wrapped in a towel—her doorbell rings. The bell sounds again. Somehow, she knows it is him, the American, and she freezes, leaned over the sink staring at her reflection. Her hair is pinned up haphazardly. Fine lines on her forehead shine with moisture. Delicate crow's feet have begun to show at her eyes and lips. She turns her head slowly from side to side, appraising her wrinkling neck. A hollow silence follows the doorbell. She turns away from the porthole she made in the fogged mirror, vaguely disappointed in herself.

She paces the apartment in the silk pajamas and pair of slippers she bought from the Uzbek vendor, pausing at the kitchen window to look through the shutter slats. The American doesn't close his shutters. She can make him out in his brightly lit kitchen with his enormous coffee cup. Maybe it wasn't Martin Tierny at her door. But she knows it was. After several more minutes' deliberation, she plucks the rose blossom from its water glass and tucks it back behind her ear. She pulls on Ursula's hand-embroidered robe and steps into her outdoor *papucs* and goes across clutching the *International Herald Tribune*.

She rings his bell, anticipation rising in her chest. He comes to the door with his sleeves rolled. Behind him, in the kitchen, he has left the water running. She holds up the newspaper, "It is one dollar."

"One American dollar?"

She eyes him uncertainly. Is he an idiot?

He is not wearing his wire glasses and squints at the newspaper. He says, "This issue is from a week ago."

She shifts her weight from one foot to the other. What is
one dollar to him?

"Sure, okay, I guess," he says, shrugging. "It's better than
nothing." He disappears inside the apartment, leaving the door
ajar.

The apartment is still furnished as it was in Mrs. Géza's
day, yet the American's presence is clear. His briefcase squats
open on the floor; boxes of books line the wall, their English
titles jumping out. A portable ironing board is propped on the
kitchen table and his ironed shirts drape the backs of the chairs.
She straightens up, hearing him coming.

"You speak English very well," he says smiling, offering
her the dollar bill.

Éva quietly clears her throat. "You also speak well."

He laughs, his teeth dazzling. "I rang your doorbell earlier. I
wanted to apologize. I was riding too fast through the cemetery.
I probably shouldn't ride through there at all."

"You tried to kill me," she says but can muster none of
her earlier fury.

"No, of course not!" He reaches out his hand. "I'm Martin
Tierny." Pausing, "And you are?"

"Éva Farkas," she tells him shyly.

At the polish flea market she comes across a used bicycle bell
and haggles for it in Russian. Nobody speaks Hungarian besides
Hungarians, except for the Uzbek. The Uzbek speaks in any

language. She takes delight in the silk pajamas she bought from
him—a bargain. Hungarians complain but shopping is not the
chore it was in Romania.

The bicycle bell wrapped in its brown paper she leaves
inside the American's door. Later, when it is surely Martin Tierny
ringing her doorbell again, she still can't bring herself to answer
it. She holds her breath foolishly, frozen, in the kitchen opening
a tin of sardines, the cat dancing at her ankles.

A few days later, on her way home from the hotel, the
bicycle bell is a bright note sounding in the sudden downpour.
She peeks from under her damp wool shawl and sees him riding across the street toward her, through sheets of rain. "Hop
on!" he shouts. "I'll give you a lift." He pulls up alongside the
curb.

She's embarrassed, reluctant. "No, no. It isn't necessary."
She glances around for shelter but already people are jam-
packed under the building overhang and there are no trees
along the boulevard.

"Come on, you're getting soaked." He reaches for her,
tugging her sleeve. He is smiling at her. "Get on."

She looks again at the umbrellaless crowd of pedestrians
pressed against the building and is struck by how gray everyone
looks compared to him. Unless she's imagining it. She knots the
shawl ends under her chin and climbs on, perched sidesaddle
on the bar between his arms. Her stomach lurches as he pedals
off and she leans back against him in the motion, laughing in
alarm. She grips the neck of the handlebar with one hand and
the bar she's balanced on with the other. He wheels along the
busy street in the downpour. The cars whiz by, spraying them.

His chest presses against her, she feels the heightening of her senses, the heat at her back. He turns down a residential street. The rain ceases. They careen through the empty, wet neighborhood, dodging puddles, through ghostlike humidity rising off the street, wheels squeaking rhythmically.

"Why don't you lock it?" she asks him, inside the vestibule.

He combs his wet hair out of his eyes with his hand. "I do sometimes," he says, shrugging. "It's just that it seems so safe here. Isn't it safe?"

"No, not really."

"You think one of the neighbors would steal it?"

"Why not?"

He makes an excuse about the combination code not working smoothly. "And besides, if someone wanted to steal it, they could just cut through the chain."

They go up the stairs together. She studies him cautiously out of the corner of her eye. They emerge on the mezzanine.

"Thank you for the ride."

"My pleasure," he replies. His eyes twinkle in the soft light. "Thank *you* for the bell."

He goes one way around the mezzanine and she goes the other. She skirts the puddles, hopping nimbly. At her door, both Levente and the cat are waiting.

"The American gave me stamps from the U.S.A.," Levente reports as they go inside. He pulls a folded-up envelope from his pocket to show her. Inside are several clipped envelope corners with postmarked stamps.

She puts away groceries, fills the kettle, and begins making sandwiches. His straw white head is bent over his treasures. Over his shoulder she can see through his thick bottle lenses, the stamp design distorted beyond recognition. "Éva *Néni*," he says, crossing his stocking feet under his seat, "will you keep my stamps safe for me?" He looks up at her, his nose twitching like a rabbit's.

Her hand alights on his shoulder. It isn't always possible to meet his eyes. She looks and she looks but he isn't there, concretely. "Of course," she tells him. "I can get you a book to collect your stamps in. Do you know how to remove the stamp from the paper?"

She fills a spare teacup with boiled water and shows him. She submerges the envelope corner with the stamp on it in the cup. The postmark is New York, New York. When the stamp comes unglued, she extracts it from the water with a pair of tweezers and carefully places it on a clean towel in the center of the table. She hands him the tweezers.

"Levente, you're left-handed?"

He is lost in concentration, ungluing another stamp, taking the stamp from the teacup, and setting it to dry. The envelope remnant curls in the hot water, the postmark on it blurred. Where was this one from? She sits down at the table with the plate of sandwiches.

"Let's eat now."

She offers him a sandwich. They discuss the American stamps displayed on the towel, comparing their attributes. He swings his feet. She will get him a pair of slippers, for when he visits.

"Does your mother mind that you come to see me?"

He nods his head slowly.

"What does she say?"

He looks her straight in the face for the first time. "She says you are a Gypsy witch."

She is impressed. "But it isn't true."

"No, *Néni*." His eyelashes are barely there, filament, spider's work. His face is narrow, with a pointy chin.

She smiles. "You are a brave boy."

Levente nods his head, hungry for the sandwich. Like a duck swallowing noodles. She refrains from saying so, the way Auntie used to.

She is stationed with her newspapers outside the Humanities building. The chubby former Russian teacher with the pocked cheeks is sitting on the steps in her winter coat, tears running down her cheeks. Her group mates crowd around her. "You must go and speak with him," they say.

"He is American. He doesn't understand the situation."

It is cold enough to see their breath. Apparently, the tearful one is in danger of failing. And they are the only group at the college taught by an American. An injustice, the student is claiming.

With the exams under way, Éva doesn't sell many newspapers. She can count on the stylish blonde from the British Council to buy the *Tribune*, also Mark Rado, a second-generation Hungarian, from Australia. Martin Tierny waves to her. Several times a week she delivers the *Tribune* to his door. He seems to have endless dollars to spare, and they talk together. She's the only neighbor who knows English.

One night when she rings he is not his usual, cheery self. He has caught a cold. She's troubled, pocketing the dollar. She walks slowly back over to her place. Next door to the American, the Fehérs' shutters are closed against the approaching winter. Down below, all the lights are out. Soon enough it will be bitter cold, the roses dormant. No one will hear with the windows closed.

Éva steeps elderberry leaves in a teapot and, cradling the pot in a towel, carries it across the mezzanine. The American opens his door wide and she steps tentatively over the threshold and sets the teapot on his little kitchen table. He is ironing shirts again.

"It's how I stay warm," he confesses.

It turns out that the American doesn't know how to operate the radiators and has been subsisting without heat, except in the kitchen where he keeps the oven door open. He also has been getting along without hot water. No wonder he is coughing.

"As if it were Romania!" she says, lighting the pilots for him.

"I haven't had time to figure it out," he says, sneezing into his sleeve.

She really can't believe him. "But you may ask me—any time."

"Okay," he says, "thank you. *Köszönöm*." He sets out two cups and saucers. "Stay, Éva. Have a seat," he tells her, removing a shirt from the back of a chair.

She sits down. He pours the hot tea. She studies the shirt he has moved to the cupboard knob. "I can press your shirts for you?"

He is liberally spooning sugar into his tea. "Can you tell I'm not used to ironing?"

"I can do it," she offers again. She reaches tentatively for the sugar spoon after he has returned it to the bowl.

"For dollars?" he asks.

"Not so many," she says, sitting up straight, sipping the tea. She looks at his face, handsome but unassuming, except for his smile, a brazen smile.

"It's nice, this elderberry," he muses over the cup.

She tells him he must drink the entire pot. It is medicinal, for the throat. Does he have a scarf to wear to sleep? She thinks of the pill bottle cat toy. Perhaps Martin Tierny could use her Tylenol?

His ringing telephone surprises her. Her apartment has no phone. He gets up to answer it. She scans the titles in the bookshelf, which stands opposite the kitchen door, coming upon *Frankenstein*. She slides the book out, flips it open, and reads the first few lines. In this instant of contact, years flap and unflap like pages in the wind.

She hears him talking on the telephone.

"Correcting papers. Or trying to. It's deadly." Pausing. "Let me call you back later. " The click of the receiver. She shelves the book. It is clear to her as he comes through the door that he has a woman. Now she's torn between his bookshelf and a desire to exit.

"Listen, Éva," he launches in again, "while you're here, can I show you something?" He takes a comic book from the top of the shelf that she hadn't noticed. It's a Hungarian kids' comic book. "I was just leafing through it," he says, "and I came across these pages."

She studies the open comic book he presents to her as they stand in his hallway. "You'd like me to translate?" she asks.

"No, I get it. I mean, these are anti-Semitic jokes, aren't they?"

She looks back at the page and nods impassively, shrugging.

"I thought so. I looked up the words."

"I must be going."

"Are you sure? What about your tea?"

"It is *your* tea, Martin!" She looks at him. "Martin, are you a Jew?"

"No." He adds, "But I'm still offended."

"Really?"

"I bought the comic book to give to the boy downstairs. He's a sweet kid."

"Yes," she says thoughtfully.

She holds open the door for him and they go inside the library. The thick quiet of books swiftly enfolds her. Absently, she takes the boy's hand. He is, as always, in disheveled clothing, poor shoes, and she feels ashamed for letting him go around like this. People must assume she is his mother. She is ruffled by how she feels—all the time now, not just lying awake late at night.

In the children's section, she looks over his shoulder at the books he picks out. The first is titled *It Is Not Brought by the Stork*. He flips through the pages.

"Can you read it?"

"A little."

He also chooses *I Never Get Letters Sent to Me*.

"Too sad?" she asks.

He shrugs.

She tilts back on her heel so that she can make out other titles. "I don't suppose you like princesses?" She peruses a book of folktales. "She is a good one, like a superhero."

"No, thank you," Levente says.

She reaches for a Winnie the Pooh book. "*Micimacko*," she shows him. "Did you read it in school?"

He nods importantly. "It's a Hungarian classic!"

She laughs. She looks around the room, taking in the stacks, feeling nostalgic.

At the desk, she checks the books out, handing over her shiny new Hungarian identification, a stitch of panic rising out of nowhere, no matter where she goes. She never had any qualms about handing over her Romanian papers.

She says to him, as they're leaving, "Now you have something else to read besides comic books."

"You don't like comic books, Éva *Néni*?"

She shakes her head. "They are just ugly jokes and games."

"And superheroes," he adds.

She takes his hand.

A few days later Martin Tierny's cold has improved and he is entertaining the blonde from the British Council. He's kind and doesn't act as if Éva is intruding. She hands him his newspaper.

He introduces Teresa Marsch but, of course, they are already acquainted from sales of English news outside the university. Teresa is delighted by the idea of home delivery of the *Tribune*. She compliments Éva's English.

"I had no idea you spoke so well!"

Éva shrugs. "I speak a little."

"You speak very well," insists Martin.

Teresa nods. "Better than some of our colleagues!"

Éva appraises the tea cups, the pastry paper from the Virág confectioner's strewn with crumbs, and an uncapped bottle of Unicum on the kitchen table.

"Martin, you should get Éva's opinion on this," says Teresa, smiling.

"Maybe you're right," he says.

Teresa is seated just inside the kitchen door. Standing over her, Éva examines her gray roots. Martin pulls out the empty chair for Éva but she doesn't move.

"Well, anyway," he says, hovering. "My students at the university are cheating and I'm not sure what to do about it."

Teresa Marsch interjects. "Perhaps it's the result of group learning under socialism?"

"They're teachers themselves," says Martin. "Why would they cheat?"

Éva hears their different accents. She also realizes she knows what he's talking about from having eavesdropped on the Russian teachers.

"Éva, any thoughts on this?" asks Teresa Marsch.

Éva is not sure what to say and states the obvious. "The students care only about passing." She can't help disliking the bewilderment on their faces. "Why should they care?" she asks, rhetorically.

"Many of them *do*," interjects Teresa.

"They should care because I care," Martin announces. He describes the offending student who came to him, begging for a passing grade. Éva pictures the chubby Russian teacher. The state will not compensate her for the course if she doesn't complete it successfully. "She's got a family," Martin says. "Her husband is a miner somewhere north of Budapest."

"Sometimes," says Teresa, morosely, "it really doesn't feel like it's our place to fail them." She takes out a packet of Marlboros and tamps it down on the tabletop.

"Whose place is it then?" asks Martin.

Neither responds. Teresa goes outside to smoke and they are alone finally.

"I was a teacher of English once," Éva offers. "A long time ago, in Romania."

"Really?"

She continues, "I didn't hesitate to fail a cheater."

"Why did you care?" he asks her.

He will never understand, and yet it is what she wanted him to ask her. "In Romania," she says, "English was an escape. Sometimes it was the only relief for me."

He looks at her curiously. "Why aren't you teaching here?"

"Here? No, I can't." She shrugs. "I work at the Best Western now. I don't mind it. It pays well, almost the same as a teacher."

"Really?"

"Yes, sure, it's an American business."

She averts her eyes. Teresa comes back inside smelling of the cold and of tobacco. She and Éva exchange a look and Éva turns to go.

As she's turning Martin catches her gently by the sleeve. "Oh, by the way, are you still interested in ironing?"

She glances halfway at Teresa, then darts back to his wide-open face. "Yes, of course. Why not?"

The American's shirts are pure cotton, and must be dampened before ironing, not unlike a Transylvanian tablecloth. They have button-down collars and it requires concentration to refasten the corners once the collar is ironed stiff. The cat is not allowed inside during the ironing because he attacks the dangling sleeves. Éva feels pleased by the sight of Martin Tierny's shirts, pressed, on hangers, over the doorknobs in her house. They exude a promise. Since Teresa Marsch has taken to coming and going, Éva is not inclined to deliver the paper. Of course, she's still pleased to make a dollar. She usually offers him a paper when he picks up his shirts. They talk on her doorstep now, instead of his. Sometimes, he comes inside for just a minute, glancing around the room as she gathers the shirts for him. "It's the same as your place," she remarked to him once.

"Yes," he murmured, taking the hangers. "I thought it looked familiar."

He can't be more than thirty-five? He's a boy compared to her. She is fifty-one. She shouldn't flirt with him.

He often asks her questions about getting around in Szeged, as if she has lived here all her life. She reminds him that she arrived only a few months before he did.

Standing in her doorway, in the afternoon sunlight in the cool November, he has the shadow of a beard and his cheeks are pink. He wants to know where he should go to buy a turkey. "I'm going to cook for some of the expats in town. Do you know about American Thanksgiving?"

She nods. Of course, she has heard of it. "It is the annual celebration of American hegemony over the native Indians." She pauses. "Everyone knows that."

He laughs. She directs him to the butcher at the ABC grocer, who carries fresh poultry.

Very early on Saturday he rings her bell again, and even though she is in her pajamas and hasn't brushed her hair out she no longer hesitates to go to him.

He's sorry to bother her so early.

"No, not at all," she tells him. She admires the sunlight on his face. "There is a problem?"

"The turkey," he blurts. "I have no idea what to do with it!"

She looks askance. "Wait one moment," she says, then softly shuts the door. A smile creeps across her face as she hastens to tie her hair back. She slips on a housecoat. He is still waiting on her doorstep, shocking in a T-shirt, no coat, and nothing at all on his feet! She eyes the broad roundness of his shoulders, his long arms. They hurry across. He has left his door open. Éva can practically see the hard-won heat escaping.

As soon as they are inside, he starts up again with apologies. "It's too early to be bothering you."

"I am up at five," Éva replies. She takes a quick survey of his apartment the way he does at hers, noting the potted fern on the bookshelf and a framed black and white photograph of a pigeon he has hung up on the wall—expecting, but not finding, signs of Teresa Marsch. His briefcase is on the floor where it usually is. One of his pressed shirts hangs from a coat hook. A new espresso maker sits on the stove.

"It's just that I've got to get this turkey into the oven," he says.

She steps into the kitchen with him. The fresh bird lies across the table unwrapped in its butcher paper. She looks at him. "You would like me to cook this turkey for you?"

He hesitates. "No, no, I mean, I don't want you to go to the trouble of it, Éva. I just, I don't know what to do. American turkeys come oven ready."

She looks at the turkey, which is nicely muscled, quite large.

He explains eagerly, "I know how to cook a turkey. I've cooked one every year, but American turkeys aren't fresh like this." He grimaces at the bird. "American turkeys don't have the head and feet."

She can't quite imagine paying for the turkey he describes. She folds her arms across her chest, her brow knitted. "You would like me to tell you how to prepare it?"

"Yes, exactly. Tell me what I'm supposed to do." He smiles at her.

She digs a meat cleaver out of one of his kitchen drawers and illustrates how to sever the neck. He jumps clear when it falls to the floor. She covers her smile with her hand.

"I'll do the rest," he says. "You can just give me instructions."

"Instructions," repeats Éva. She removes the feet and innards and wraps them up with the neck to take home with her. Then she seats herself, folding her hands on her lap. While she directs his trimming of the bird she looks around his kitchen. The narrow cupboard is ajar and she can see it is well stocked. She notices the toaster. Then her eyes alight upon the microwave. She stares at it.

"I saw a microwave demonstration in the Centrum," she blurts out. "Did you buy it at the Centrum?"

"In Budapest," he tells her, "the prices are actually better for things like microwaves, appliances in general."

She admits, "I've never used one."

"Would you like to try it out?"

He suggests she warm up the leftover chicken soup in his fridge. She presses the START button and steps away, bumping into him accidentally.

He smiles down at her. "I promise there's nothing to be scared of."

"I know, I know that," she says, sidestepping. "I understand how it operates. It's completely possible, not so risky." The buzzer goes off and she is startled. Now he seems amused. She blushes, sweeping invisible crumbs from her skirt. Her shoulder brushes against his as he shifts his weight. She holds very still, asking in the quiet, "How old are you?"

"How old are *you*?" he counters, reaching for the microwave door.

"Too old," she tells him, taking the soup bowl he hands her.

She sits at the table drinking the soup while he spoons the stuffing into the turkey. He appears to know what he's doing despite having never seen real poultry. The stuffing contains sausage and chestnut and bread crumbs. "Éva," he says, looking over at her as she sips her soup. "You're Romanian and Hungarian? How does that work?"

She says, "I'm not Romanian blood, but I'm citizenship. It's not so unusual." She watches him struggle to thread the needle. "Let me sew it?" she says, reaching.

"You're a lefty," he remarks, watching her stitch up the turkey.

"Well, but I can use either," she says, switching the needle into her other hand to show him.

"Ambidextrous!"

She smiles.

"You don't like to talk about yourself, do you?"

She quickly shrugs. "Well, it isn't so important." Tying off her knot, she sets the needle aside. He opens the oven door and they slide the heavy pan in. He has long, refined fingers. She watches him wipe the steam from the lenses of his glasses on a dish towel and carefully put the glasses back on. His modern wire frames are unlike anything available here. He focuses in on her.

"But you were born here, in Szeged."

"Yes," she pauses, getting up to wash her hands at the sink. "May I?" She squeezes past him. When she turns the water off, he hands her a towel. Glancing up cautiously, she says, "My father was Hungarian. And my mother was Jew." She is certainly not used to volunteering this information, but it washes over the American. He is not capable of judging her, at least not with regard to her past. And when she looks at him, she can't see her reflection the way she can in everyone else.

"It must be hard to come back here after having lived your whole life somewhere else," he says.

She shakes her head. "The situation is much better here. Opportunity." She checks herself. She doesn't want to feed him lines.

"How was it you grew up in Romania, anyway?"

"The war," she pauses. "It was the war."

He reheats a bowl of soup for himself in the microwave and sits down with her. He talks about his mother, who died two years ago. The soup is her recipe. At Thanksgiving, his mother always cooked glazed carrots, but he likes to roast carrots— parboil them and nestle them in with the turkey for the last fifteen to twenty minutes.

Éva listens intently, copying his inflection in her mind. "I'm doing all the talking again," he remarks, but she knows he will go on. That is not American, that is men. Anyway she doesn't want him to stop. She wants to know everything about him. She thinks he has artist's hands.

"You're welcome to join us later on," he says, changing the subject. "For Thanksgiving. Teresa's coming and the Americans in town."

She shakes her head. "I'm busy."

He switches into momentary earnestness. "I monopolized your Saturday morning, Éva. What can I do to thank you?"

She's certain he's not talking about dollars. Anyway, she knows what she wants. "I could borrow a book perhaps?"

He brightens, pleased. "By all means. What do you like to read?"

Together they survey his hallway bookcase.

"I like to read this," says Éva, reaching out promptly.

"Mary Shelley?" He eyes her. "It's not exactly *Frankenstein* from the movies."

She clutches the paperback. "I don't know the movie," she replies. She feels flushed, looking up from the page. "It was a long time ago when I read it the first time. In Romania, another life!" He smiles at her. He can have no idea of it and that's his privilege.

They are saying good-bye, Martin still chattering with the door open. There is a loud noise behind her down in the courtyard. Ágnes's door flies open. They glimpse her thick foot only, booting Levente's backside. He lunges out the door, landing on the cold bricks as the door slams.

"What was *that*? Is he all right?" Martin steps outside

Levente looks up at them in his glasses. She waves him up.

She says quickly, "His mother beats him when she's drunk. You haven't seen?"

Martin shakes his head. "I wondered, but . . ." his voice drifts off when Levente appears at the top of the stairs. The boy walks slowly over to them, his coat unbuttoned. The cat trails him, cautiously, on this side of the mezzanine.

"Come to my apartment, Levente. I have fresh bread." He is colorless even in the cold. She rests a hand gently on his shoulders. She looks at Martin. With a rush of emotion, she is up on tiptoe, whispering in the cool air near his ear. "You must help me rescue him!"

She and the boy go into her apartment with the cat. "There is that toy he will chase, a pill bottle." She suggests, "Have a

look under the radiator for it." While the boy plays with the
cat, she warms up food. Then she calls him to the table. "Let's
wash our hands," she says, lighting the pilot at the sink. His
little fingers keep dropping the bar of soap. She steps in to help,
lathering his hands for him, rinsing them and patting them dry
in a fresh towel.

"Sit down, Levente. I'm sure you're hungry."

"Yes Éva *Néni*." He slides into the smaller of the two chairs.

"Why did she throw you out like that?"

For a moment, he doesn't say anything. "Sometimes she
tells me to go. But today is so cold." He has a nervous habit of
wrinkling his nose, perhaps to keep his glasses in place.

"What will you do?" she asks, biting her lip.

He shrugs again. "She will fall asleep watching TV. She
won't even notice me."

"What about your sister?"

"My sister?" He looks up for a second. "My sister doesn't
have to go."

"I'm sorry," Éva says, feeling daft. She ladles the soup.
She sets the bowl down in front of him and brings the bread.

Shame grips her later that night, reading *Frankenstein*. When
Victor Frankenstein abandons his deformed creation he is con-
sumed in guilt, but he never takes responsibility. She remembers
how it plagued her when she first read it. She is not Levente's
mother. But the conflict remains, unabating, a rose thorn in her
forefinger. She rationalizes, is afraid. In the book, the monster
resigns himself to self-destruction, as if peace can be found

only in extinction. She gets up out of bed and shuffles down the hallway into the kitchen. She peeks between the shutter slats. Downstairs, Ágnes's light is out for a change. The whole building is dark but she can see Martin has left his shutters up again, his window glistening.

He will be traveling to Istanbul for the holidays. He is making the trip with other American teachers, "friends from Budapest," he tells her. He stops by her flat one afternoon to ask if she will bring in his mail and water his plant while he's away.

"I'm turning forty on Christmas Eve."

She's pleasantly surprised. "There's only a decade dividing us!"

He gives her his key and several dollars in advance. He's encouraging her hustling, paying her at every turn—not that she wishes he wouldn't, not exactly.

"Don't mind the pigeons on the balcony," he tells her.

After he's gone to Turkey she ventures across with his key. There is no mail for him today and the fern doesn't need a drink. She glances out the window, taking in the view. She decides to use his espresso maker. She pours a steaming black thread of coffee into a porcelain cup. She carries it with her through the closed double doors into his living room and perches on the arm of the couch, sipping the espresso. She reaches for one of the English-language newspapers on the coffee table—headlines from Mikhail Gorbachev's resignation. The Soviet Union has ceased to exist. It's a new day. If it wasn't so hard to fathom she might trust in it.

Tossing the paper aside, she goes into his bedroom. He has pushed the two single beds together. A green striped duvet is balled up next to the pillows. She resists the urge to make up the bed like a chambermaid at a hotel yet she can't help collecting the stray clothes on the floor as if they were Ursula's. She pauses in front of the open wardrobe, catching his scent.

There is a flurry of activity outside on the balcony. Stepping closer to the balcony door she sees the birds. He has built a pigeon coop. Sheets of screening enclose the stucco balcony. He has left the hinged roof open. An automatic seed dispenser is just now strewing grain onto the floor.

She recalls seeing him carrying in the window screening. He mentioned he was feeding birds on his balcony. She gropes for the light switch on the wall, knowing it is there. On the shelves in the bedroom there are veterinary supply and first aid kits and several books on raising birds, homing pigeons, racers.

The doves alight on the rail as the feeder tosses grain, hopping onto a small wooden platform in order to poke their way inside, one by one, through a canvas flap door. She counts ten birds, pale gray with dark collars. She has never much cared for pigeons. They were the bane of the wheat farmer and their incessant mourning brings memories of her broken jaw, recovery on the couch at Irini's. She looks on as a hen with an unusual mark on her head, small and circular like a drop of ink, sweeps her tail feathers indiscriminately. Two cocks with puffed-up chests spar over her with quick jerking necks. Tiny molting feathers splash up around the blustery birds—a few moments of flapping wings before peace returns and they are strutting about in small circles again. The little inkspot flies up and out to perch in the beech tree for the night.

Before Éva turns off the light to leave, she notices on the night table, beside a shiny pile of Hungarian coins that he apparently has no need for, the copy of *Frankenstein* that she returned to him. Is he some kind of post-Communist spy?

She hurriedly washes out the espresso maker in his kitchen, attempting to restore the status quo. Her disquiet fades by the time she is back at her place, looking aimlessly around her own rooms.

"Look, *Néni*," says Levente, holding up the postcard. "It is for me, from the American!"

She opens the door, encouraging him in from the cold.

"Look at the Turkish stamp, *Néni*!"

"So colorful!" she agrees. "And large! Very special." Martin has printed Hungarian words on the card: *Hello Levente! Good trip! From Martin.* "It's a good addition to your collection," says Éva.

Levente holds it out in front of him studying it for a minute.

"Will you remove it right now?"

"Yes," he affirms. "I am ready."

She fills a bowl of warm water and he sits at her table looking almost earnest, dipping the corner of the card in until the stamp comes loose. He fishes out the stamp, setting it to dry. Behind him, at the counter, she is chopping garlic. He goes to get the envelope of his stamps from his shelf in her living room. It is when he returns and she glances at him appraisingly that she sees the burn mark on his ear lobe.

She quietly gasps. Why is she surprised? She goes to the
sink and washes her hands. In her medicine cabinet, she finds
the calendula ointment, the scent recalling Irini's poultices.

"This will cool it," she tells him, dabbing the earlobe carefully. "So there's no infection."

He flinches.

"I'm trying to help," she whispers, hating how hollow it
sounds. She brings out his Szilveszter presents before he leaves.
He will be gone the whole next day to Kecskemét with his
mother and sister. He seems pleased with the stamp album.
Together they eat the chocolate-covered cherries.

She recriminates herself for being no better than Mrs. Géza,
but the pigeon coop has become filthy in his absence and she
has no plans for New Year's Day. She steps cautiously out onto
the balcony with the broom and a bucket and mop. She thought
that the birds had all flown after feeding, but as she is wring-
ing the mop she feels something touch down on her shoulder
and freezes, startled. Her eyes strain to see the hen that has
landed there. Will it poke her eyes out if she slowly turns her
head and looks at it?

"Good day, little Inkspot," she says softly, pausing. "I am
Éva."

His train was due twenty minutes ago. Éva's anticipation is
so intense she can barely sit still. Her darning needle flies. At
the sound of the doorbell she flings the sock aside and hops

up from the couch, pausing to smooth her hair before going
to the door.

"Martin, you have a beard!"

He kisses both of her cheeks in Hungarian greeting and
she feels his whiskers. She offers him his apartment key, warm
from her hand clenching it inside her pocket. "I bought you
some milk with the money you gave me. It's in your fridge, and
bread, since the shops are already closed." She looks him over.
He is tanned and looks windblown and free as usual. He is
toting a worn rucksack on his shoulders.

"It's good to see you, Éva."

"Yes," she murmurs in agreement.

He's turning to go, his key in hand. "You know," she says,
hesitantly, "during Communism, people like you were arrested."

He looks at her quizzically. "Like me? Americans?"

"Pigeon-heads," she tells him.

He grins.

The color rises in her cheeks. "Forgive me. I was snooping
like a typical Hungarian neighbor."

"How are my birds? I missed them."

"The boys have been fighting over the little female. She
incites them."

"Yes," he says.

"You are training these birds?" she asks warily.

He laughs. "Not for espionage, I promise!"

He has showered and combed his hair and beard. They have only
ever sat down at his place. At hers, they hover in the entryway,

but now he is bearing gifts, Turkish tea and halva. She invites him in.

"I'll just fill the kettle, we'll try out the tea?"

"Sure, if it's no problem. You're not busy?"

She shakes her head, echoing him, "No problem."

She shows him to her spotless kitchen table. "Sit down, Martin." She busies herself opening the tea, slicing the halva.

"What can I do, Éva?" he asks, shifting in his seat. "American men like to help."

"Really?" She eyes him. He is utterly sure of himself. "They like to do the cooking and the cleaning?"

"Some do. "

She unwraps the halva, carefully cutting it. Behind her, on the stove, the kettle sounds and she swivels, her skirt rustling against his chair. She turns off the flame, lifting the kettle.

He's enthusiastic about Turkey—the delicious food, the warm weather. "I wore a T-shirt and flip-flops."

She marvels at the thought. Szeged is in a cold snap.

He isn't looking forward to the start of the new term. Not all the students are plagiarizers and cheaters but enough to make him feel even more hopeless than usual correcting papers. "At least I can finally tell Ibolya Kovács from Ildikó Kovács since Ibolya died her hair that henna color."

"Russian red," she says. Ursula's had been a quieter henna.

"Ibolya Kovács is the university magistrate's daughter. Teresa Marsch says I shouldn't fail her."

"Teresa Marsch?" she cautiously asks. "Did she go with you to Istanbul?"

He shakes his head, looking at her evenly. "Maybe if she wasn't a smoker." He pauses. "Or a boring expat like myself."

In Istanbul, he tells her, he met up with another American, a travel writer for an American publisher, and this second American told him that he should try writing a guidebook on Budapest.

"For tourism," he says, prompting her. "A travel guide. You work at the Best Western, Éva, you must have some idea of what I'm talking about."

She nods uncertainly, reaching for another piece of halva. It is so sweet. She should eat only a little.

"Don't you think it makes sense now that the region is opening up?" he goes on, his eyes glittering with interest. "Not a coffee table book, but something with good information—hotel listings, restaurant reviews, that sort of thing."

Who is this man? Her eyes drift to his dark beard, his Adam's apple poised to swallow. His shirt she ironed herself. He wears a brown V-neck sweater over it, like an intellectual. His damp hair has begun to curl in the warmth of her kitchen. She is generous with the heat because for the moment it is included in the rent.

"You know, Éva," he says to her, "I was thinking you might give me a few Hungarian-language lessons?"

She laughs. "You will sound like a peasant if you learn from me."

He shrugs. "I don't mind."

She can't believe him. "I will fail you if you cheat." Then she leans in. "Martin, why did you come to Hungary?"

"To meet you," he says charmingly.

She asks him suddenly, "Are you CIA?"

He laughs, claiming the birds are a hobby. "We had a pigeon loft on the roof of our building growing up. My father trained pigeons in the army. A few of his birds were honored for distinguished service. I have a photograph."

"Yes, I know it," she says.

"That bird carried a crucial message hundreds of miles over forbidding terrain in Italy. One leg and part of its wing were shot off but it survived the mission. Pigeons are survivors."

She thinks fleetingly of Stefan Siminel's father, who gave his life for pigeons. She can still see the bird's shadow in the corner of the movie screen.

Martin says that he never had any interest in homers while his father was alive. "We weren't close. He died when I was young. My parents were older. They adopted me."

"Oh?"

He nods, looking across the little table at her. He offers, "I have Hungarian blood in me."

"Really?"

"Kovács was my surname, I think. The name was about the only piece of identification that turned up in the church records."

"It's a common name," Éva says. "Smith."

He nods. "Yes, I discovered that. The Szeged phone book alone must have a hundred Kovács."

"And there are the rest without a telephone," she murmurs. She studies his face, his thick lips, the rounded tip of his nose. Maybe he looks older with the beard. "You have come to search, Martin?"

"I think I'm just escaping," he says smiling.

"Escaping from America?" she asks, in surprise. "What are you escaping, Martin?"

He smiles, shrugging. "An unresolved life."

She is bewildered, fallen silent.

"And what about you, Éva? You still haven't told me why you came back to Hungary."

She looks away. "To meet you, I think."

1991

HE IS LATE. She opens the door when she finally hears him knocking. He looks stricken.

"Martin?"

He blurts out, "My bicycle was stolen!"

She pulls him in out of the cold, her small hands encircling his arm. She is wearing a silk head scarf and a white apron around her waist.

"Right out in front of the Ping-Pong pub, where I always park it." He is shaking his head.

"It's unfortunate," she says. She gives him a tissue to wipe his nose. "It was a nice bicycle."

"I'm such an idiot. I left it unlocked."

"No, Martin."

He removes his eyeglasses and wipes the moisture with a second tissue. His arrogant expression falls away, his naked face now vulnerable. "I hope you haven't been worried. I'm sorry I'm late. I'd have phoned, I mean, if you had a phone."

"A telephone? No, no," she laughs a little. "It's a five-year wait for a telephone. Really, Martin, it's no problem." She has adopted his inflection, "no problem."

"It *is* a problem," he insists. "I deserved it. I was conducting a sociological experiment."

She pauses. "An experiment?"

"I'm an idiot."

She shakes her head.

"It's just that it seems so safe here."

She clears the vegetable peelings off the table and pours out a bowl of tomorrow's soup. "Here, Martin," setting down the soup and a spoon. She slices bread.

"I'm sorry I missed my first Hungarian lesson," he says.

"It's no problem," she tells him again. She watches him drinking the soup. Then she shows him the schoolboy's notebook in which she has written out pages of different dialogues. The first lesson is Greetings and the Weather.

He flips through the notebook looking a little bewildered. "I hope you're not too strict," he jokes.

She eyes him brightly. "You don't like strict?" She leans in and combs a lock of hair back with her fingers. He is too vain for a hat.

He catches her wrist and presses his lips to the back of her hand. "*Kezít csókolom,*" he says softly. It is a traditional greeting: I kiss your hand.

"That's too formal for me, Martin."

He pushes back in his seat and slips his other arm around her waist and pulls her to him so that she sits on his lap. She surprises herself, relaxing into him.

"I can't stop thinking about you. I stare at your door when you're not at home, Éva. Sometimes I wonder if it's something in the water since I've given up boiling it." He tilts his head back to look at her. She runs her middle finger slowly over the curve of his jaw.

His hands slide up her back and then to either side of her face. His grip tightens and he draws her mouth to his.

They are interrupted by the shouting outside. It is pitch black through the window. They stare into each other's eyes, listening. When they go out onto the mezzanine, they can see dark shadows downstairs and they can hear the blows of the beating.

"Stop, stop it!" Martin shouts down over the railing. Perhaps she is startled by his foreign voice. Their eyes have adjusted and they can see Ágnes's hard face squinting up at them, the glint of the gold in her ears. She is holding Levente by the coat collar. They are returning home from somewhere. Now she drags him up the stoop along with her shopping bag and they catch the shuffle of his pencil legs scrambling after her. She unlocks the door, the light goes on inside the apartment, and Ágnes's beefy form looms in the doorway before she slams the door shut, the light swallowed up. The cool evening surrounds them on the mezzanine.

"It's late, Martin." She stands behind him. She reaches out. He turns and pulls her to him.

She catches her breath and then releases it. She says quietly, "I dream of poisoning her."

"Why doesn't anyone go to the police?"

"The police, Martin? The police will harass me about my status."

"But you're not here illegally, Éva. You said you were born here. They'd have no reason." He looks down at her. "What can they do to you?"

"Well, they can do anything." She lets go of him, arms dropping. "They don't need a reason, Martin."

He shrugs in exasperation. "Maybe it's okay to beat your child in Hungary."

"Okay? I hate that word. 'O-k,'" she snaps back.

He leans on the railing, sighing. "You're right, it's late."

She stands in front of the mirror, plaiting her hair, coiling and pinning it up, contemplating the bold streaks of silver that appeared since she stopped dyeing it red, after Markowitz's death. She doesn't mind the skunk look but wonders what Martin thinks. She turns sideways and stands straighter, lifting her chest. She is still slim, with muscular calves and pretty ankles and small tough feet. She steps into her boots, the heels worn down on the instep, and pulls on her coat, wistful for her shawl waylaid in the darning basket. Then she hears his knock. He has asked her to "go out on a date." It is a new idiom for her.

"Hi, Éva."

"Hi, Martin." Buttoning her coat, she steps out onto the mezzanine.

"Do you play Ping-Pong by any chance?" he asks.

She eyes him tentatively. "Sure, of course. It was a Communist sport."

It is another cool evening. They head down the stairs but the light shuts off in just a few seconds, due to István Géza's stinginess. Martin reaches for her hand in the darkness. He pulls her to him at the bottom of the stairs, his lips finding hers. Her back presses up against the wall. The light flicks on again as someone enters the building. They pause in each other's arms as Ágnes goes past in the vestibule, reeking of alcohol.

"She casts a spell over us," Éva murmurs.

Martin says nothing until they are out on the street. "I went to the police. But they barely speak English, Éva." At the corner, he takes her hand as they cross on the green light.

The pub used to be a subterranean dive, but the new owners have installed tile and refurbished the bar and also set up a Ping-Pong table. The nightly tournaments draw a large crowd and a number of talented players. Modest gambling takes place on the sidelines.

She is a hummingbird in flight. The pub crowd tightens around the table. She is trouncing the reigning player, a thin, long-haired university student named Csaba. He leaps with long arms to return her serve and attempts a smash but she scoops and lobs it and his drive stroke ends at the net. Her cheeks are flushed, her delicate nostrils flaring. She is cool and calculated, sharp and quick, deflecting bullets with a pen-hold grip. Csaba makes a show of inspecting her paddle afterward, and she offers to switch paddles with her next opponent. After several matches her control of the table remains unchallenged. She pockets her winnings, giving up her paddle, searching for Martin's beaming face in the crowd.

"Éva, you're an Olympian!" he exclaims.

She laughs, slumping into the chair beside him, out of breath. "Not really. I played in Masters only."

"You're full of secrets."

She reaches for the shot glass he offers.

"Like, what about those gold teeth?" he asks.

She pretends not to hear him, swallows the shot, her lips pouting. "I could play either hand at Ping-Pong," she says. "If you were ambidextrous, you could survive life during Communism." She looks around at the pub life. "But I'm all worn out by now." He reaches for her and she looks at him curiously. "Don't you think I'm too old for you, Martin? You are my student, after all."

They try to converse in Hungarian for a while. She teaches him a Hungarian saying, "Old hen and young carrot make good soup." He orders another round. When he helps her with her coat, later, she falls back into his arms, laughing. "It was me against the Hungarians again, Martin!" She looks back fleetingly at the Ping-Pong table. They climb the stairs to the street. She links her arm with his and they walk along the riverside, past the glittering disco boats full of Arab dental students. They turn off onto cobblestones, weaving their way through an elegant neighborhood of the left bank.

As they are crossing the unlit plaza of the Centrum department store a shadow runs out at them. A young boy with a crazed look on his face waves something in his hand—a dead pigeon. He holds the carcass by the wing and shakes it in their faces. More kids ambush them from the other side, Gypsy boys, six or seven of them. Éva wastes no time in defending herself—striking out, swatting with her hands, clawing her way through the horde. Martin, behind her, towers over the scrum. He rips the pigeon out of the boy's hand and waves the carcass back at them. The boys guffaw at his audacity, parting like sheep. Martin and Éva hurry out to the avenue, where the gang retreats because of the taxis parked under the streetlamp, the drivers who throw stones at them. One of the boys calls out, "Sir, Madam, our pigeon, we need our pigeon!" and Éva insists, tugging at Martin's sleeve until he tosses it backward, toward the little hands reaching from the black.

They go to her place. He is easy, kissing her hand as they go up the stairs. She slips out of her boots and he helps her out of her coat and stays there, stroking the back of his fingers along her neck while he takes the pins out of her hair.

"You should wear it down," he says, "like this." He runs his fingers through it. His hands rest on her shoulders, his forehead presses against the back of her head.

"There is a zipper there, Martin," she whispers in the quiet.

He unzips her dress. Finding the hem, he slips his hands under the skirt, easing it up over her head. She shivers in her threadbare slip, hair falling to her shoulders, and turns to kiss him. Finally, she pulls away. Pressing the back of her hand absently to her lips, she takes him by the hand, into the bedroom.

The rawness deepens, her muscles tense against his, her mouth drinks him in. At last, he enters her. He pushes up on his arms and she arches her head back straining for release.

Lying in the tangled duvet, later, his face still shining with heat in the light from her cemetery candles, he tells her she is beautiful and she reminds him he isn't wearing his glasses.

They share a glass of water. She asks him if he's ever been in love before and he shakes his head, reaching to finger one of her curls gone haywire.

"And what about you?"

She pauses. "Once."

Outside somewhere they can hear the tom. She is up on one elbow, peering at him beneath the sheet. "But didn't you say you weren't Jewish, Martin?"

"I'm not."

"Really? Do all American men look like you?"

"Only the circumcised ones," he says, after a moment.

"I didn't know." Her eyes fall across his smooth chest.

"I'm your first American, apparently." He adds fetchingly, "And you're my first Hungarian."

"I am a Jew." She remembers she has told him already; it isn't news. The remaining candle stub sputters and burns out. She curls up on her side and his body cradles hers from behind, and they lie like crescent rolls in the baker's window.

Inside the cavernous vestibule of the Guttenberg Street synagogue, Éva says good afternoon to the old Jew seated behind a small folding table. She tries to appear like a tourist. "Thank you," she murmurs, taking the information pamphlet he hands her. She fishes inside her purse for coins for the donation plate.

In several languages, including English, the pamphlet describes the synagogue's history. She lifts her eyes and looks around—on the anterior walls, black-and-white photographs from 1944 document the sanctuary piled high with boxes and crates. Not long after she'd gotten out, the Nazis occupied, a ghetto was erected, and the synagogue was turned over for war effort storage.

She stands in front of a large marble plaque listing the local victims of the Holocaust.

"Are you looking for someone?" the old Jew asks her. He has been following her around.

She shakes her head without turning to look at him. A moment later, she concedes, "My mother."

"Who is she?"

"She's not here," she says. "She was never claimed with the other Farkases."

The old Jew sneezes and blows into a handkerchief. "You can apply for the engraving," he says. "There's no fee involved, rich Americans are paying, like Tony Curtis."

"Perhaps . . . ," says Éva, folding her arms across her chest. She steals a look into his watery eyes.

"Do you want to go in?" he asks, indicating the sanctuary door.

She follows him up the carpeted step and he opens the door for her. Her breath catches in her throat as she steps inside. Her eyes lift to the painted dome ceiling. She turns slowly, taking in the enchanting turrets and cupolas. Once it was a castle.

A vast stillness surrounds her. Sunlight floods in through the stained-glass panels on either side of the sanctuary, pastel rays touching down in the center aisle. She stares at the ghostly altar in the distance. The sanctuary is so desolate that the dust has come to life; between the rows of wooden seats, tiny pinpoints dance in the streaming light. Her hand is fizzing for the first time in years. She gropes her way to a seat.

It was here, outside, that she saw her mother raped. She is caught in the clutch of it.

She gets up abruptly and exits the building, holding her breath so she won't inhale the tangy sap. The evergreens are pungent in the late spring, different than in her memory, and she recollects that it was winter when they smuggled her out. She remembers a coat with a secret pocket in it. She is striding briskly home, fleeing, feeling chased, down Béke Street to quiet Josika.

By now it is late in the day, the sun behind the buildings. As she comes up the street she sees Martin and Levente in the pigeon loft. He has been inviting Levente in recently. She can hear the tapping on a tin can. Birds flutter down from branches, the roof.

Upstairs, she finds Martin's door unlocked and lets herself in. A cool breeze comes from the back of the house, the balcony door wide open. She slips off her shoes. She can hear them talking.

"If you let her go, she will come back?" Levente has asked.

"Yes."

"Why will she come back?"

"She wants to." Martin sounding sweet in Hungarian. "She wants."

"To come home?"

"Yes, yes."

She lingers in the shadow of the bedroom. She can see Levente on the balcony, holding a dove. "She is so nice," Levente murmurs, softly stroking the crest with his forefinger.

Something inside Éva is unfurling, layers giving way. She turns around and slips back out of the apartment.

The cat is waiting. She opens the door and scoots in without him, pulling the door closed. She hangs up her coat, then pours a saucer of milk and slips it outside her door. He has grown into a handsome tom, but she can't let him in because he is on the prowl and stinks up the place.

She washes her hands at the kitchen sink, then fills the kettle. She is lost in thought, waiting for the boil. Over her head, strings of pepper and braided garlic dangle from the ceiling pipe.

The kettle blows, rousing her. She squelches the flame and steeps a glass of Turkish tea, watching the sugar cubes dissolve. Then she goes to collect the application for the engraving from the pocket of her coat and sits down to fill it out.

The roosting pairs on Martin's balcony link beaks and amorously preen. They are bringing in nesting materials. Soon the eggs arrive, then all the hatchlings. They seem to grow overnight. The birds feed their newborns milk, Martin says. There is an old Hungarian recipe called bird's milk, made with eggs. Auntie used to serve it in the spring.

"They both make the milk," Martin adds. "The mothers *and* the fathers."

"*Fantastikus!*" Levente cries.

"Yes," says Martin, nodding enthusiastically. He turns to Éva, says, "There's an equal division of labor in the pigeon pair. The male and the female take turns keeping the nestlings warm and fed."

"Is that so?"

When Levente leaves, she stays. They make love sideways on his bed. She straddles him, feeling her body in his hands, breasts spilling from his fingers. After, she watches him move from the bed and stand at the balcony door, wearing just his eyeglasses. There is only a bit of daylight.

"I saw Levente's mother downstairs today. He must have been at school," Martin says. "She was taking the little girl out in the stroller. It was cute. They were sharing a pastry."

"Yes," Éva says softly. "She loves her daughter."

"We have to do something."

"I'm afraid she will kill him if anyone interferes." She turns away from him, admitting this.

"Éva, I need you to translate."

She nods, looking back at him, chagrined.

"Let's go back to the police tomorrow."

Her eyebrows jump. "Tomorrow?"

"Éva, you have to stop peeking through your fingers!"

She is cross with him for saying this, even if he's correct. What can he know of it? She begins hunting down her strewn clothing, hastily getting dressed.

The semester ends. Martin has given all the Russian teachers 4s and 5s whether or not they deserved it. He begins traveling with his birds, training them for sport. He dreams of entering an international pigeon-racing competition. Anything is possible. He convinced her to part with his old bicycle box cardboard for the construction of a bird carrier. She is worried he'll get arrested for spying and has made him promise not to release the birds in sight of any train stations. Often she and Levente wait together for the birds' return. Martin has converted his Hungarian lesson notebook into a flight record book and the pages are filling up with Levente's strangely shaped letters and numbers.

One Saturday when the birds are flying and Martin is gone, Ágnes entertains a boyfriend in the courtyard, the same *srác* who sometimes works under the hood of a rusty Lada parked on the street. Ágnes is serving him lunch on a folding table in the sunshine. The children are already seated in front of bowls of soup. Éva is heartened by the appearance of domesticity. She lingers, hanging laundry. Martin has left her his key as usual and she snuck her load into his washing machine.

Suddenly, she hears Levente's scream. He has fed his bread to the pigeons. Their chair legs scrape the bricks. Ágnes is dragging him. They disappear from sight and now she hears them coming up the stairs. Ágnes comes out into the light of the mezzanine, gripping Levente by the neck. Ágnes whips off his eyeglasses and hoists him in her arms. She dangles him upside down over the railing, holding him around the legs. He is an ingrate! He should beg her for forgiveness. And he begs.

Éva runs across, swinging a damp dish towel over her head like a flail. "Put him down, Ágnes Sas!"

Ágnes drags Levente back up and sets him down in front of her, like a shield. Éva stops short. Levente looks stunned. Ágnes is breathing heavily from exertion, the heaving shoulders of a bull. Her skin is oily with sweat. "Keep your whip to yourself, fucking Gypsy," says Ágnes, shoving Levente toward the stairs.

"You stain your soul," Éva says.

Ágnes spits over her shoulder as they pass.

"I will go to the police," Éva threatens, hollowly. When they have gone inside downstairs, she collapses against the wall of the building. She unlocks Martin's door and slips inside. Standing apprehensively at the kitchen window, her heart pounding in her chest, she fears for Levente's life. She is surprised to see them all going out twenty minutes later, Levente pushing the stroller.

She lies down on Martin's bed in her dark red sweater with patched elbows, wool skirt, and stockings, drawing her knees up and wrapping her arms around.

A couple of hours later Martin climbs gingerly into the bed with her.

"It's you," she stirs. "I didn't hear the birds fly in yet."

"There was this couple on the train," he whispers in her ear, "in the seat opposite me. They kissed the whole way from Budapest to Szeged. I didn't want to stare but I couldn't help it. No one else in the car took any notice."

She chuckles and rolls into him. "You are a prudish American." He pulls her closer, but then she remembers and sits up.

"Martin, let's go to the police."

She tells him what happened earlier. He reaches to fasten the button of her blouse that has come undone. Her hair is still loose, and when she goes into the bathroom to splash cold water on her cheeks she sees in the mirror a softness that pride usually conceals.

"I brought you a milkshake," he calls.

She brightens. "From Burger King?"

Martin loves to hate Burger King, but he has introduced her to milkshakes, which he claims are more delicious in Hungary than in America because they are made with real ice cream. She hears him retrieving the giant-size cup from the freezer.

The sound of the policemen knocking ricochets back and forth in the courtyard and brings most everyone in the building to their windows. Downstairs, Ágnes finally opens up. The police go inside and a while later emerge with Levente. They escort him out of the building.

Béla Barát seems to think it is István Géza who brought in the authorities. Mrs. Fehér says she learned the housing council had put Ágnes's flat up for sale.

"István wants to buy it."

Éva feels momentarily wrapped up in this camaraderie, gossiping with the neighbors on the mezzanine. "It was the American," she tells them. "He has been complaining to the police for weeks."

They look skeptical. "Yes, but István Géza has a nephew in the police force," says Béla Barát. "I think that was him, the younger one, who was knocking."

Inside, Martin is at the stove cooking eggs. "István Géza is getting the credit," she tells him.

Martin shrugs. "Maybe he deserves it. The social worker said there was another complaint already on file. Maybe it was István Géza."

Éva is biting her fingernails. "I wonder where they are taking Levente?"

"We will find out."

It's true he had impressed her with his perseverance at the police station and then at the welfare agency. She had stood beside him translating, trembling, her gloved fingers clinging to the counter.

A few days later Ágnes moves out of the building. She and the *srác* load a trunk and several bags onto the top of his Lada and drive off, the little girl seated on Ágnes's lap. István Géza comes the same Saturday to clean out the apartment. He carries in a ladder and bucket of paint.

Éva and Martin are not admitted at the orphanage while Levente's case is under investigation. The warden talks with them through the gate. A pudgy woman with pretty eyes, she wears a housecoat and slippers on her feet.

"In a few weeks, come back," she tells them. "You can apply to visit."

On the bus ride back into the city they stop at a red light. On the corner opposite where the bus is standing, restoration of an old bank is under way, an art nouveau gem. The building is lined with scaffolding but it is possible to see fragments of the facade, the original detail rediscovered beneath the leaded blackness. Éva stares out. The light turns and the bus roars through the intersection.

"The warden seemed sympathetic, didn't she, Martin?" she asks, turning to him.

"You mean nice? I guess so."

"I hope she doesn't keep the chocolate bars for herself."

"Oh, Éva."

"I'm so afraid for him, Martin."

He nods, reaching for her hand.

Five weeks go by and Levente's case is still open. She is swimming the breaststroke back and forth in the crowded pool when she sees him. He stands with a group of kids that have just come onto the pool deck. They are lining up to go into the water and there he is, striking in his red swim trunks. The orphanage warden emerges from the changing room, wearing a bikini under her housecoat and a whistle on a string around her neck. At the pool steps, Levente hands the warden his eyeglasses before stepping cautiously into the water.

Treading water in the middle of the pool, Éva can see how much he has grown. He appears to have gained a couple of kilos. He splashes and bobs with the other kids in the sparkling water. Éva notices the warden, sitting on the grass reading a magazine. She climbs out of the pool. Wrapping a towel around her, she walks over.

"Do you remember me? Levente Sas's neighbor?"

"Sure," says the warden, blowing cigarette smoke out the side of her mouth. "I remember you—with the American boyfriend."

Éva gestures toward the pool. "Levente looks well. Can I say hello to him?"

The warden eyes her. "It's just as well that he forget you, no? His case has been open so long now. I thought it would close quickly since the mother wants nothing to do with him."

The warden puts her cigarette out in the dirt. Her jiggling arms
and protruding belly are darkly tanned. She looks at her watch.
"His life with her is in the past." She gets to her feet with some
effort and stands squarely, looking at Éva. Levente's eyeglass
strap dangles from the warden's pocket. "Unless you are interested in adoption, what's the point of it?"

"Well, but I was his neighbor. How could I adopt him?"

The warden shrugs. "Are you single or married?"

"Single."

"Under age forty-five?"

Éva sighs.

Turning away, the warden blows her whistle and walks
off. Éva looks on as Levente climbs out of the pool, puts on his
glasses, and is herded into the changing rooms.

The heat does not lift after dark. Martin, wrapped in just a towel,
is seated in a chair on the mezzanine. Éva draws the razor across
his skin. She wears a sleeveless blouse, her hair combed straight
after her swim. "He looked well," she is saying. "Healthy." She
swallows hard, thinking of Levente. She soaps Martin's chin
with the brush. "The water was perfect."

No one at 72 Josika is sleeping. Lights and televisions
are on and all the windows are open. Down in the courtyard,
Mr. Fehér and his elder son play chess by candlelight. The cat
appears and rubs against Éva's ankles.

"The warden thinks we should leave off." She adds, "Unless
we want to adopt."

He looks up at her. "Don't we have to be Hungarian?"

She glances at him tentatively as she rinses the blade. "Hm, yes, one of us does." She tips her head to the side, studying his jawline. "Hold still," she says as she continues to shave him. After a minute, she shows him in the mirror—the handlebar mustache and pork chop sideburns she has left there. "Look, you are a Hungarian now!"

He laughs at his reflection and they look together into the mirror. She shaves him clean in another minute. "This is how I like my Martin Kovács," she says, wrapping his face in a towel. "I will just trim the curls?" She brandishes the scissors, stepping between his knees.

He slips his arms around her waist. "Is this haircut ever going to end?"

Across the mezzanine, Béla Barát has come out to smoke. They can see the burning tip of his cigarette. But it is too hot to go inside. She sets down the scissors. Martin pulls her closer.

"You can dispense of your Puritan roots a little?" she asks him, in a whisper. She pulls his towel away.

He runs his fingers through her damp hair.

She is on her knees, kissing with murmuring lips. "You know, we meet the criteria if we get married, Martin. You are young enough, and I have Hungarian citizenship."

"Married," he whispers, his fingertips pressing helplessly on her head.

"Yes," she says.

*   *   *

Lying awake in the heat that night she confides her plan to travel to Kraków.

"I know it's the past. I have no business, really." She contemplates his shadow in the dark beside her. "My mother didn't make it to Auschwitz, but I have to see for myself what it was. Ever since I went to the synagogue I've been thinking I must do it."

"You didn't mention you'd gone to the synagogue."

She feels exposed and turns over.

"You could release a few birds in Kraków," he suggests, his voice coming closer. "It's a ritual at cemeteries." His finger draws a slow spiral on her back.

"They will fly all the way home from Poland?" she asks, swallowing the lump in her throat.

"Farther," he says.

She rolls back to him, folding in against his chest, closing her eyes inside his embrace. The thought of going has put noise in her brain, but she hears him nonetheless—a bicycle bell in the rain.

"We make good soup," he tells her, in his rudimentary Hungarian.

At the end of the month she moves in with him. There is no use in paying two rents.

She has not been able to sleep aboard a train since her hysterectomy many years ago now, but still she is grateful for the semiprivacy of a sleeper car, which Martin paid for. She stows the bird carrier safely at the end of the overhead bunk, then climbs up, stretching out her legs. There is one other occupant of the compartment, a freckled Lithuanian, who has claimed the low bunk. The Lithuanian has donned pajamas for the overnight journey and wears a hairnet. She is sitting up in bed with an English-language workbook.

Éva tries to get comfortable but it isn't possible. Once the journey is under way the lights inside the train go out. A little while later, the young woman down below begins talking in her sleep. After a few minutes, Éva peers over the side of the bunk in disbelief. It is unnatural: she rambles nonstop! Here and there her Lithuanian is spotted with English. "I am fine. How are you?" and "Mon-day. To-day is Mon-day." Éva stares down from her bunk at the round, pale face, the eyes sealed shut over babbling lips. She resists throwing one of her boots down.

Over this long night of gibberish, fear takes hold of her. She presses her stocking feet against the bird carrier at the bottom of the bunk. She imagines gripping the handle with her toes, lifting off, escaping with her charges through the ceiling of the train.

In Kraków, several groups of tourists board the local along with her. Numb from no sleep, the bird carrier on her lap, she stares wearily out of the window as the landscape changes to countryside. The harvest is over. The hay has been baled. Soon the train pulls in to the small station at Oświęcim. Taxi drivers descend on the disembarking passengers, calling out in English—"Auschwitz? You want to go to Auschwitz? Five dollar to Auschwitz?"

She elbows past the taxi drivers, shaken. In the train station bathroom, she feeds the doves.

The local bus approaches the former concentration camp across the flat land. The bus windows are brown with mud. She hugs the bird carrier. The bus stops at the site and she and two Canadians with enormous backpacks disembark. Old wooden barracks line the road alongside the vast compound of brick buildings. The trees are beginning to lose their leaves.

She stares across the road, at the front gate, the wrought-iron proclamation, ARBEIT MACHT FREI. It is unmistakable from the few photographs she has seen. She grasps the bird carrier and, breathing deeply, makes her way inside the entrance.

The silent brick buildings of the compound display the personal belongings of Auschwitz's victims—hills of relics: clothing, shoes, toys, books, eyeglasses, human hair. The former gas chambers overflow with broken Zyklon B cannisters. A few of the buildings are empty, cavernous spaces—her own hurried footsteps filling her ears. Why has she come? What is the point? She doesn't remember. All nerve has been sucked out of her. She is small as a mouse. Nothing scurries in the shadows.

Outside in the dusty yard she retches. Wiping her mouth on her sleeve. She opens the bird carrier. Two of the three doves don't hesitate upon release, but the little hen is trained to wait for a kiss on her tiny head. It takes Éva a moment to remember. She is staring at the little bird hopping up and down on the edge of the carrier. Then slowly she reaches out, gathering up the hen, and delivers a soft kiss. She tosses the bird up after the others. Craning her neck, envious of their flight. They disappear from sight. All life evaporated, a blank sky. She looks warily around at the brick buildings, which appear almost two-dimensional, like cutouts. Frightened by this desolate stage, she closes up the empty carrier and hurries away.

The return trip, Kraków to Budapest, is a notorious smuggler's route. To her dismay, she shares a compartment with a family transporting fox stoles. The smugglers spend the journey concealing the furs down their children's pant legs and sleeves in anticipation of the Hungarian customs. The compartment reeks of the canned meat they spread on their sandwiches. Éva's disgust mounts as the hours pass under a flickering fluorescent bulb. When she reaches to turn off the light, the father of the family blocks her, placing his big square hand over the switch—as if they are less suspicious with the light on! She seethes, telling herself she will inform the officials, but later, when customs finally appears, she can't bring herself to speak.

In the women's lavatory in Nyugati Station, Budapest, she gives herself a sponge bath at the sink. She is so relieved to be back! She buys herself a milkshake at Burger King. Her gums tingle as she sucks the icy concoction through a straw aboard the express back to Szeged. She reads the headlines of a newspaper left behind on the seat. Inflation is rising, along with unemployment rates, since the end of Communism. For the first time, in Hungary, there is homelessness. Always in the news is the question of compensation for those who suffered during the Communist and Fascist regimes. Monetary compensation? She wouldn't say no to it. As the train travels south over the great plain, she gazes out at the fields of sunflowers, blocks of palpitating color like brilliant quilt squares. She feels as though she is moving along a deep seam, repairing.

Occasionally, a bird does not return. Twice before this has happened to Martin. There are more and more telephone wires going up and, of course, raptors. A thunderstorm, too, can throw a flier off.

They spend her first night back lying awake, listening for the hen's return. The other two fliers have come home safely.

"I'm so sorry," Éva whispers, clinging to him in the darkness. "I'll never forgive myself."

"Stop, Éva, please."

"But she was your darling." She pictures the little bird perched on Martin's shoulder. He had trained her to eat out of his shirt pocket. "We should never have tested the homing instinct!"

"Shh, Éva, you're exhausted." He strokes her head on the pillow, over and over, and it soothes. She sleeps far into the next afternoon beneath his striped duvet, and when she awakes he brings in one of his giant mugs and she sits up against the pillows and drinks the hot chicken soup, his mother's recipe, and watches him tending the birds on the balcony.

Two days later she is reading in the bedroom when she hears the flapping on the landing board. "Martin! Come look who it is!"

The dove is covered in blood. Her breast has been torn open and the stomach is obscenely exposed. Astonishingly, she is hopping around with fiery eyes.

Martin scoops up the bird. "Who did this to you? A hawk, an owl?" He turns to Éva. "Take her while I get the vet kit."

Éva holds out her hands, horrified by the blood-encrusted feathers. She feels a tiny, pulsing heart against her fingers.

They assess the gash under a lamp. The wound isn't fresh and will require careful cleaning and then stitching. "I can do it, Martin," she says.

He looks at her hopefully.

"I'll get my reading glasses."

Martin holds the bird still while Éva anesthetizes around the gash, dabbing with an American cotton ball that leaves no traces. They have covered the bird's head, calming her. The hen is perfectly still in Martin's hold. Éva sterilizes several needles over the stove, and then she sits down for the surgery under the fluorescent light.

Once the area is washed she can see better. "The tear is in three places. I'll sew top to bottom." She feeds the needle into the flesh, delicately, not wanting to disturb the congealed blood. The first stitch is the most difficult to make, but once it holds she feels confident, manipulating the needle in either hand.

Afterward Martin removes the silk scarf covering the bird and they both smile at the sight of her still blinking bright red eyes.

*   *   *

A patch of Lenten roses blooms in the snow outside the Szeged orphanage. They go up the stone steps. Even the orphanage is under renovation. Martin takes her hand, dodging the plasterers on stilts. They follow the warden down the corridor. Martin holds the bird carrier. Levente is waiting in a special room for new adoptions. There is comfortable furniture, toys lying around.

She swallows nervously. "Levente?"

He is wearing pleated pants, a button-up shirt, and a neck scarf that is part of the orphanage uniform. He greets them formally, as he's been coached, kissing Éva's hand and shaking Martin's. He has had a haircut in anticipation of their arrival and flaxen slivers still cling to his collar. Éva dusts the stray hairs with her fingertips, then reaches to hug him.

"You've grown," Martin says, opening his arms, beckoning him.

Levente steps from Éva to Martin, slowly, like he is just learning.

They sit awkwardly on plastic chairs. Éva pulls apart a chocolate bar to share. In pursuing the case with the orphanage, they have had to confront Levente Sas's history, the fact that he was born of rape. Ágnes Sas has forfeited her parental rights. There were many weeks, and many years before, leading to this day. Éva is fearless. She wears a silver-plate wedding band to match Martin's. The marriage was a means to an end, that is her viewpoint, but Martin seems changed, anchored by it. He wants to buy property in Szeged.

Martin slides the bird carrier across the floor to Levente. "Here's another old friend. Do you want to release her?"

They gather together at the tall window. Martin unlatches the cover and Levente reaches in for the dove.

"She likes a good-bye kiss."

"I remember," Levente says. He touches his lips to the crown feathers. With an unfamiliar grace, he thrusts his arms out, tossing the bird up. In an instant, the dove is airborne. "Look at her go, Éva *Néni!*"

The pigeon ascends over the tiled rooftops.

"Let's race her home," Éva says.

Martin collects the empty bird carrier and Éva brings Levente's little suitcase. Hurrying out, down the orphanage steps, they each take one of the boy's hands. Now they run, laughing, up the street.

Acknowledgments

I HAVE TRIED to remain true to history in the creation of this fiction, drawing on many excellent sources. The following books were most useful for background: *Kiss the Hand You Cannot Bite* by Edward Behr, *The Politics of Genocide: The Holocaust in Hungary* by Randolph L. Braham, *The Hooligan's Return* by Norman Manca, *The Jews of East Central Europe Between the World Wars* by Ezra Mendelsohn, *Notes from the Other Side of Night* by Juliana Pilon, and *The Return* by Petru Popescu. Any discrepancies of fact that I encountered in my research and that were part of my story I have posited from the character's point of view. The villages of Crisu and Ticu are fictional, named after small rivers. The geography is otherwise factually represented. All characters and plot events are products of my imagination and any real life resemblance is unintentional.

My story would not have been possible without the assistance of dear friends Erzsébet Barat and Paula Fekete. Köszönöm szépen Bereczkiéknek, magyarországi családomnak

Pécsen. I am grateful to the Fekete and Balaj families of Arad, Romania, and to Maria Tóth. I also could not have done without the assistance of my long time first-readers Jessica Lynch Alfaro and Anna Headly. I thank Rachel Manley and Mary Soyer for their unflagging support and my mother for teaching me to swim the long distance. Thanks to my large and extended family, to my friends and colleagues, anonymous readers at www. doctormama.blogspot.com, and my contacts in the Fall River Pigeon Racing Club.

I appreciate my affiliation with the following institutions: Kenyon College, University of Michigan, U.S. Peace Corps, University of Szeged (formerly Jozsef Attila University), Franklin W. Olin College of Engineering, and the MFA program in Creative Writing at Lesley University.

Finally, I thank Claire Dunnington, my fearless agent Vicky Bijur, my exceptional editor Elisabeth Schmitz, and everyone at Grove/Atlantic.

SMUGGLED

CHRISTINA SHEA

ABOUT THIS GUIDE

We hope that these discussion questions will enhance your
reading group's exploration of Christina Shea's
Smuggled. They are meant to stimulate discussion, offer new
viewpoints, and enrich your enjoyment of the book.

More reading group guides and additional information, including summaries, author tours, and author sites
for other fine Black Cat titles, may be found on
our Web site, www.groveatlantic.com.

QUESTIONS FOR DISCUSSION

1. As the book progresses from wartime Hungary to Communist Romania, what are the similarities? Is it poverty and hunger or fear of brutal authority that grinds the people down more?

2. From a flour sack to a haystack to fox furs, smuggling and hiding of people and things pervade the book. Talk about the incidents when characters are driven to subterfuge.

3. What is the quality of Anca's mind? Would you call it a shifting balance between headstrong bravery and paranoid diffidence? Give examples of these conflicting impulses, starting from her childhood.

4. Does it surprise you that Éva, witness to her mother's brutal assault, and later as Anca, victim herself to multiple attacks, can bring herself to trust anyone?

5. How are Gypsies and Jews linked thematically in the story?

6. Is it fitting that Éva/Anca develops an affinity with outsiders? Talk about Crin, the Gypsy boy (pp. 53–54) and Irina and Levente, the albino boy in Szeged.

7. "Bunica was always irreverent. She refused to feel threatened by the Stalinist cultural regime, which by now had reached the villages" (p. 56). Is irreverence a trait of survival? "Going

to church was an act of protest that Bunica never tired of"
(p. 57).

8. Tennis and table tennis as team sports begin as salvation
   for Anca but end in disenchantment. Why?

9. What is Anca's attitude toward being Jewish? What is her
   experience of being treated as a Jew? Do you think she will
   reclaim this part of her heritage?

10. How does Éva, herself a refugee, become a caregiver again
    and again?

11. Are there good marriages in the novel? Whose? Which are
    the relationships that reaffirm the power of love, loyalty, or
    at least friendship? What are the degradations that often
    doom love in the book?

12. "Her banished self, the isolated past, was a dense forest. She
    felt its pull" (p. 107). As Anca begins to identify Peter in Roma-
    nia, what are the risks to redeeming her "banished self"?

13. After Anca's maimed hand is restored to her, Peter's room-
    mates "hypothesized that the deformity was also a psychic
    injury," and Peter concurs. "You are living a lie here. We
    should get married" (p. 115). How do these issues work out?

14. Is there any hint about what makes totalitarianism thrive
    in Europe? Is it only fear that keeps people in their places,

often ignoring the brutalizing and slaughtering of whole populations? Is there a different fear, a paranoia of enemies around the fatherland worse than the occupiers? What fuels the youth groups?

15. How does the Éva of post-1990 Hungary differ from the Anca of Romania she has been for nearly fifty years? Is there a new authenticity she is granted? Can you describe it? "She is rapidly coming up for air after Communism" (p. 211). How does Éva react to this disorienting feeling?

16. "If you were ambidextrous, you could survive life during Communism" (p. 271). What does "ambidextrous" mean for Éva/Anca? Later in Szeged, how does she use her negotiating skills with the banana seller? (p. 209) How does she shrewdly supplement her income? What are other ways she has of feathering her nest? How do we regard Éva for cutting corners at this point in her life? Do you censure, or admire her ingenuity? What other characters have contrived to scratch out income in unusual ways in the book?

17. By the end, has Éva made peace with her childhood and adult lives? What evidence is there? Or, like perhaps most post-war, post-trauma victims, will she cope by drawing a curtain over the horrors?

18. "What are you escaping, Martin?" "An unresolved life" (p. 265). Describe Martin. Even as an American, what do he and Éva share in their "unresolved" lives?

19. What new aspects does Martin Tierny bring into Éva's life? How much laughter have we heard in the book before?

20. "Something inside Éva is unfurling, layers giving way" (p. 276). What is it that releases her from her distrust? Martin? Levente? A combination?

21. "It is never too late to be what you might have been." This is a mysterious quotation attributed to George Eliot, but do you find it apt for *Smuggled*? Does the ending catch you by surprise? Does it seem credible? Why? Or why not? Do you think Éva's experiences have been such that can make this resolution work?

SUGGESTIONS FOR FURTHER READING:

Stones from the River by Ursula Hegi; *Balzac and the Little Chinese Seamstress* by Dai Sijie; *Those Who Save Us* by Jenna Blum; *The Invisible Bridge* by Julie Orringer; *The Hooligan's Return* by Norman Manea; *Purge* by Sofi Oksanen